Dᴉꜱɴᴇʏ
MULAN'S ADVENTURE JOURNAL

The Palace of Secrets

Cleary - Innocente - Urbinati - Cardinali

DARK HORSE BOOKS

The Palace of Secrets – Mulan's Adventure Journal
Story by Rhona Cleary for Book on a Tree, London
Art by Agnese Innocente (comics pencils), Gaia Cardinali (comics paints), and Ilaria Urbinati
(watercolor illustrations) for Book on a Tree, London

Historical and cultural background supervision by IW Group, Los Angeles – New York – San Francisco
Lettering by Alta Fedeltà, Milan
Cover, comics, and diary page design by Red Spot, Milan

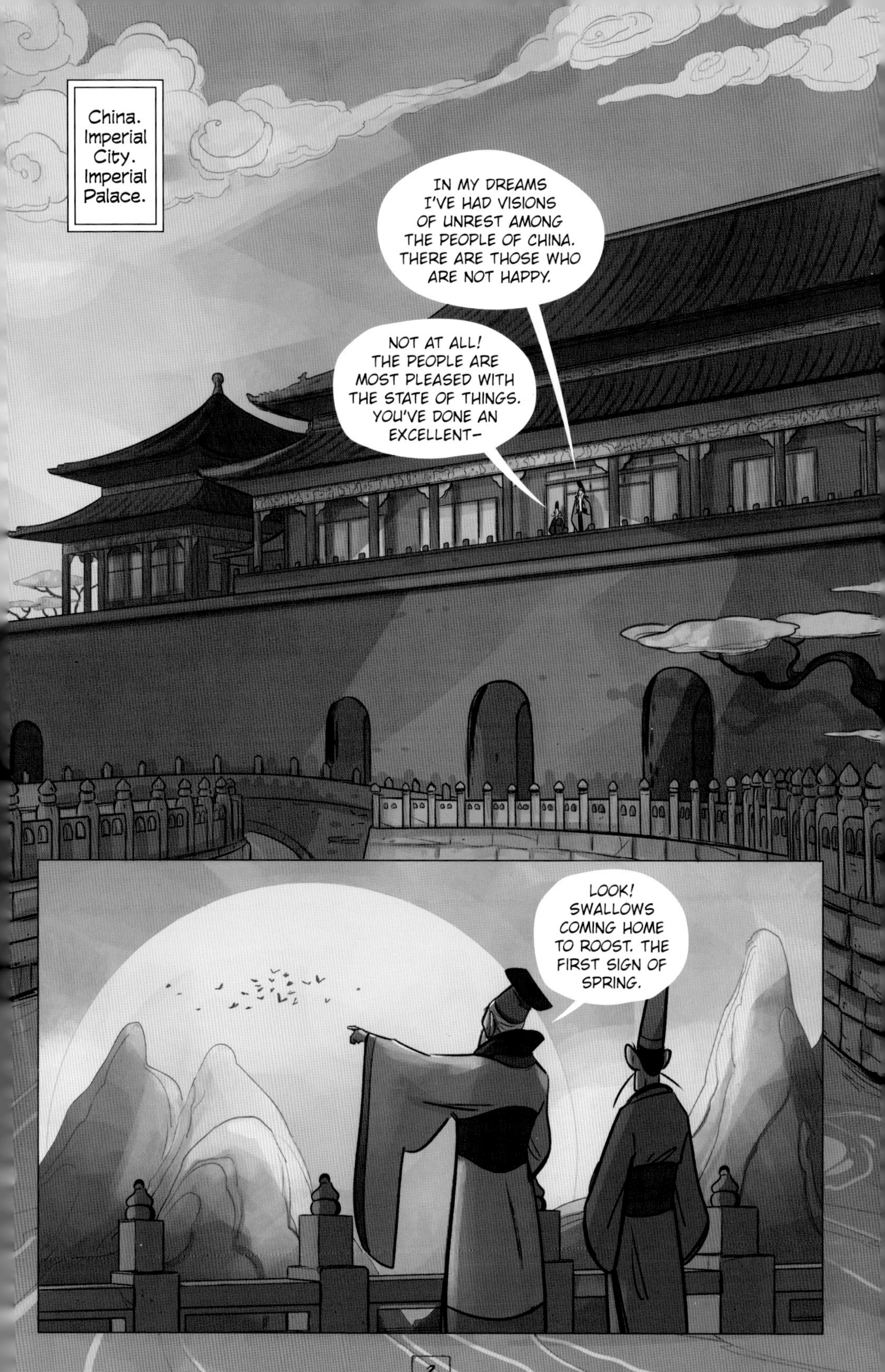
China. Imperial City. Imperial Palace.
IN MY DREAMS I'VE HAD VISIONS OF UNREST AMONG THE PEOPLE OF CHINA. THERE ARE THOSE WHO ARE NOT HAPPY.
NOT AT ALL! THE PEOPLE ARE MOST PLEASED WITH THE STATE OF THINGS. YOU'VE DONE AN EXCELLENT–
LOOK! SWALLOWS COMING HOME TO ROOST. THE FIRST SIGN OF SPRING.

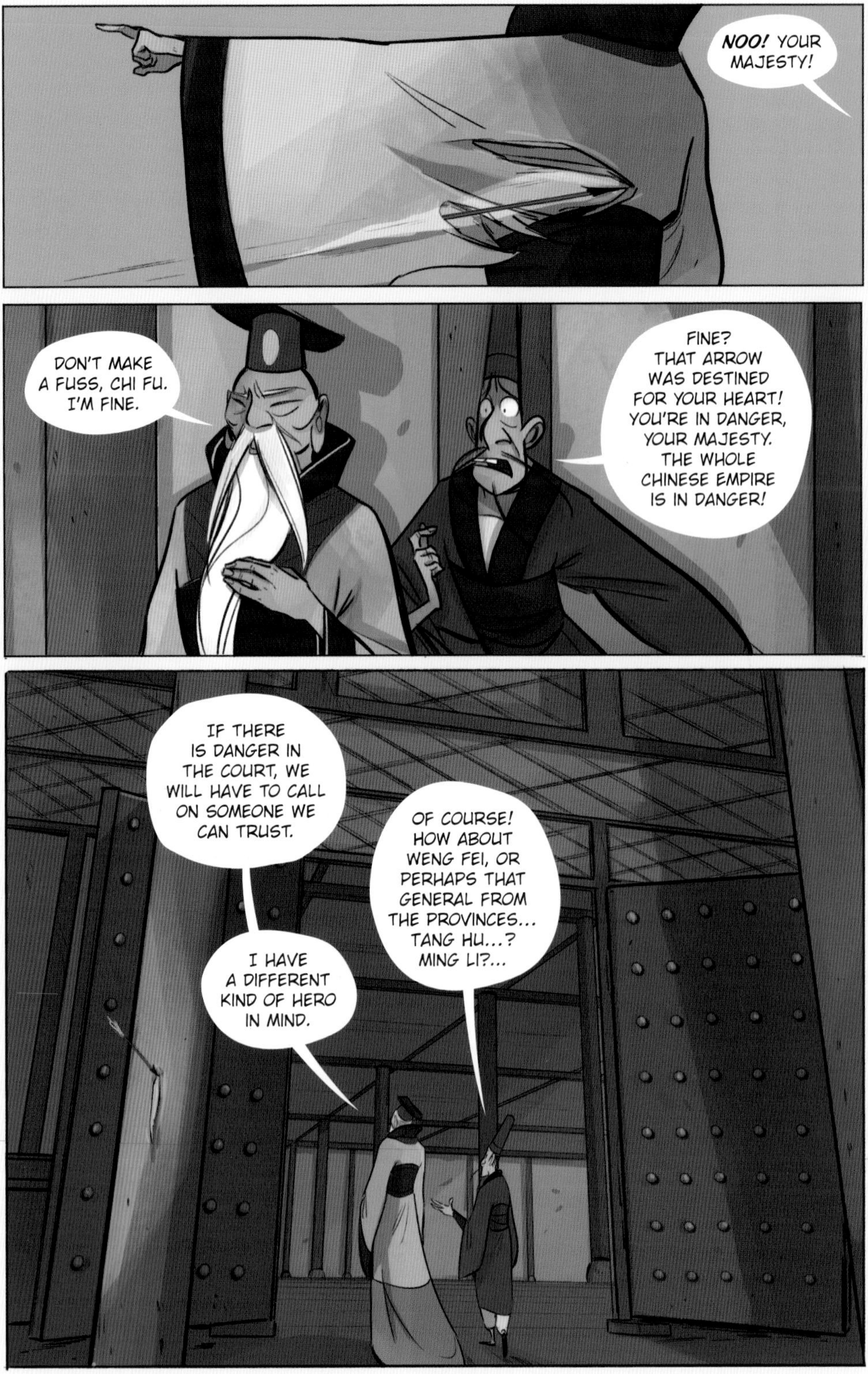
NOO! YOUR MAJESTY!
DON'T MAKE A FUSS, CHI FU. I'M FINE.
FINE? THAT ARROW WAS DESTINED FOR YOUR HEART! YOU'RE IN DANGER, YOUR MAJESTY. THE WHOLE CHINESE EMPIRE IS IN DANGER!
IF THERE IS DANGER IN THE COURT, WE WILL HAVE TO CALL ON SOMEONE WE CAN TRUST.
OF COURSE! HOW ABOUT WENG FEI, OR PERHAPS THAT GENERAL FROM THE PROVINCES... TANG HU...? MING LI?...
I HAVE A DIFFERENT KIND OF HERO IN MIND.

It's an exciting time to be back home, with preparations
for the Spring Festival underway. The whole household
is buzzing with activity as we sweep away the past year's
bad luck and prime for the new year's good fortune.

I'm happy to see Mother and Father and Grandma again
after being away, but I must confess I miss feeling
like a part of something bigger than me.

I miss the open skies, the excitement
of the actions, waking at dawn
with a sense of purpose...

MULAN!!!

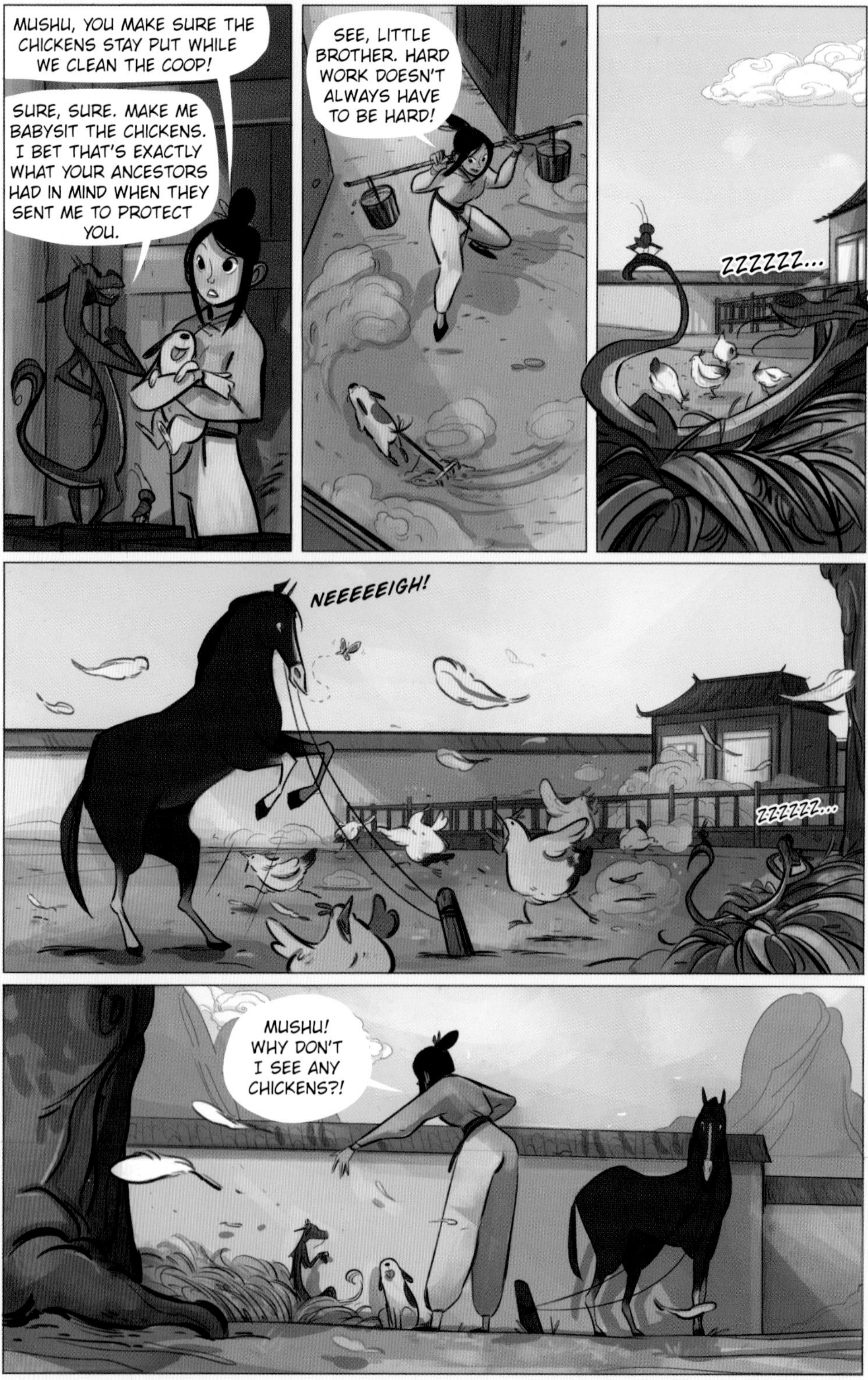
MUSHU, YOU MAKE SURE THE CHICKENS STAY PUT WHILE WE CLEAN THE COOP!
SURE, SURE. MAKE ME BABYSIT THE CHICKENS. I BET THAT'S EXACTLY WHAT YOUR ANCESTORS HAD IN MIND WHEN THEY SENT ME TO PROTECT YOU.
SEE, LITTLE BROTHER. HARD WORK DOESN'T ALWAYS HAVE TO BE HARD!
ZZZZZZ...
NEEEEEIGH!
ZZZZZZ...
MUSHU! WHY DON'T I SEE ANY CHICKENS?!

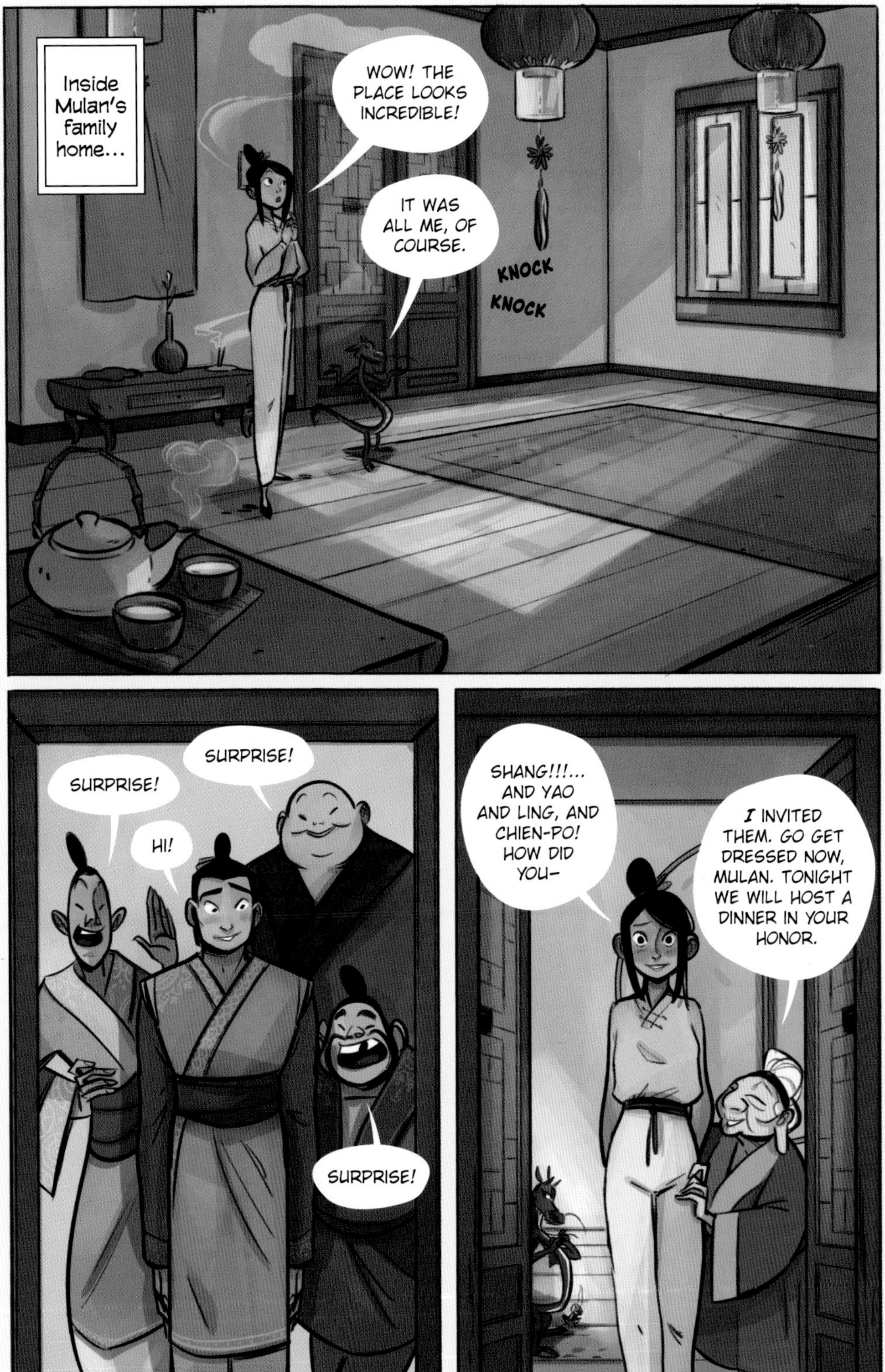
Inside Mulan's family home...
WOW! THE PLACE LOOKS INCREDIBLE!
IT WAS ALL ME, OF COURSE.
KNOCK
KNOCK
SURPRISE!
SURPRISE!
HI!
SURPRISE!
SHANG!!!... AND YAO AND LING, AND CHIEN-PO! HOW DID YOU–
I INVITED THEM. GO GET DRESSED NOW, MULAN. TONIGHT WE WILL HOST A DINNER IN YOUR HONOR.

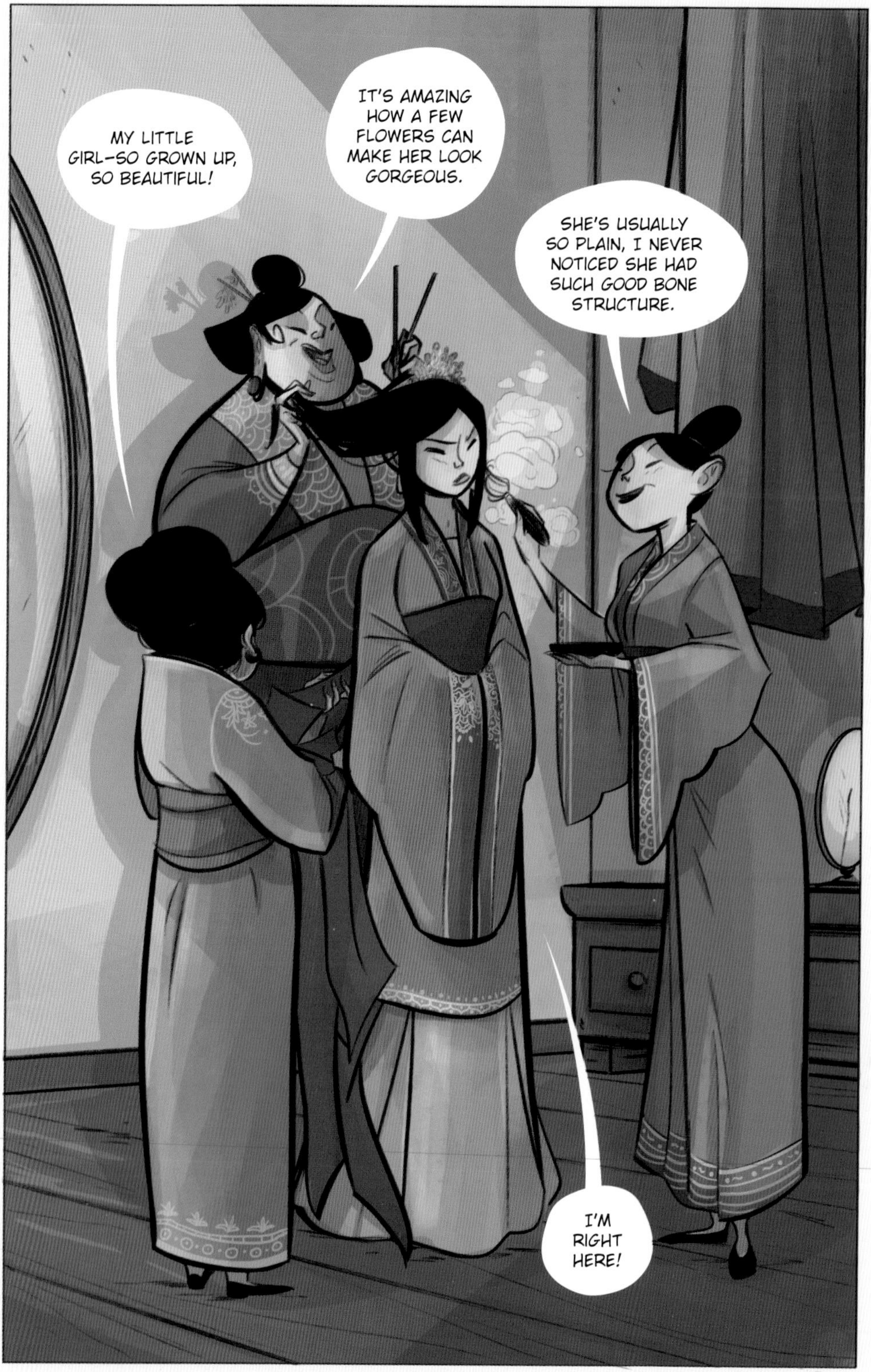
MY LITTLE GIRL—SO GROWN UP, SO BEAUTIFUL!
IT'S AMAZING HOW A FEW FLOWERS CAN MAKE HER LOOK GORGEOUS.
SHE'S USUALLY SO PLAIN, I NEVER NOTICED SHE HAD SUCH GOOD BONE STRUCTURE.
I'M RIGHT HERE!

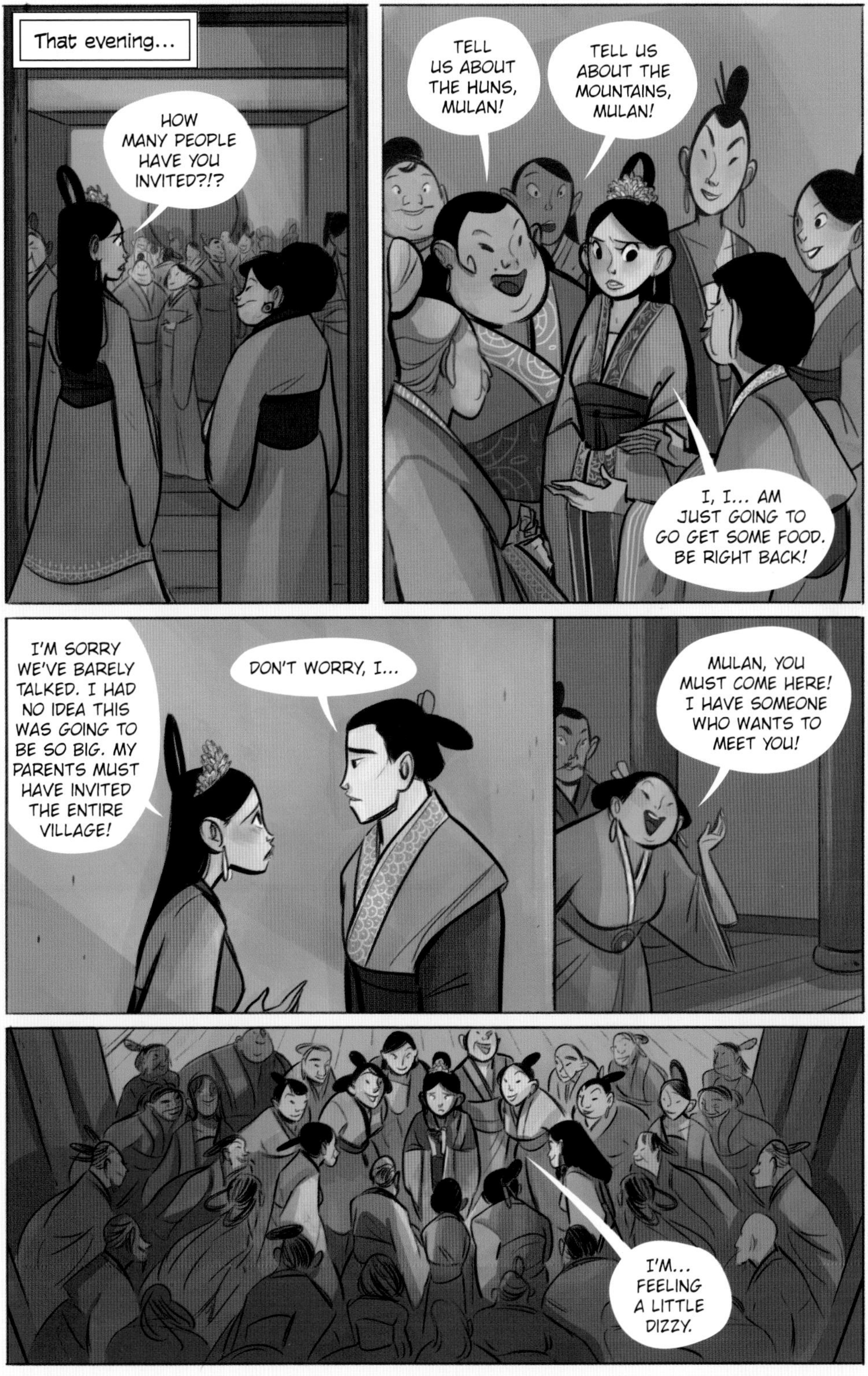
That evening...
HOW MANY PEOPLE HAVE YOU INVITED?!?
TELL US ABOUT THE HUNS, MULAN!
TELL US ABOUT THE MOUNTAINS, MULAN!
I, I... AM JUST GOING TO GO GET SOME FOOD. BE RIGHT BACK!
I'M SORRY WE'VE BARELY TALKED. I HAD NO IDEA THIS WAS GOING TO BE SO BIG. MY PARENTS MUST HAVE INVITED THE ENTIRE VILLAGE!
DON'T WORRY, I...
MULAN, YOU MUST COME HERE! I HAVE SOMEONE WHO WANTS TO MEET YOU!
I'M... FEELING A LITTLE DIZZY.

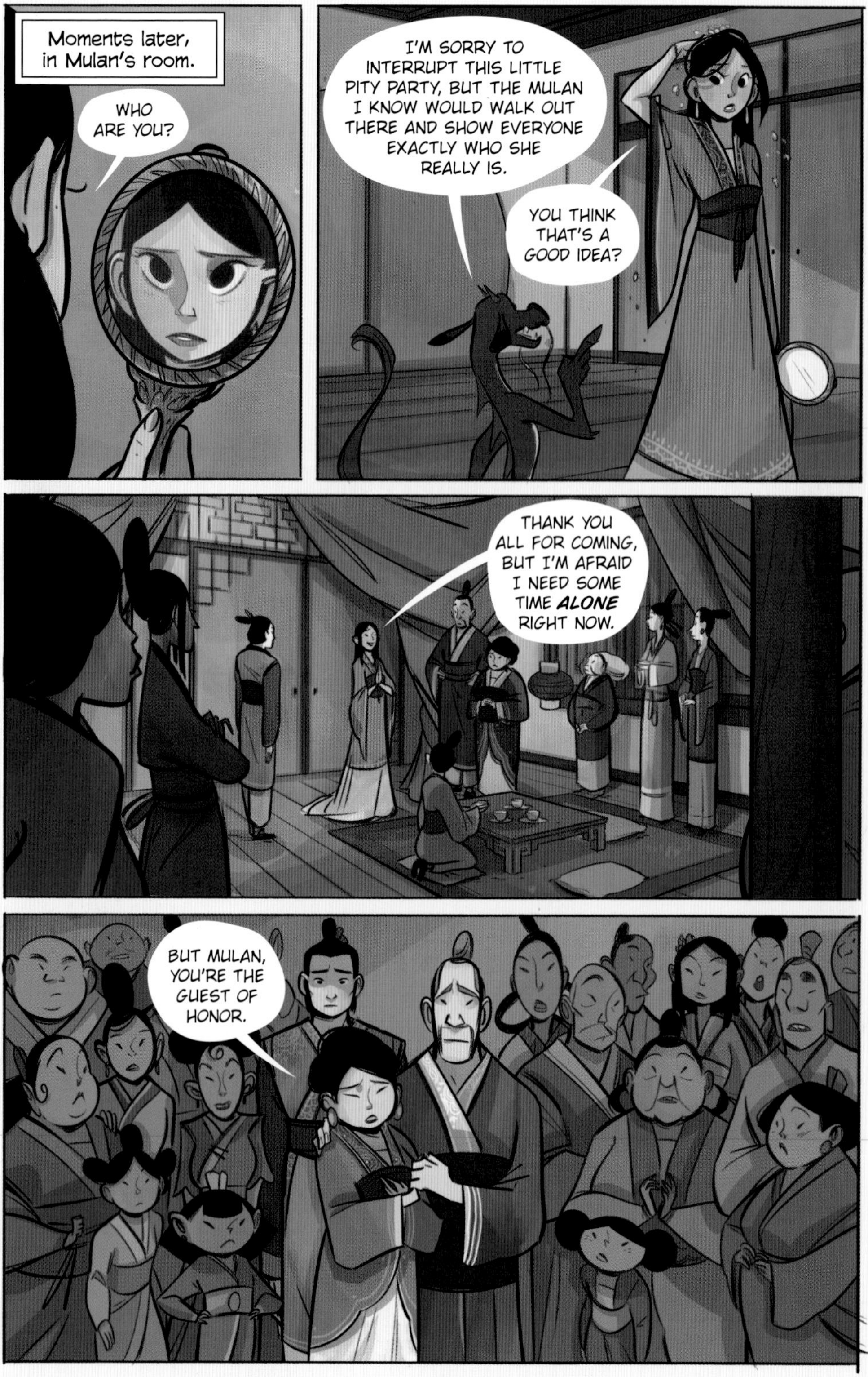
Moments later, in Mulan's room.
WHO ARE YOU?
I'M SORRY TO INTERRUPT THIS LITTLE PITY PARTY, BUT THE MULAN I KNOW WOULD WALK OUT THERE AND SHOW EVERYONE EXACTLY WHO SHE REALLY IS.
YOU THINK THAT'S A GOOD IDEA?
THANK YOU ALL FOR COMING, BUT I'M AFRAID I NEED SOME TIME ***ALONE*** RIGHT NOW.
BUT MULAN, YOU'RE THE GUEST OF HONOR.

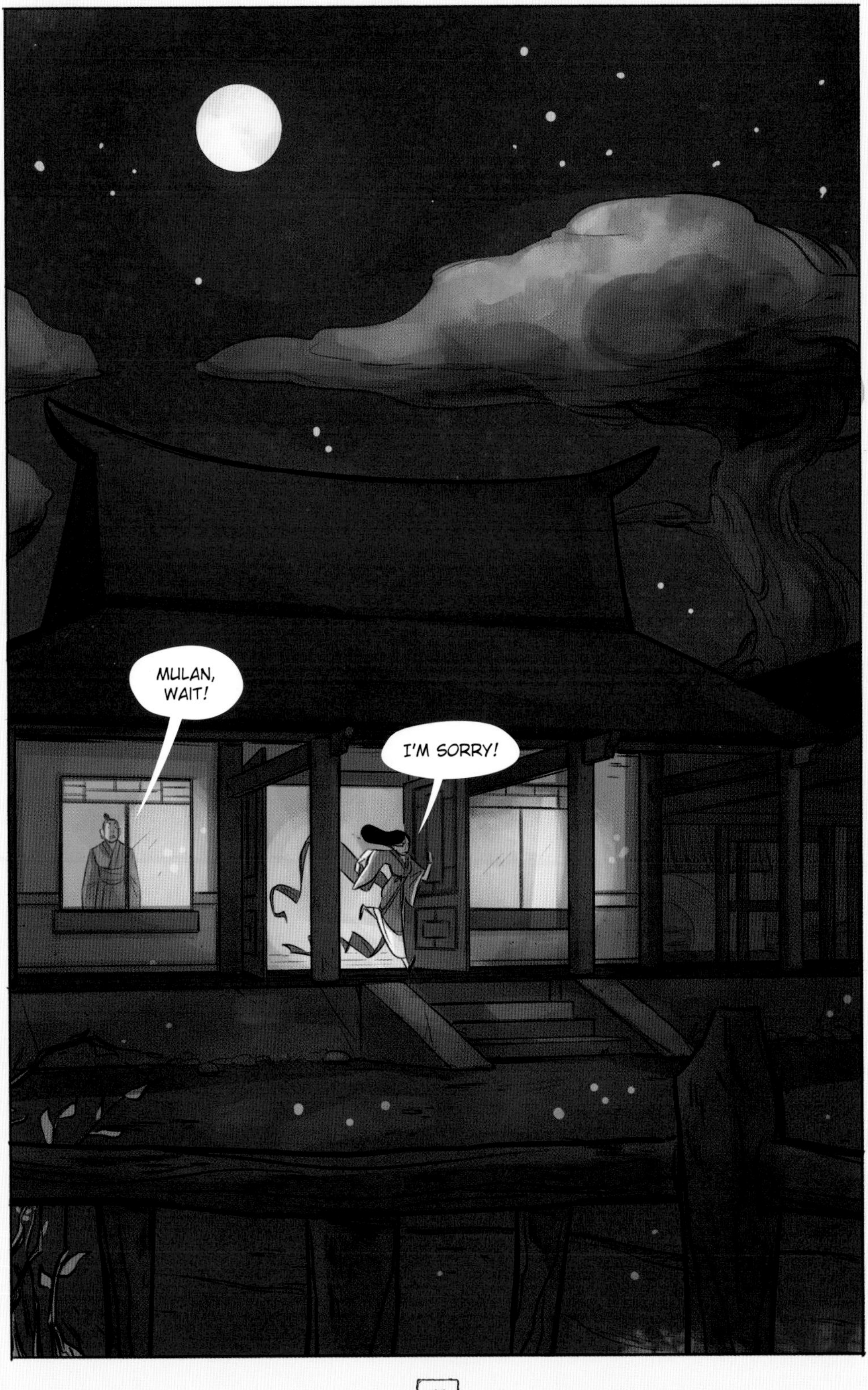
MULAN,
WAIT!
I'M SORRY!

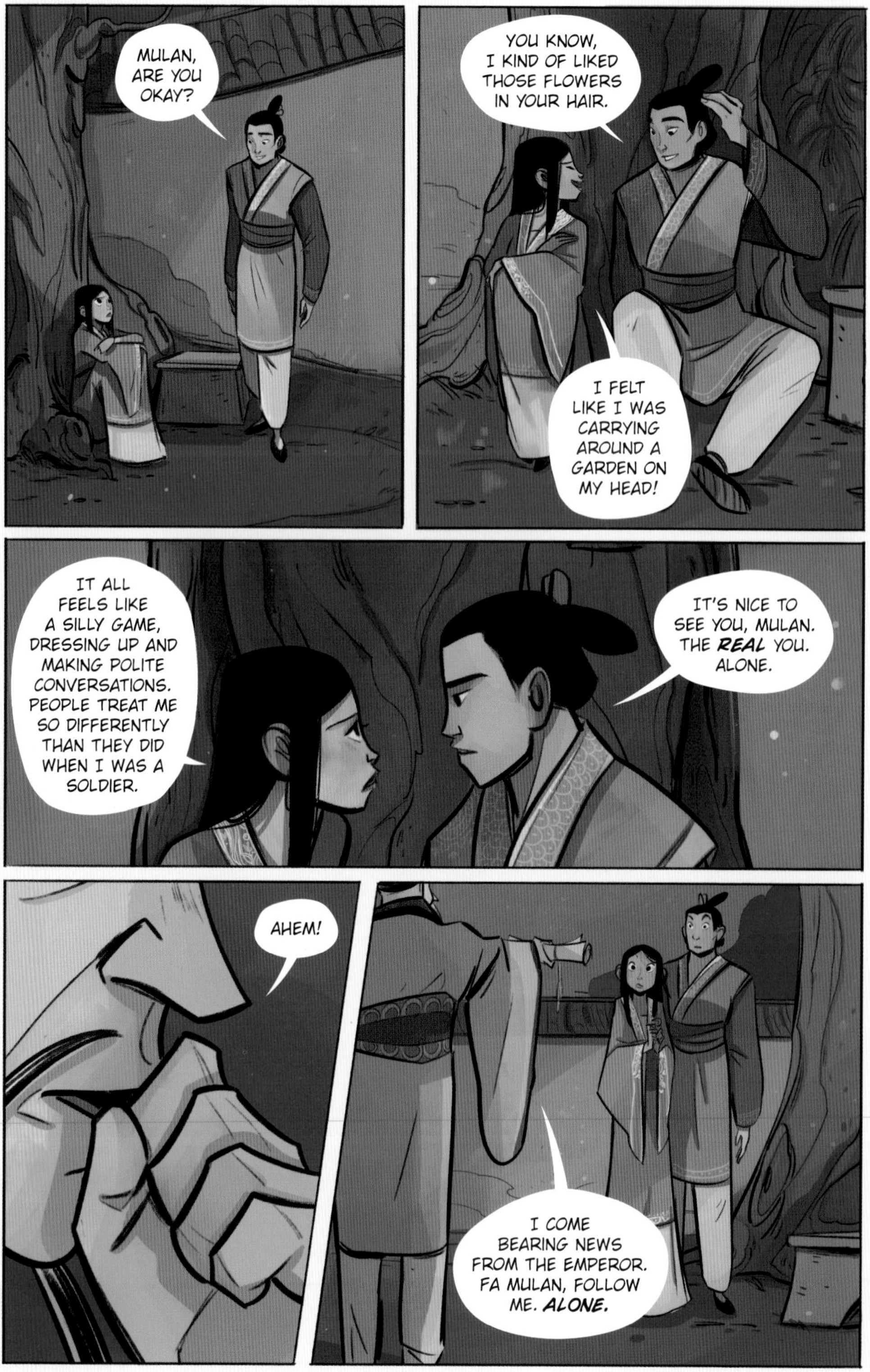
MULAN, ARE YOU OKAY?
YOU KNOW, I KIND OF LIKED THOSE FLOWERS IN YOUR HAIR.
I FELT LIKE I WAS CARRYING AROUND A GARDEN ON MY HEAD!
IT ALL FEELS LIKE A SILLY GAME, DRESSING UP AND MAKING POLITE CONVERSATIONS. PEOPLE TREAT ME SO DIFFERENTLY THAN THEY DID WHEN I WAS A SOLDIER.
IT'S NICE TO SEE YOU, MULAN. THE *REAL* YOU. ALONE.
AHEM!
I COME BEARING NEWS FROM THE EMPEROR. FA MULAN, FOLLOW ME. ***ALONE.***

I, the Emperor of China,
request your participation
in an important mission.

China is in a moment of upheaval.
The palace is beset with hidden dangers,
and my own life has been threatened.

I know you are trustworthy, brave,
and a master of disguise, which makes you
the perfect person to infiltrate the court and
uncover the source of these threats on my life.

You will tell your family that
I have summoned you to the Imperial Palace
to honor you as a national hero during
the Spring Festival.

You may bring one family member with
you as an official companion to the palace
for the celebrations.

This matter requires your utmost discretion.
You must tell no one about the true
purpose of this visit.

The Emperor

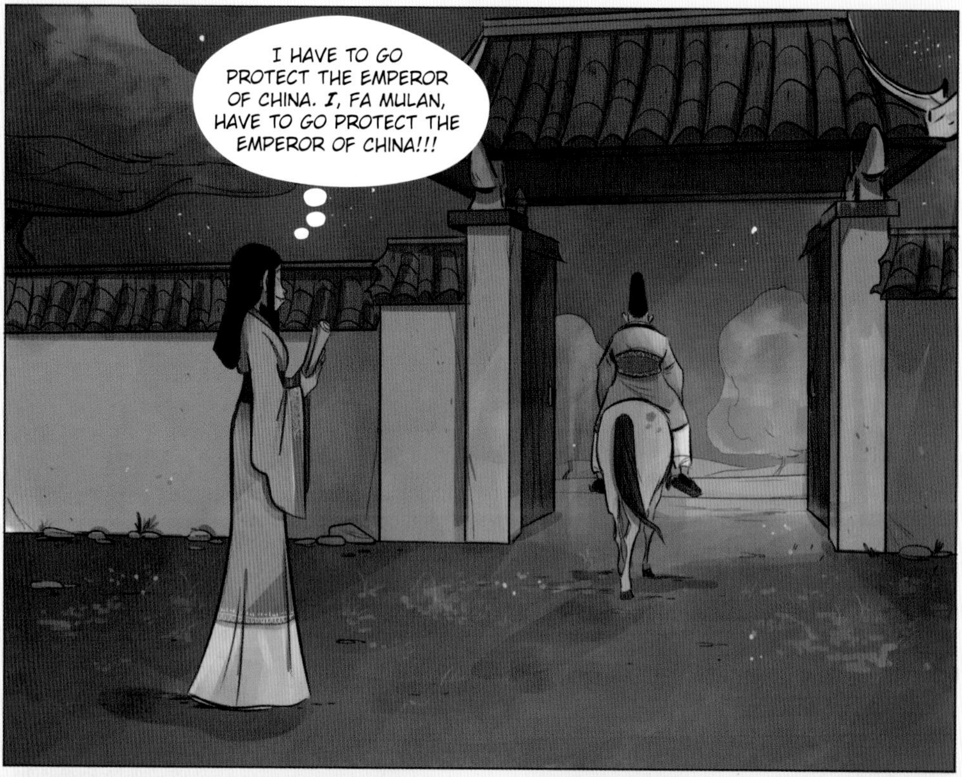
I HAVE TO GO PROTECT THE EMPEROR OF CHINA. *I*, FA MULAN, HAVE TO GO PROTECT THE EMPEROR OF CHINA!!!

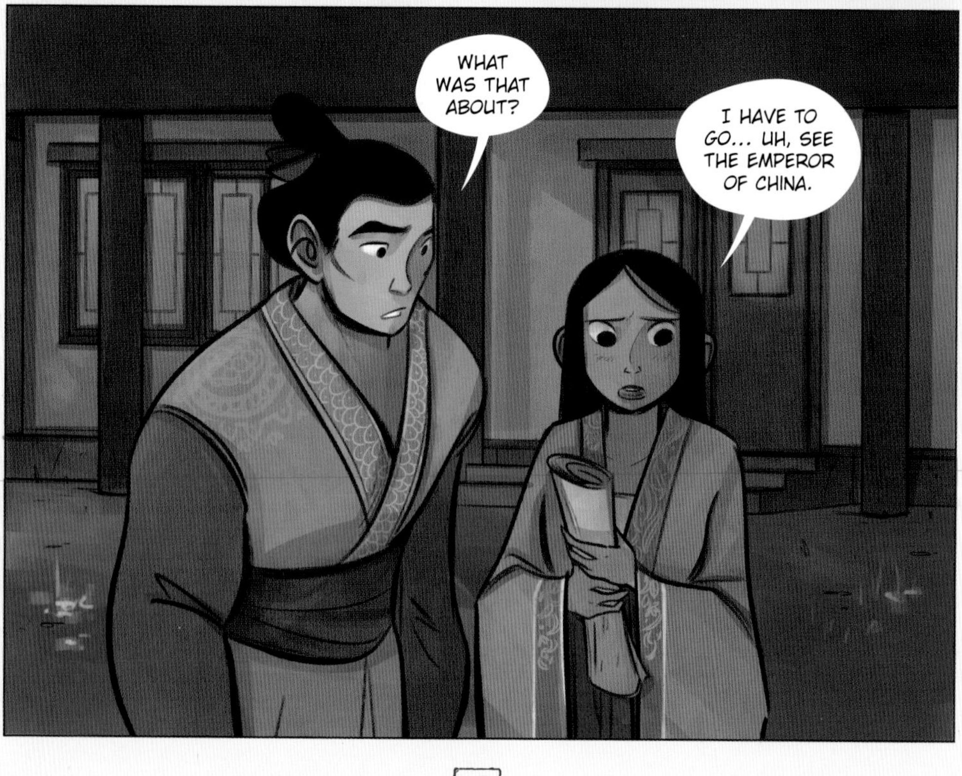
WHAT WAS THAT ABOUT?
I HAVE TO GO... UH, SEE THE EMPEROR OF CHINA.

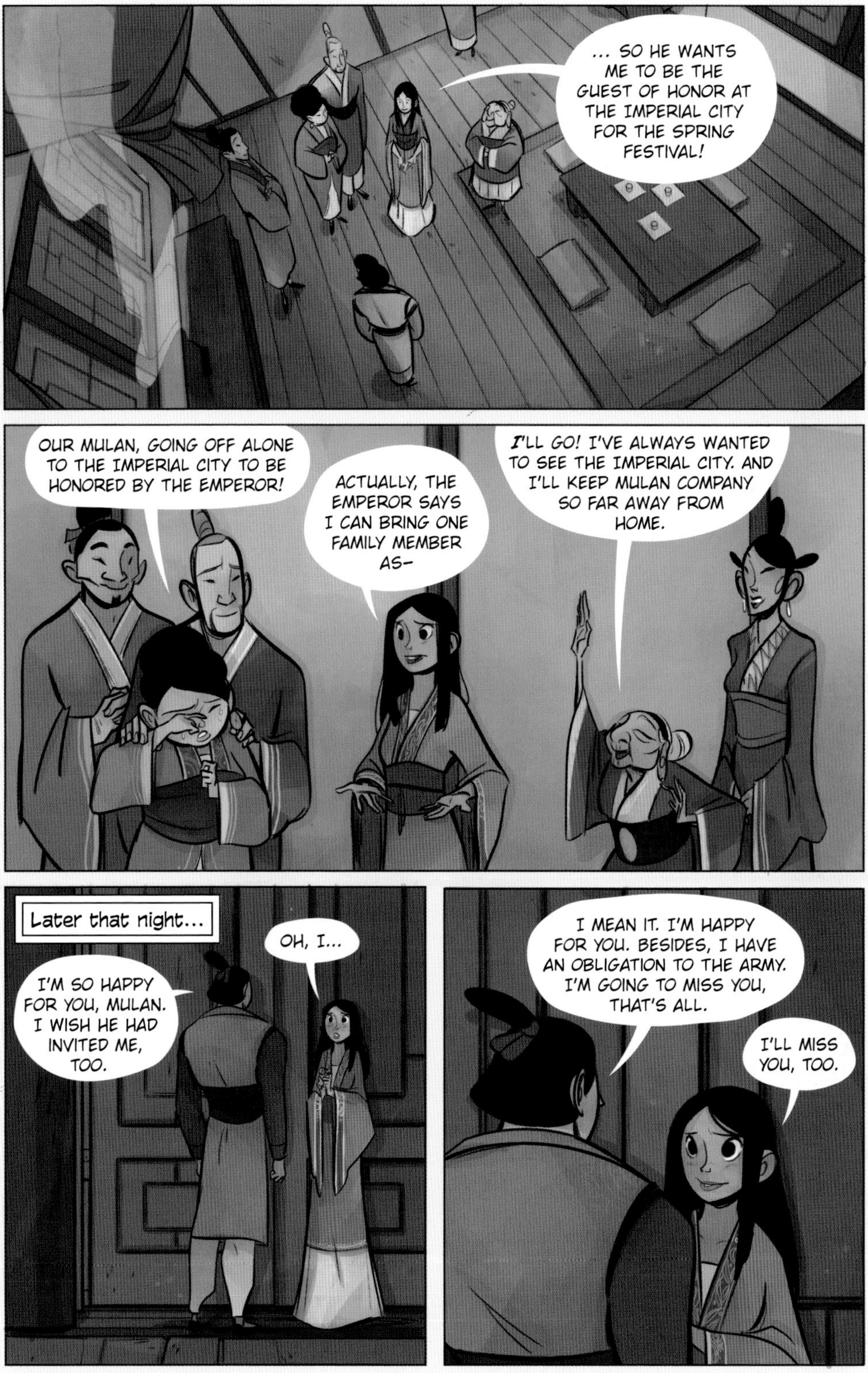
... SO HE WANTS ME TO BE THE GUEST OF HONOR AT THE IMPERIAL CITY FOR THE SPRING FESTIVAL!
OUR MULAN, GOING OFF ALONE TO THE IMPERIAL CITY TO BE HONORED BY THE EMPEROR!
ACTUALLY, THE EMPEROR SAYS I CAN BRING ONE FAMILY MEMBER AS–
I'LL GO! I'VE ALWAYS WANTED TO SEE THE IMPERIAL CITY. AND I'LL KEEP MULAN COMPANY SO FAR AWAY FROM HOME.
Later that night...
I'M SO HAPPY FOR YOU, MULAN. I WISH HE HAD INVITED ME, TOO.
OH, I...
I MEAN IT. I'M HAPPY FOR YOU. BESIDES, I HAVE AN OBLIGATION TO THE ARMY. I'M GOING TO MISS YOU, THAT'S ALL.
I'LL MISS YOU, TOO.

I know I should be sleeping, but I'm just so excited and nervous, I can't even stay still. Tomorrow Grandma and I will be leaving for the Imperial City.

I'm sad to leave Mother and Father after being home for such a short time, but I'm proud to be able to fulfill my duty to China. Grandma will be with me, so I know I'll never be lonely.

My welcome home party was a disaster, and getting out on the road again will be good for me. It's nice to be home, but sometimes I feel a little trapped here.

I'm going to miss Shang, too. I'm happy I was able to see him, even if only for a short while.

It's an incredible honor to be personally invited by the Emperor to protect him. I just hope I can live up to his expectations!

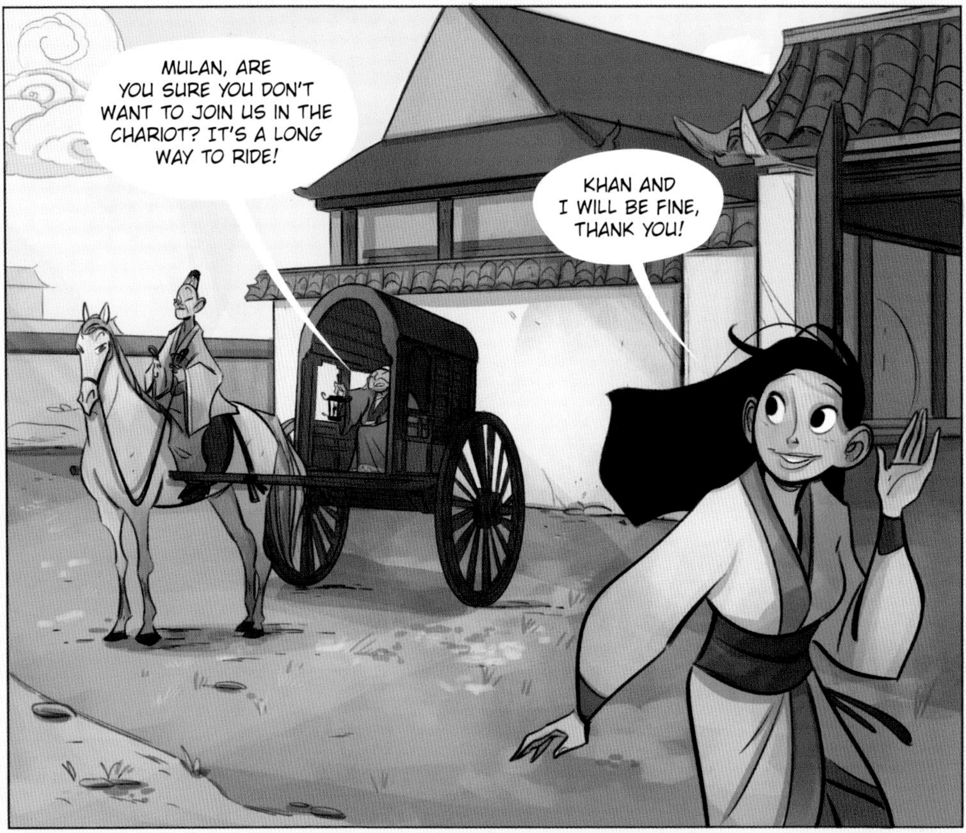
MULAN, ARE YOU SURE YOU DON'T WANT TO JOIN US IN THE CHARIOT? IT'S A LONG WAY TO RIDE!
KHAN AND I WILL BE FINE, THANK YOU!

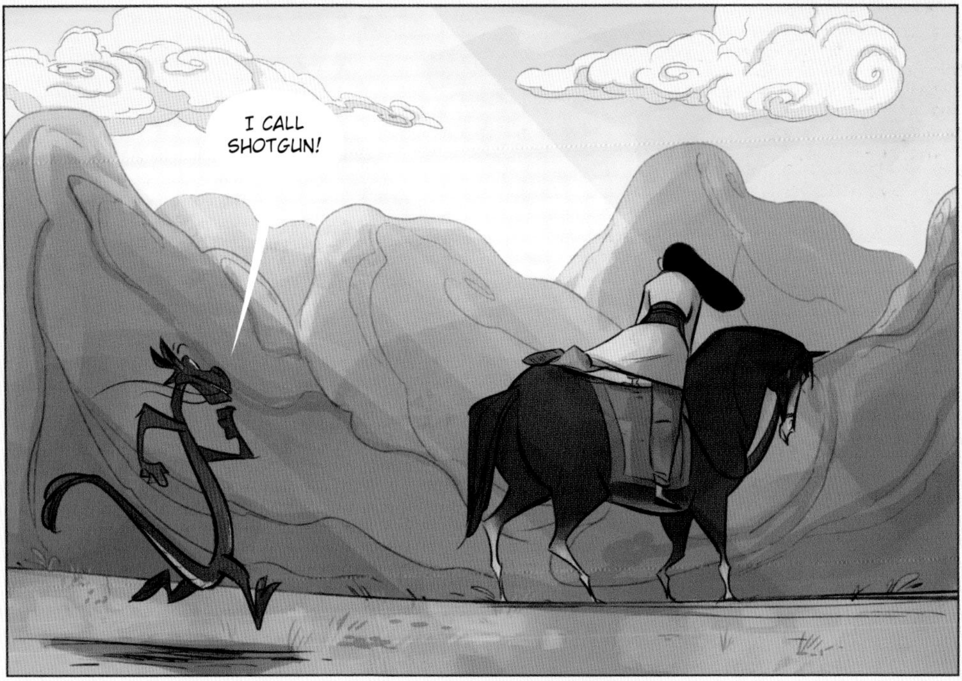
I CALL SHOTGUN!

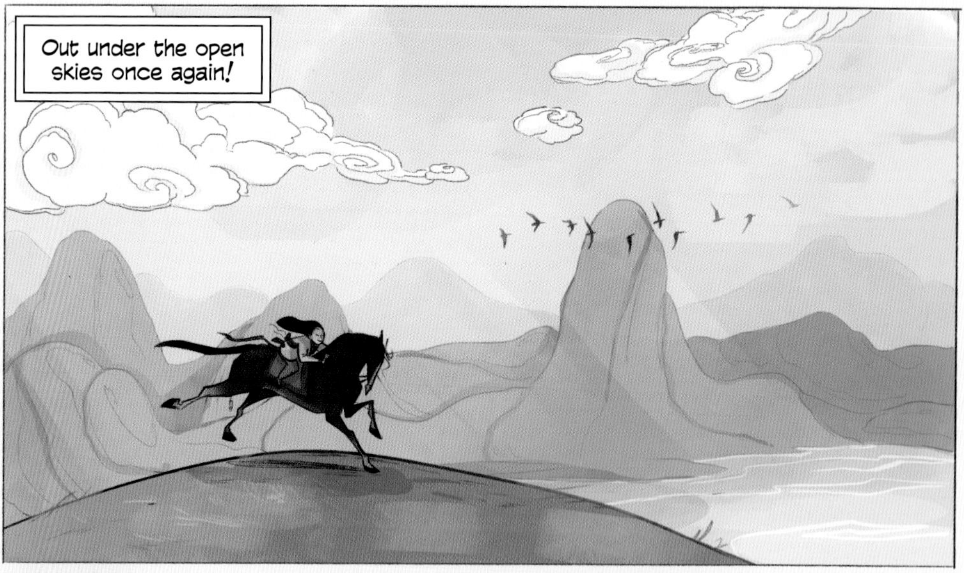
Out under the open skies once again!

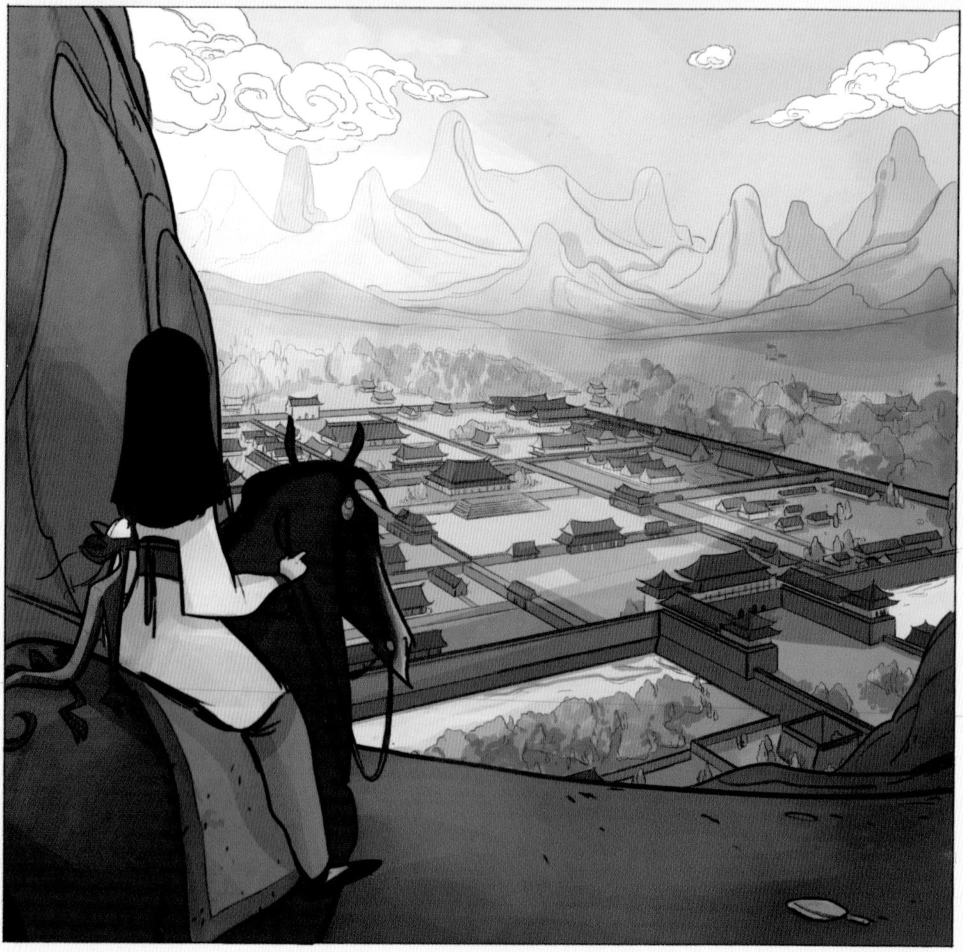

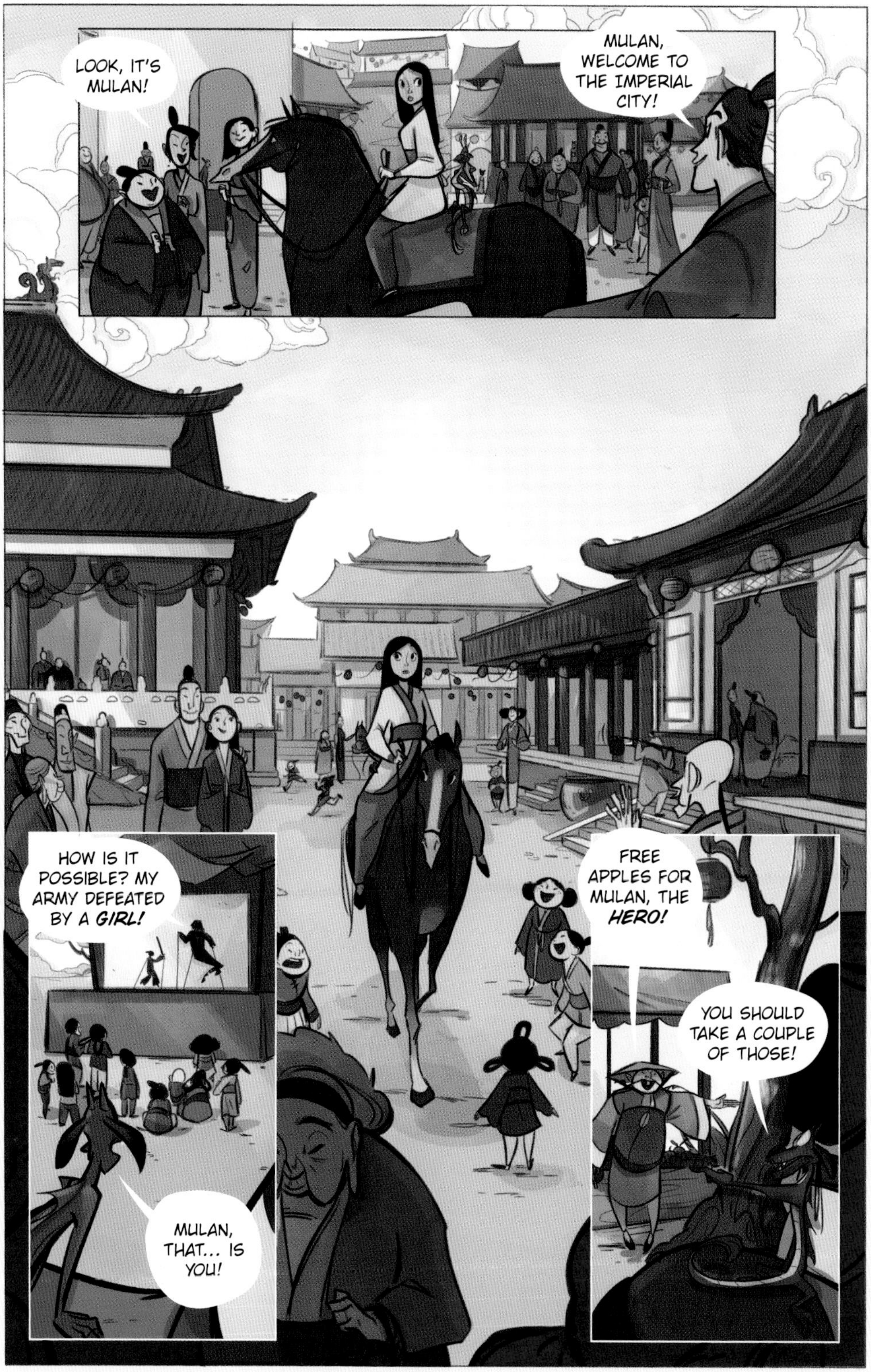
LOOK, IT'S MULAN!
MULAN, WELCOME TO THE IMPERIAL CITY!
HOW IS IT POSSIBLE? MY ARMY DEFEATED BY A GIRL!
MULAN, THAT... IS YOU!
FREE APPLES FOR MULAN, THE HERO!
YOU SHOULD TAKE A COUPLE OF THOSE!

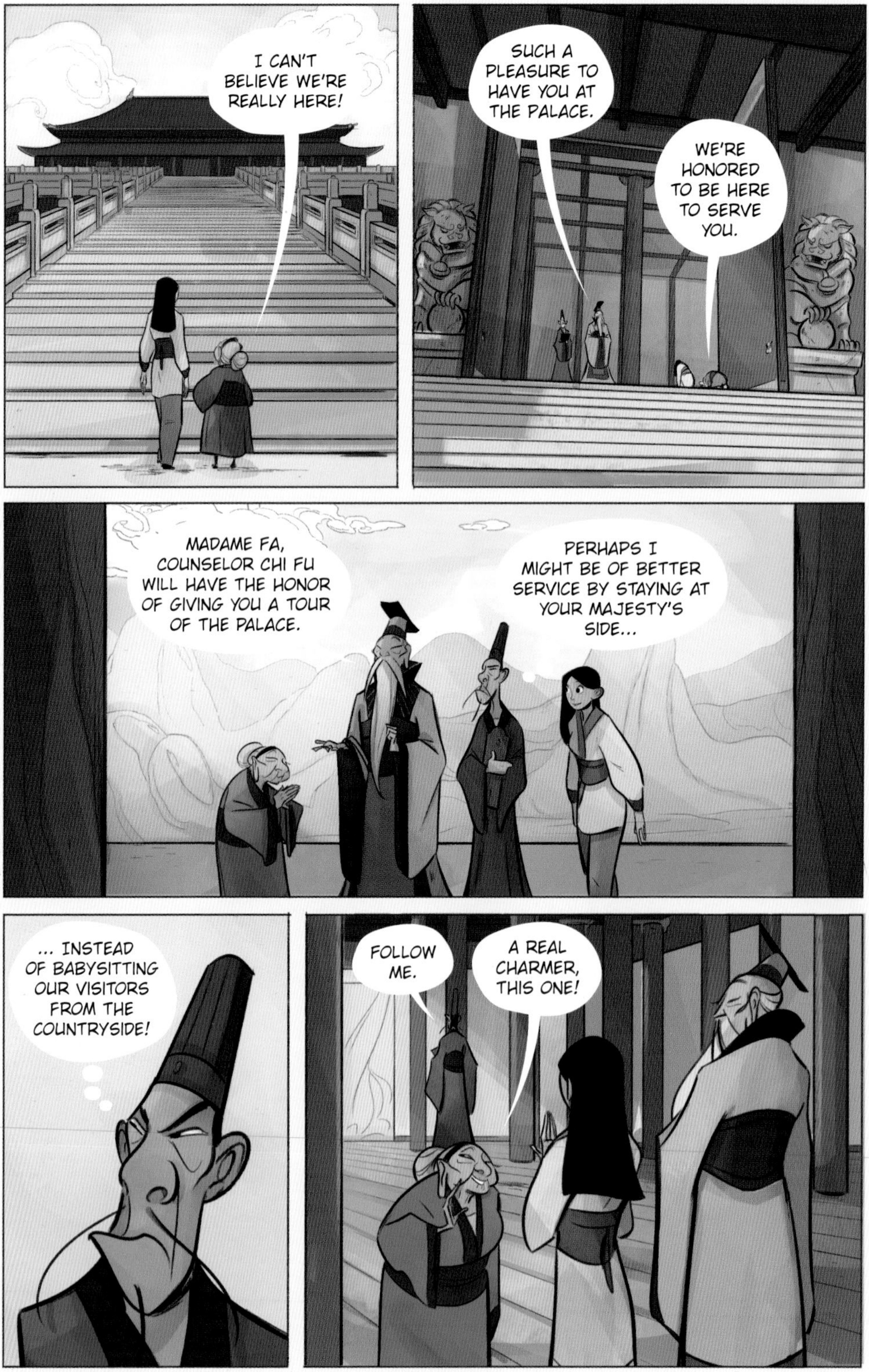
I CAN'T BELIEVE WE'RE REALLY HERE!
SUCH A PLEASURE TO HAVE YOU AT THE PALACE.
WE'RE HONORED TO BE HERE TO SERVE YOU.
MADAME FA, COUNSELOR CHI FU WILL HAVE THE HONOR OF GIVING YOU A TOUR OF THE PALACE.
PERHAPS I MIGHT BE OF BETTER SERVICE BY STAYING AT YOUR MAJESTY'S SIDE...
... INSTEAD OF BABYSITTING OUR VISITORS FROM THE COUNTRYSIDE!
FOLLOW ME.
A REAL CHARMER, THIS ONE!

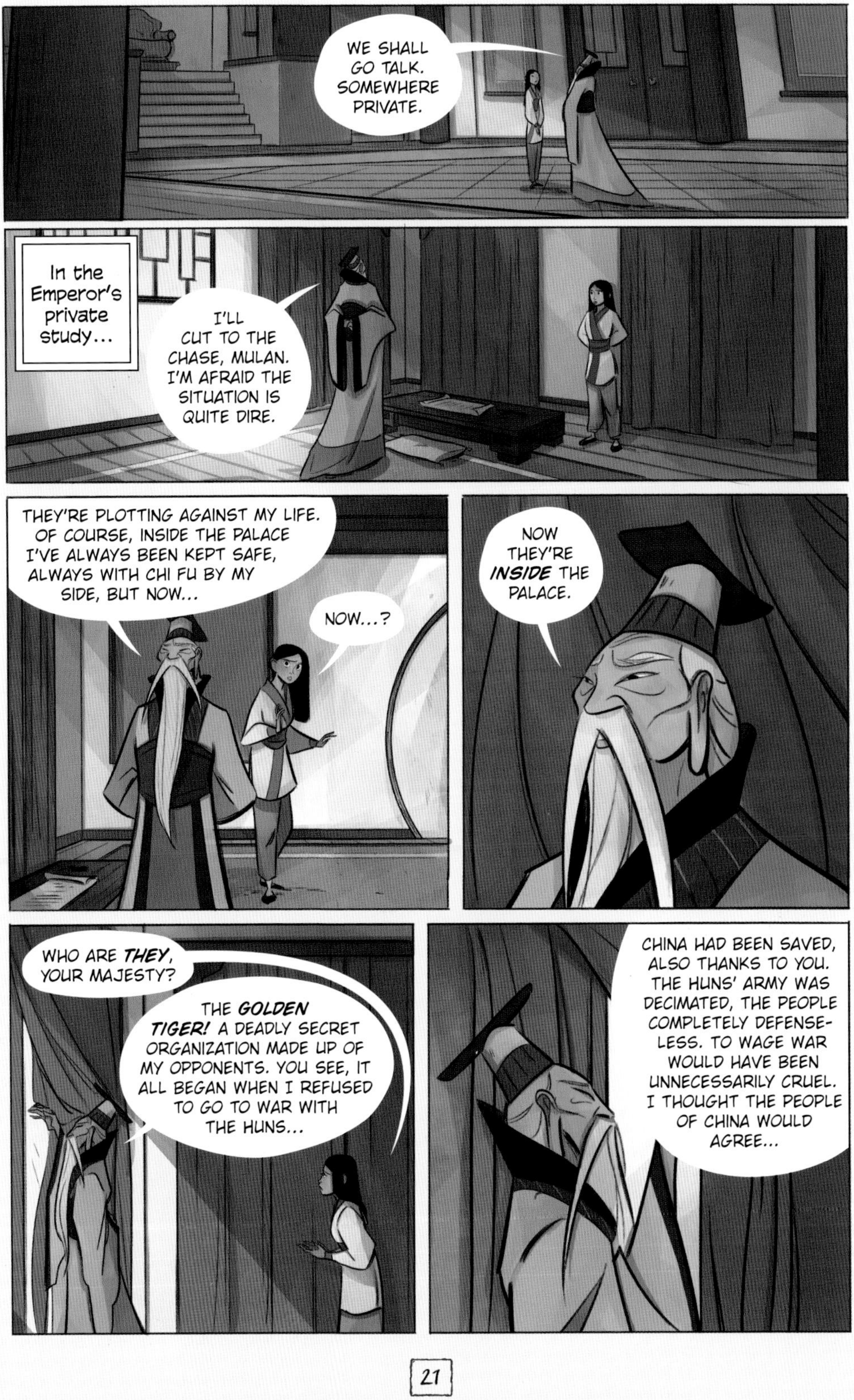
WE SHALL GO TALK. SOMEWHERE PRIVATE.
In the Emperor's private study...
I'LL CUT TO THE CHASE, MULAN. I'M AFRAID THE SITUATION IS QUITE DIRE.
THEY'RE PLOTTING AGAINST MY LIFE. OF COURSE, INSIDE THE PALACE I'VE ALWAYS BEEN KEPT SAFE, ALWAYS WITH CHI FU BY MY SIDE, BUT NOW...
NOW...?
NOW THEY'RE *INSIDE* THE PALACE.
WHO ARE *THEY*, YOUR MAJESTY?
THE ***GOLDEN TIGER!*** A DEADLY SECRET ORGANIZATION MADE UP OF MY OPPONENTS. YOU SEE, IT ALL BEGAN WHEN I REFUSED TO GO TO WAR WITH THE HUNS...
CHINA HAD BEEN SAVED, ALSO THANKS TO YOU. THE HUNS' ARMY WAS DECIMATED, THE PEOPLE COMPLETELY DEFENSELESS. TO WAGE WAR WOULD HAVE BEEN UNNECESSARILY CRUEL. I THOUGHT THE PEOPLE OF CHINA WOULD AGREE...

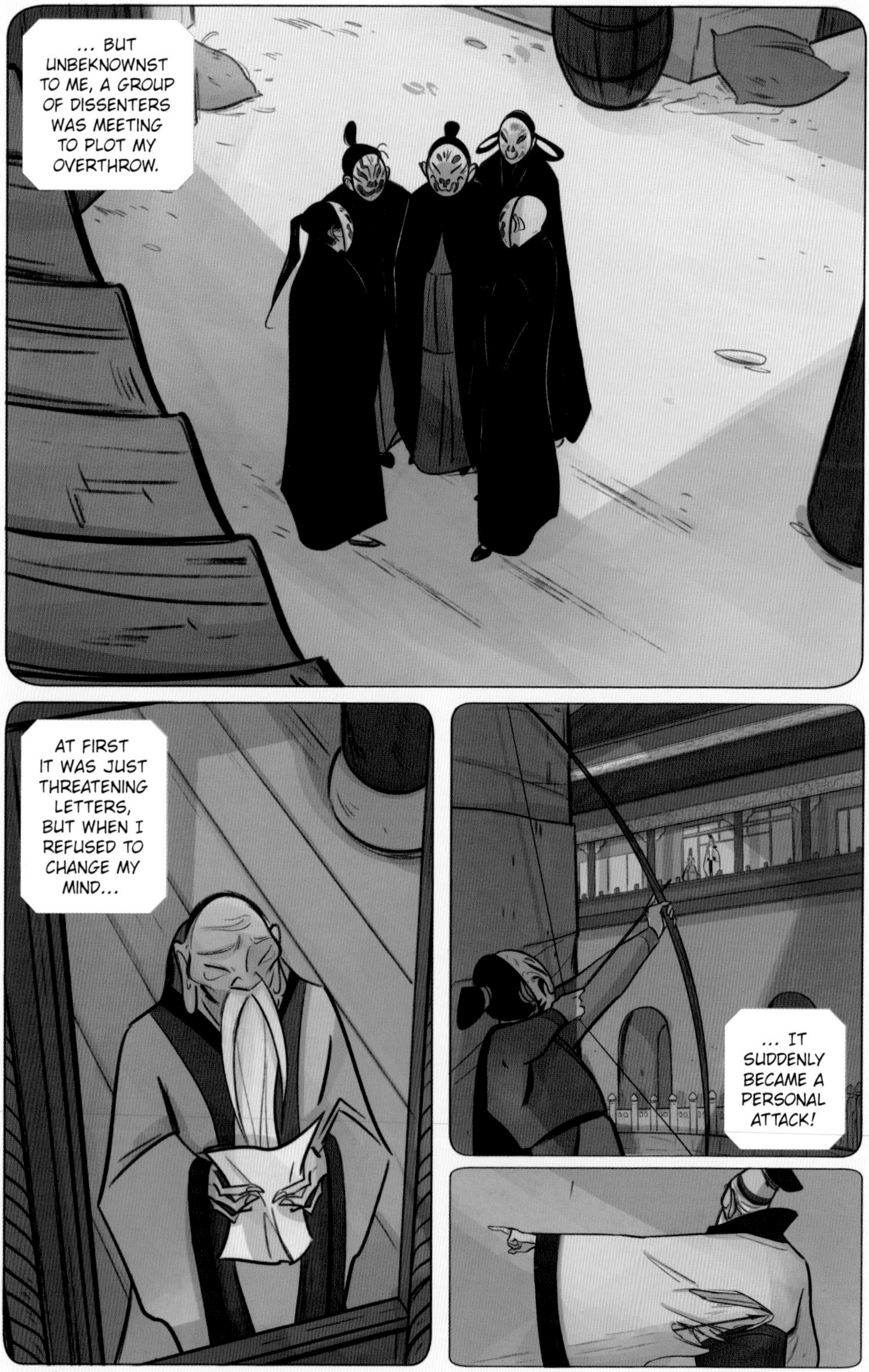
... BUT UNBEKNOWNST TO ME, A GROUP OF DISSENTERS WAS MEETING TO PLOT MY OVERTHROW.
AT FIRST IT WAS JUST THREATENING LETTERS, BUT WHEN I REFUSED TO CHANGE MY MIND...
... IT SUDDENLY BECAME A PERSONAL ATTACK!

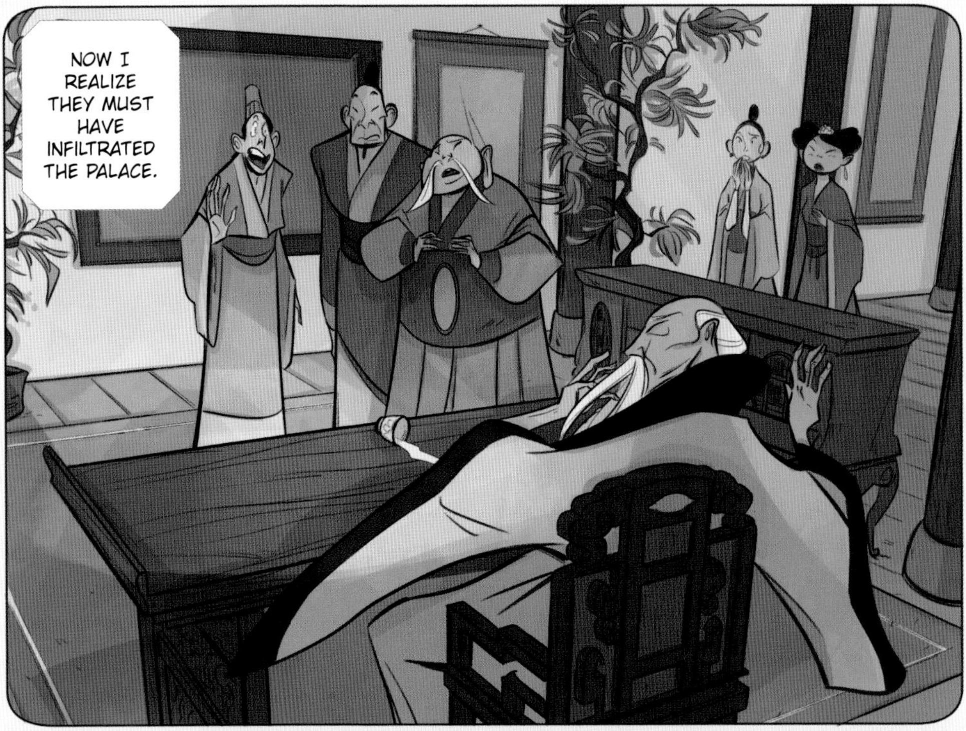
NOW I REALIZE THEY MUST HAVE INFILTRATED THE PALACE.

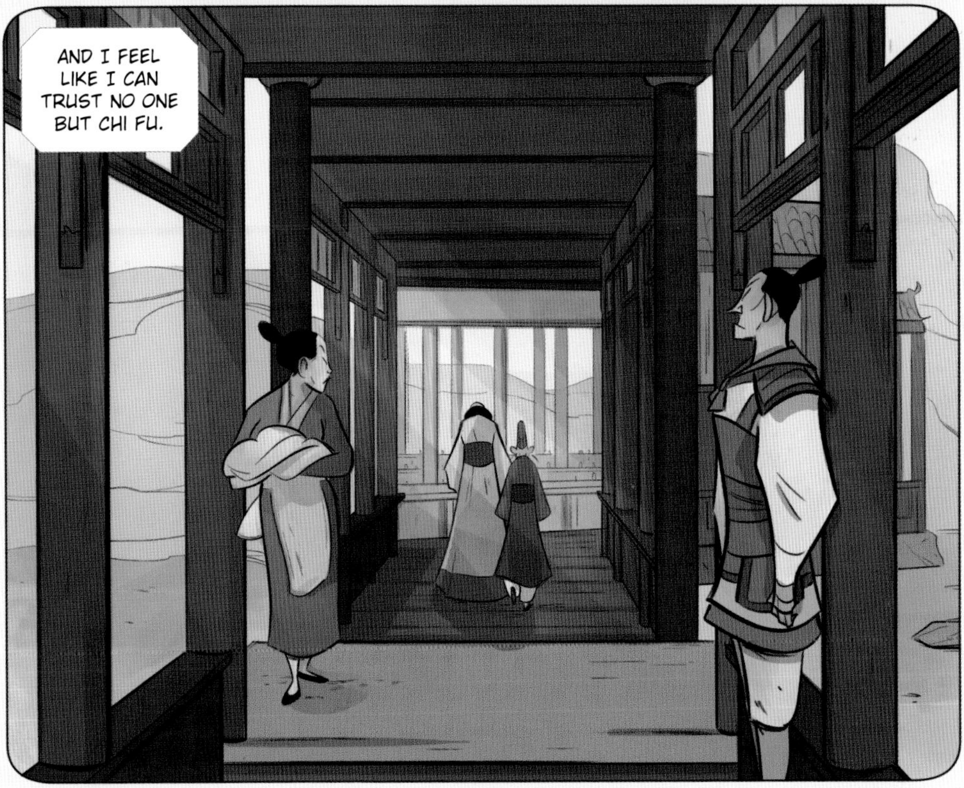
AND I FEEL LIKE I CAN TRUST NO ONE BUT CHI FU.

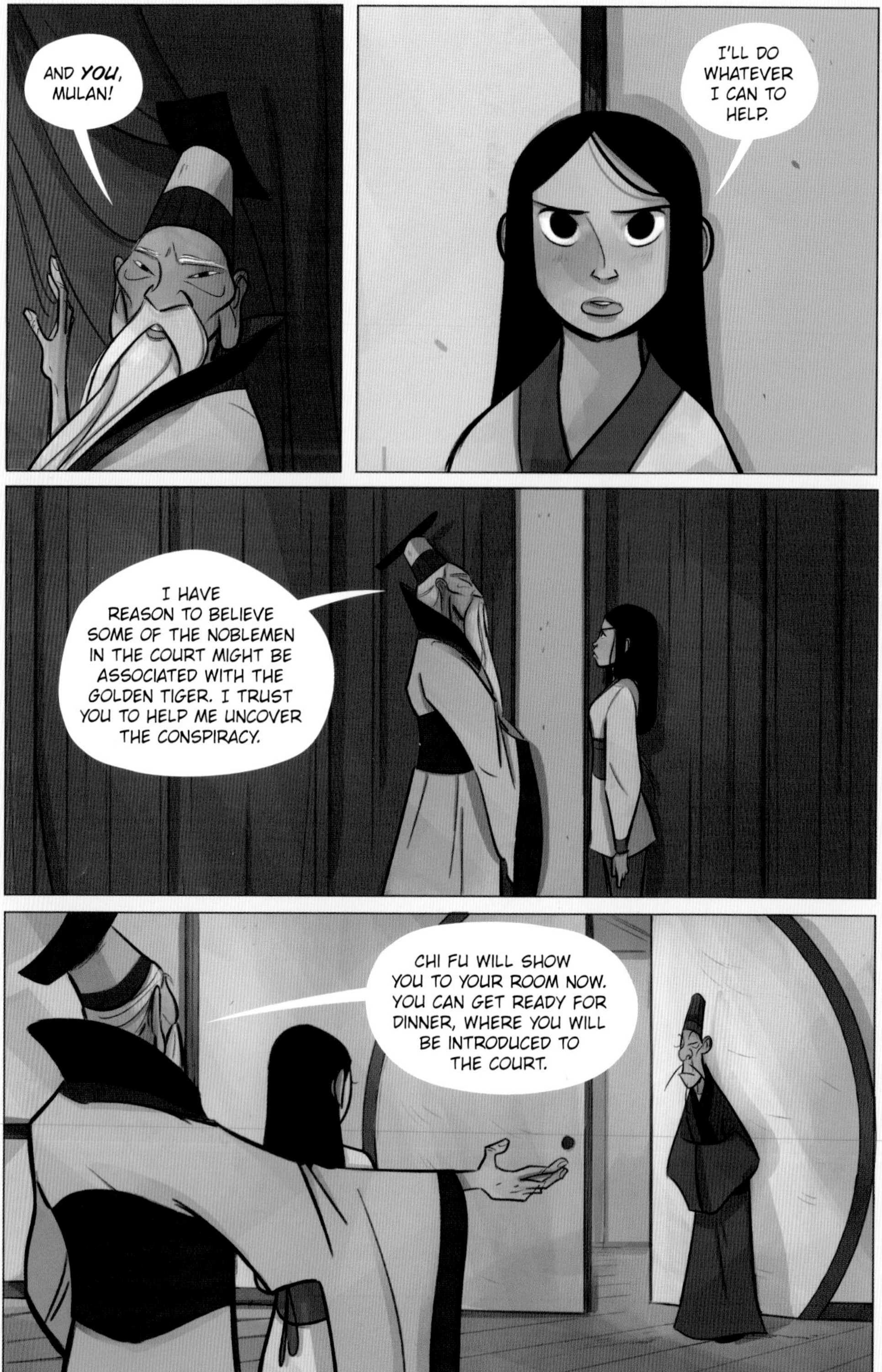
AND *YOU*, MULAN!
I'LL DO WHATEVER I CAN TO HELP.
I HAVE REASON TO BELIEVE SOME OF THE NOBLEMEN IN THE COURT MIGHT BE ASSOCIATED WITH THE GOLDEN TIGER. I TRUST YOU TO HELP ME UNCOVER THE CONSPIRACY.
CHI FU WILL SHOW YOU TO YOUR ROOM NOW. YOU CAN GET READY FOR DINNER, WHERE YOU WILL BE INTRODUCED TO THE COURT.

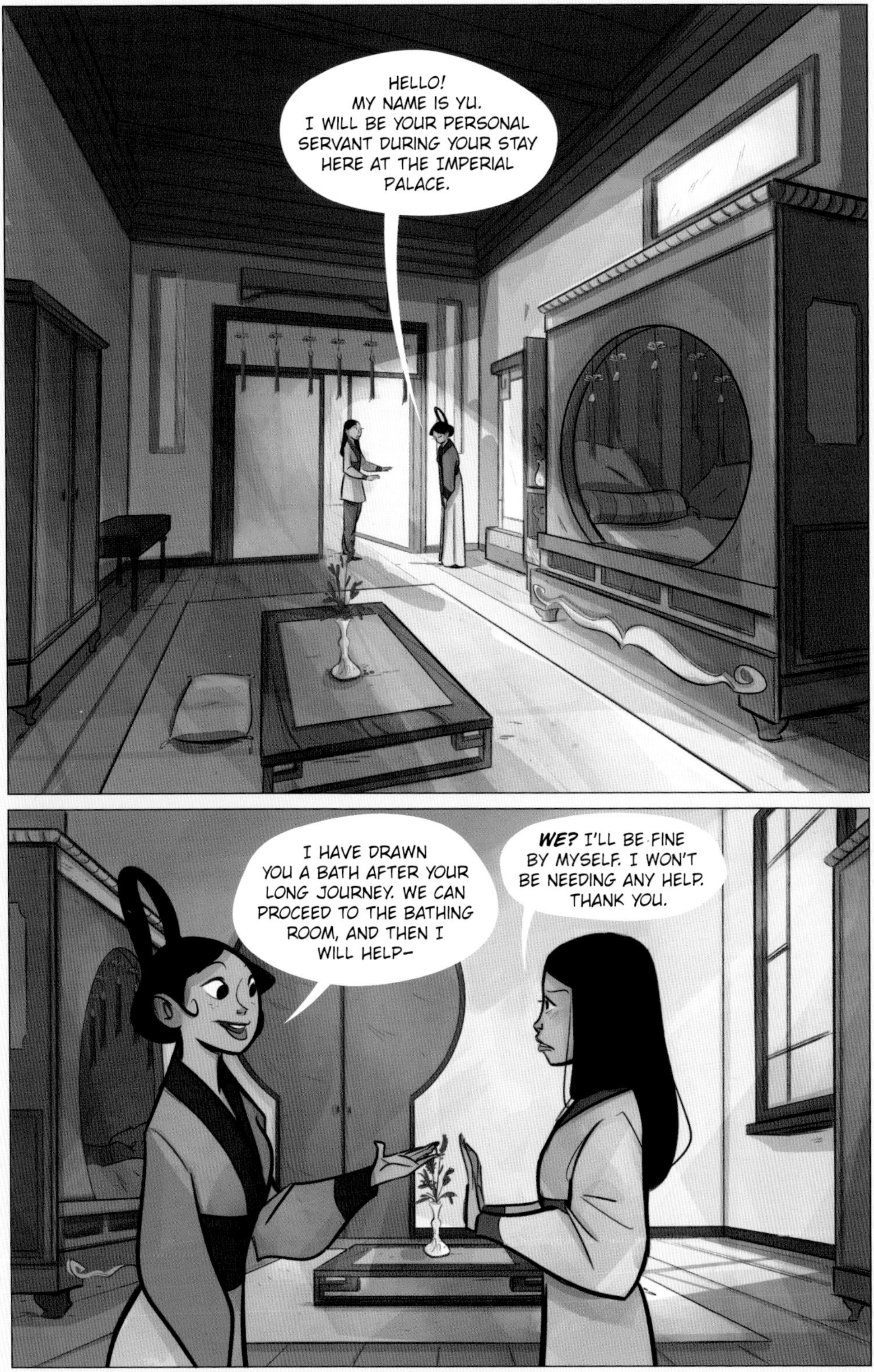
HELLO! MY NAME IS YU. I WILL BE YOUR PERSONAL SERVANT DURING YOUR STAY HERE AT THE IMPERIAL PALACE.
I HAVE DRAWN YOU A BATH AFTER YOUR LONG JOURNEY. WE CAN PROCEED TO THE BATHING ROOM, AND THEN I WILL HELP–
WE? I'LL BE FINE BY MYSELF. I WON'T BE NEEDING ANY HELP. THANK YOU.

I never could have imagined that I would end up as a guest at the Imperial Palace, but here I am. My bedroom is huge: You could fit Mother and Father's entire house in this bedroom alone!

The whole palace is decked out for the Spring Festival with fresh flowers and red lanterns everywhere. But even with all this beauty around, inside the palace you constantly feel under siege. There are guards everywhere.

Hearing about the Golden Tiger has me a little on edge. I'm glad Grandma is here with me. It already looks like the Emperor and Grandma will get along well. She seems more comfortable here than I am!

And then there's Chi Fu. I'm not sure I'm ever going to get on that guy's good side. He hasn't even fallen for Grandma's charms yet—and that's saying something!

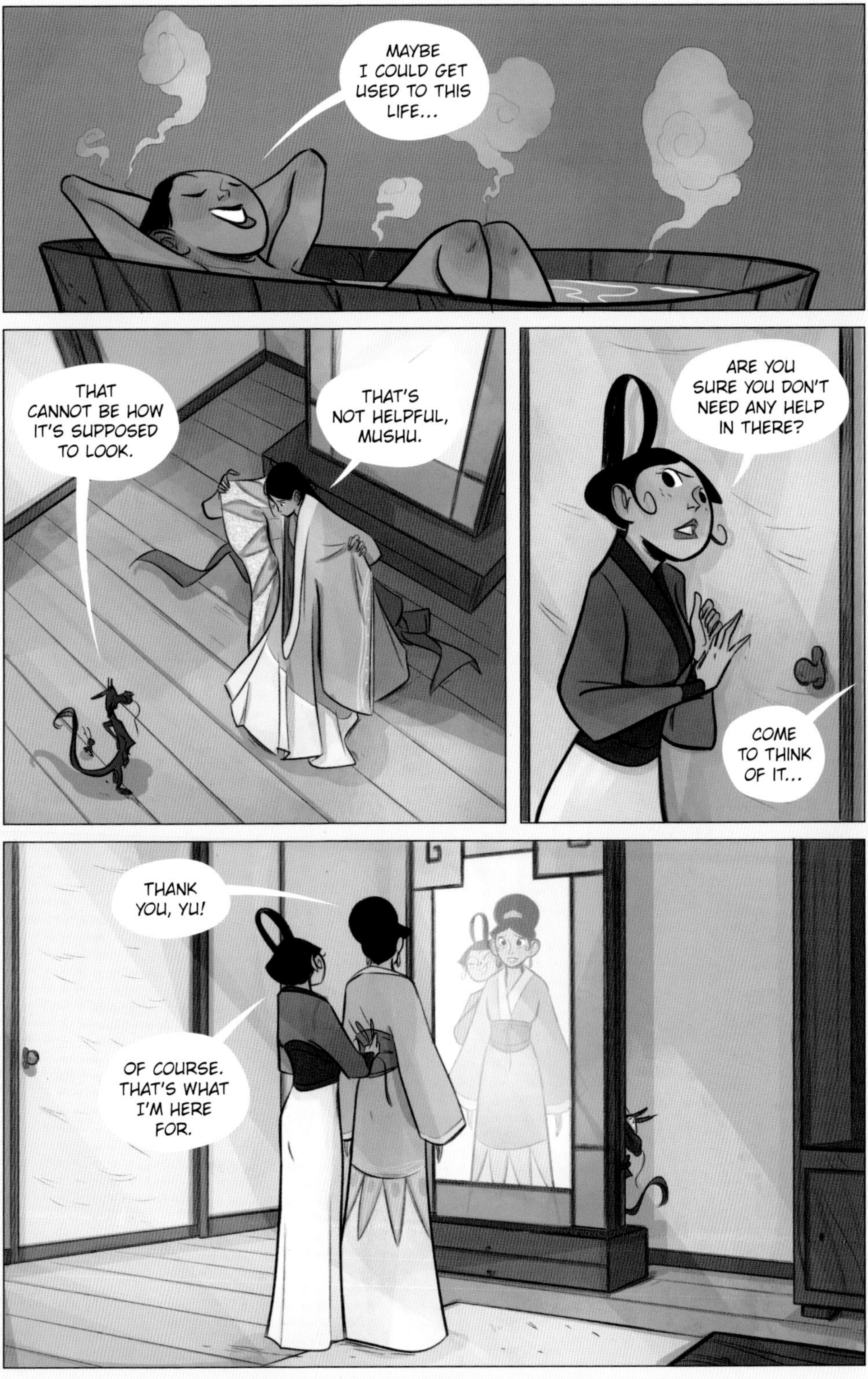
MAYBE I COULD GET USED TO THIS LIFE...
THAT CANNOT BE HOW IT'S SUPPOSED TO LOOK.
THAT'S NOT HELPFUL, MUSHU.
ARE YOU SURE YOU DON'T NEED ANY HELP IN THERE?
COME TO THINK OF IT...
THANK YOU, YU!
OF COURSE. THAT'S WHAT I'M HERE FOR.

I was less nervous going into battle with the Huns than I am about going to this dinner full of noble people tonight. I fear that everyone is going to laugh at me and tell me I don't belong here. If it wasn't for Yu I don't think I would have even managed to get into my formal robe!

I know the Emperor must think highly of me or he wouldn't have invited me here. I just don't want to let him down.

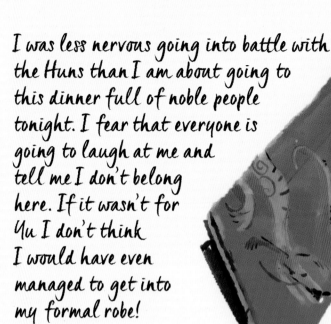

I have to remind myself that the real reason I'm here is to protect the Emperor, not to wear fancy dresses and makeup, and bow to people. Of course, I have to do all of those things, too... Wish me luck!

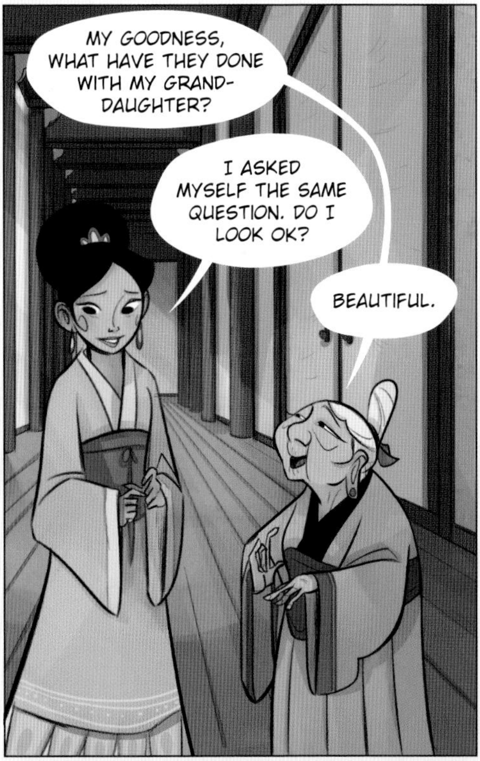
MY GOODNESS, WHAT HAVE THEY DONE WITH MY GRAND-DAUGHTER?
I ASKED MYSELF THE SAME QUESTION. DO I LOOK OK?
BEAUTIFUL.

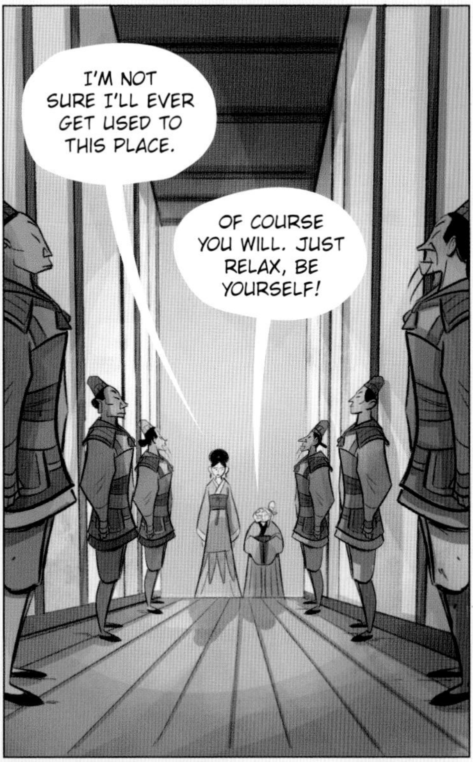
I'M NOT SURE I'LL EVER GET USED TO THIS PLACE.
OF COURSE YOU WILL. JUST RELAX, BE YOURSELF!

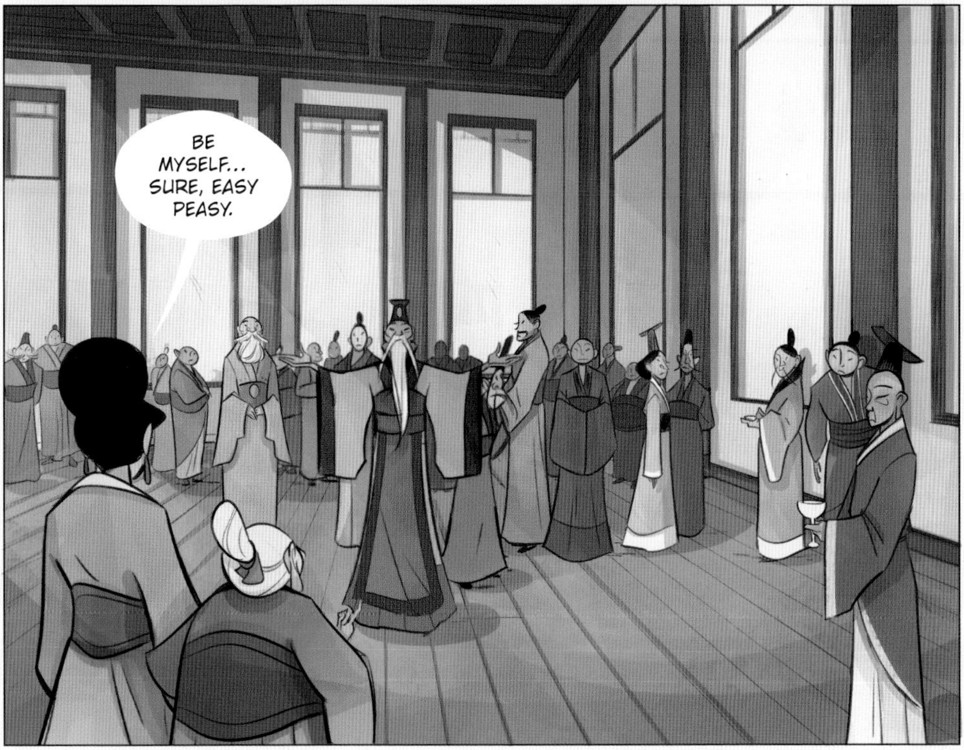
BE MYSELF... SURE, EASY PEASY.

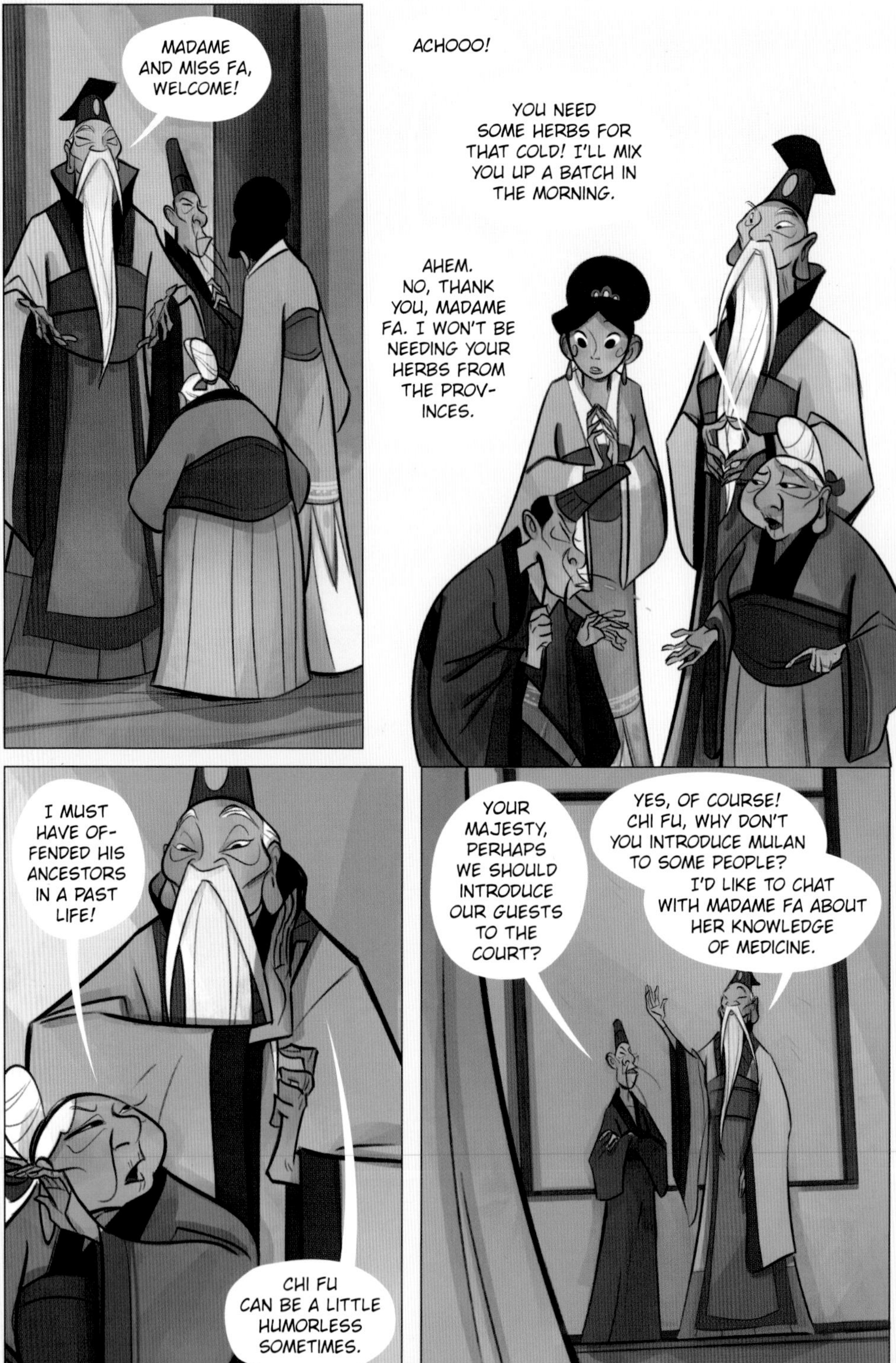
MADAME AND MISS FA, WELCOME!
ACHOOO!
YOU NEED SOME HERBS FOR THAT COLD! I'LL MIX YOU UP A BATCH IN THE MORNING.
AHEM. NO, THANK YOU, MADAME FA. I WON'T BE NEEDING YOUR HERBS FROM THE PROV-INCES.
I MUST HAVE OF-FENDED HIS ANCESTORS IN A PAST LIFE!
CHI FU CAN BE A LITTLE HUMORLESS SOMETIMES.
YOUR MAJESTY, PERHAPS WE SHOULD INTRODUCE OUR GUESTS TO THE COURT?
YES, OF COURSE! CHI FU, WHY DON'T YOU INTRODUCE MULAN TO SOME PEOPLE?
I'D LIKE TO CHAT WITH MADAME FA ABOUT HER KNOWLEDGE OF MEDICINE.

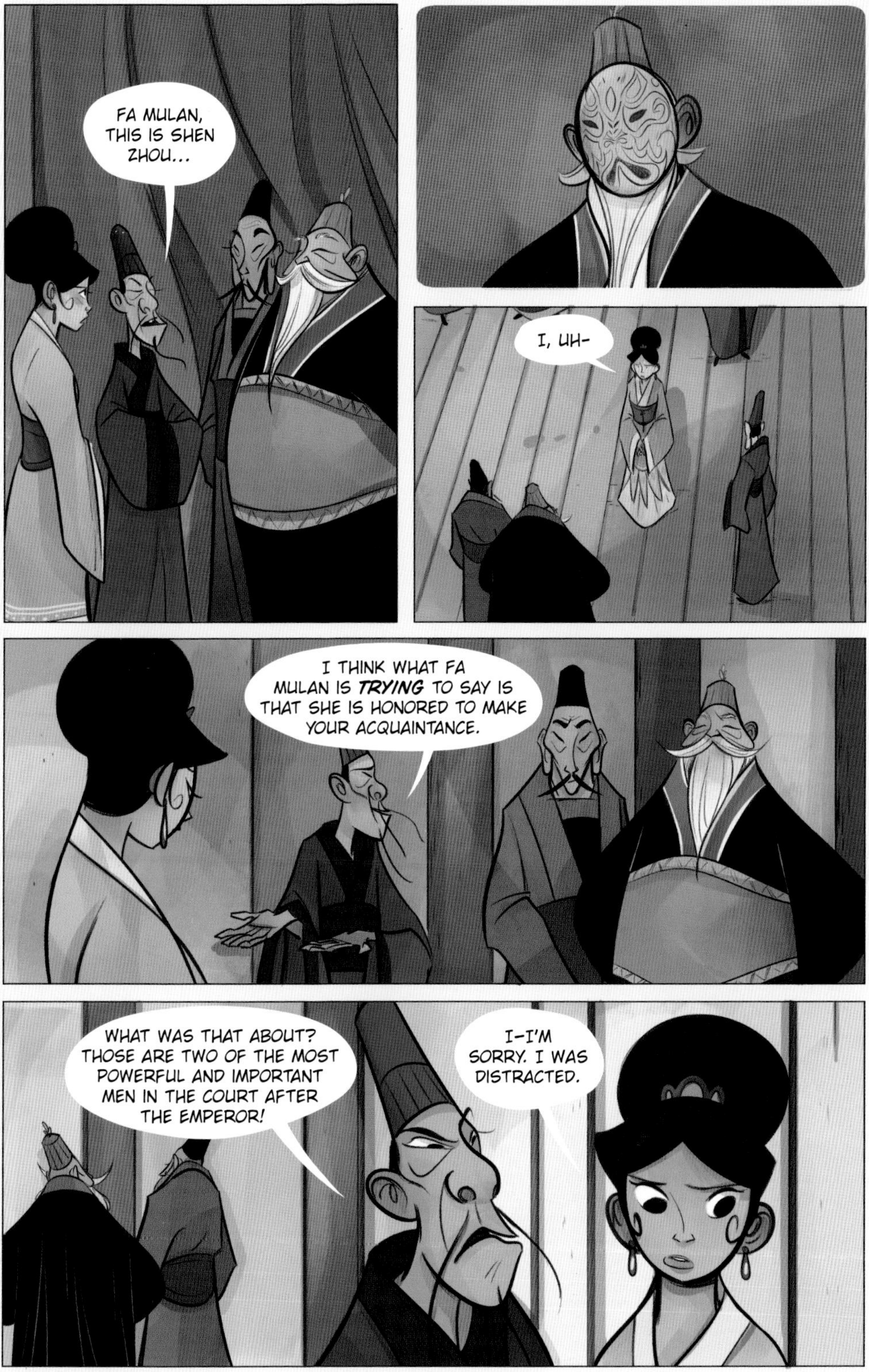
FA MULAN, THIS IS SHEN ZHOU...
I, UH-
I THINK WHAT FA MULAN IS ***TRYING*** TO SAY IS THAT SHE IS HONORED TO MAKE YOUR ACQUAINTANCE.
WHAT WAS THAT ABOUT? THOSE ARE TWO OF THE MOST POWERFUL AND IMPORTANT MEN IN THE COURT AFTER THE EMPEROR!
I-I'M SORRY. I WAS DISTRACTED.

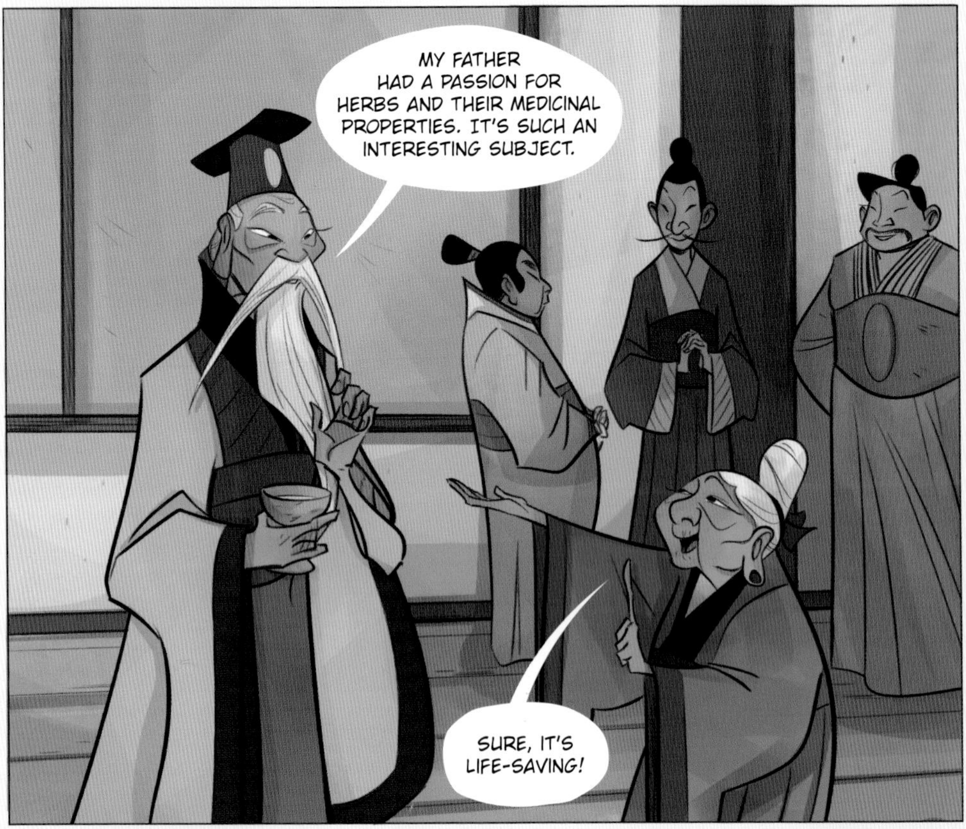
MY FATHER HAD A PASSION FOR HERBS AND THEIR MEDICINAL PROPERTIES. IT'S SUCH AN INTERESTING SUBJECT.
SURE, IT'S LIFE-SAVING!

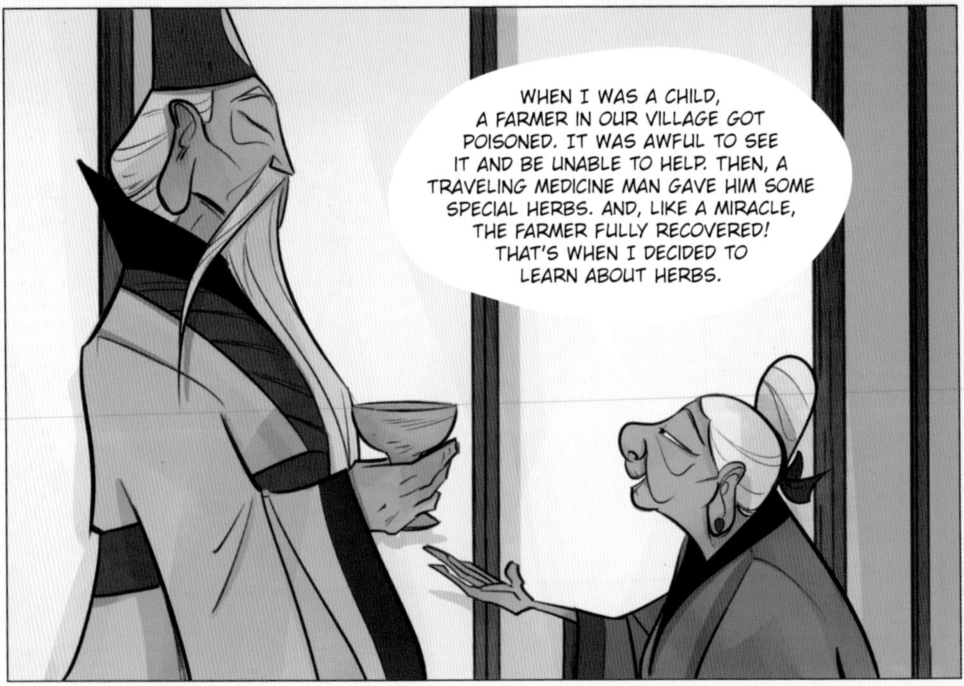
WHEN I WAS A CHILD, A FARMER IN OUR VILLAGE GOT POISONED. IT WAS AWFUL TO SEE IT AND BE UNABLE TO HELP. THEN, A TRAVELING MEDICINE MAN GAVE HIM SOME SPECIAL HERBS. AND, LIKE A MIRACLE, THE FARMER FULLY RECOVERED! THAT'S WHEN I DECIDED TO LEARN ABOUT HERBS.

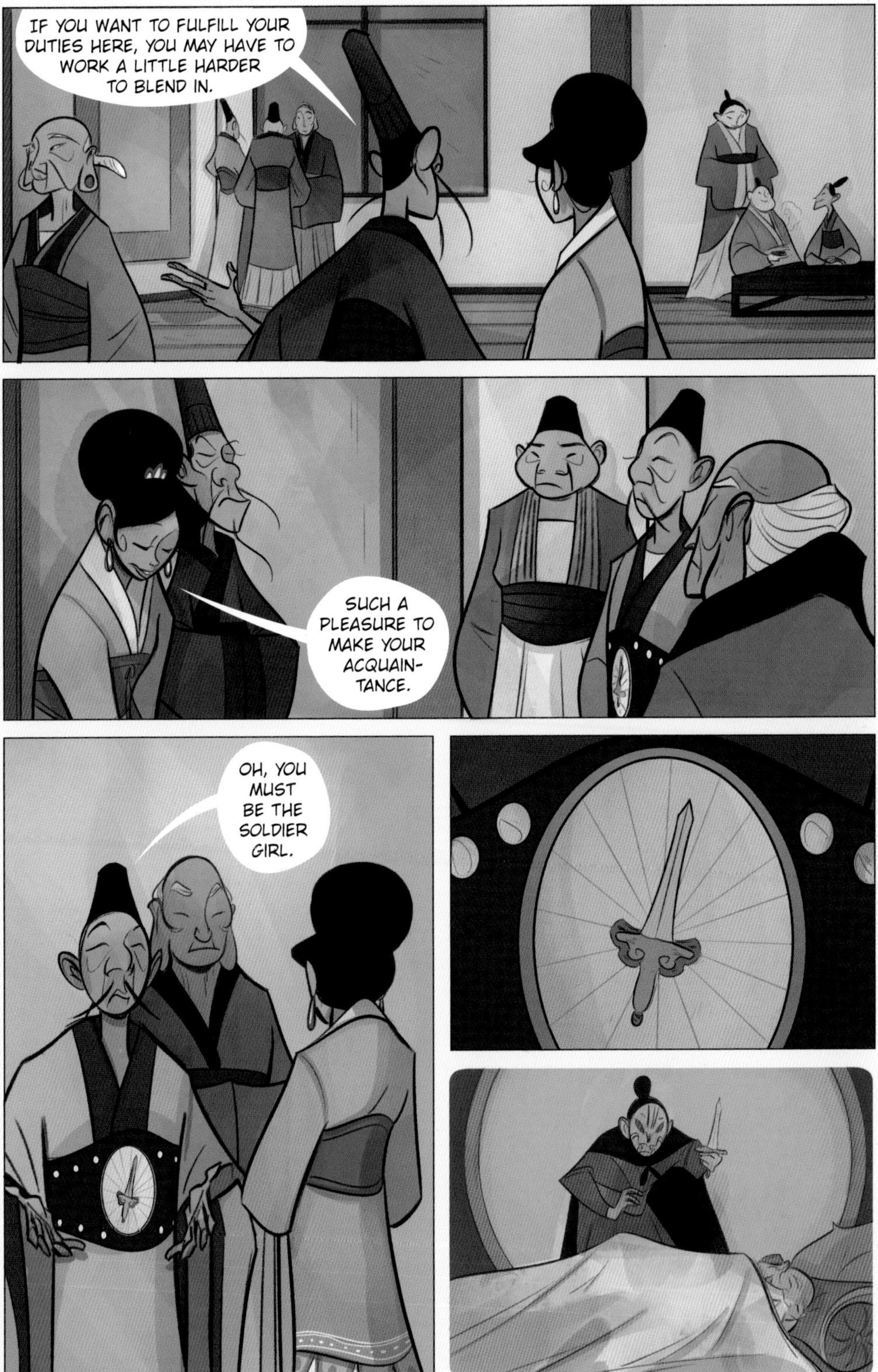
IF YOU WANT TO FULFILL YOUR DUTIES HERE, YOU MAY HAVE TO WORK A LITTLE HARDER TO BLEND IN.
SUCH A PLEASURE TO MAKE YOUR ACQUAIN-TANCE.
OH, YOU MUST BE THE SOLDIER GIRL.

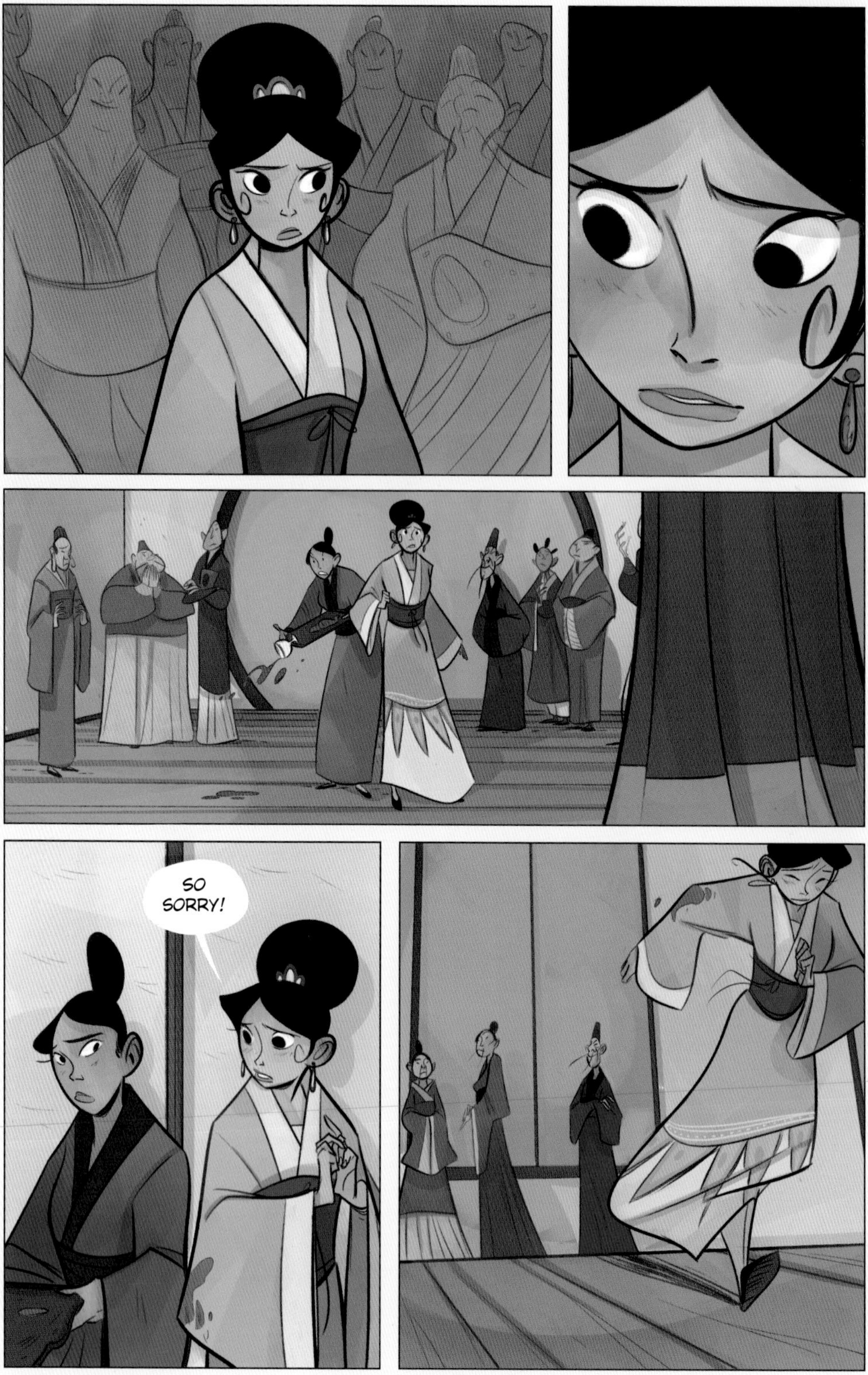
SO SORRY!

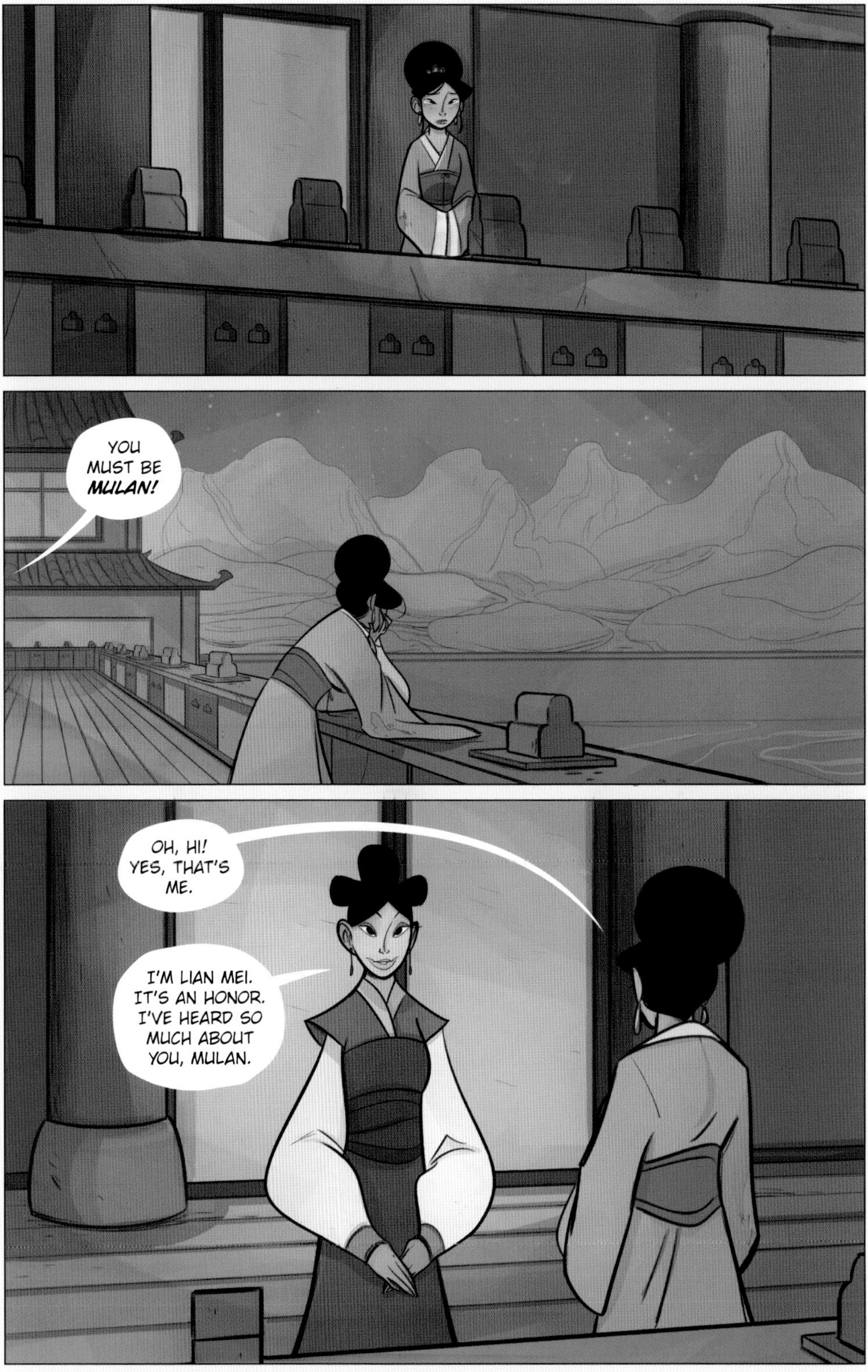
YOU MUST BE MULAN!
OH, HI! YES, THAT'S ME.
I'M LIAN MEI. IT'S AN HONOR. I'VE HEARD SO MUCH ABOUT YOU, MULAN.

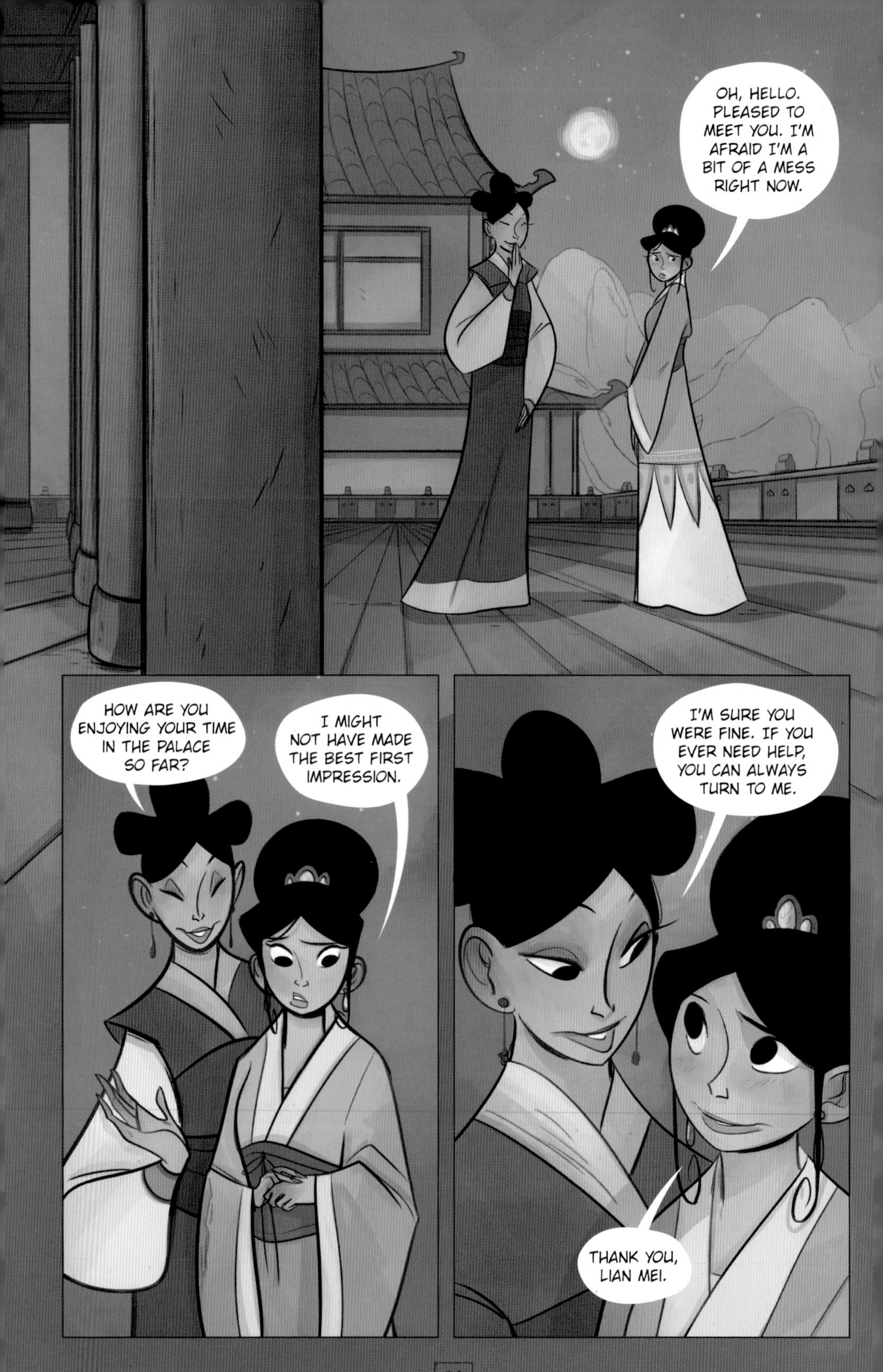

OH, HELLO. PLEASED TO MEET YOU. I'M AFRAID I'M A BIT OF A MESS RIGHT NOW.
HOW ARE YOU ENJOYING YOUR TIME IN THE PALACE SO FAR?
I MIGHT NOT HAVE MADE THE BEST FIRST IMPRESSION.
I'M SURE YOU WERE FINE. IF YOU EVER NEED HELP, YOU CAN ALWAYS TURN TO ME.
THANK YOU, LIAN MEI.

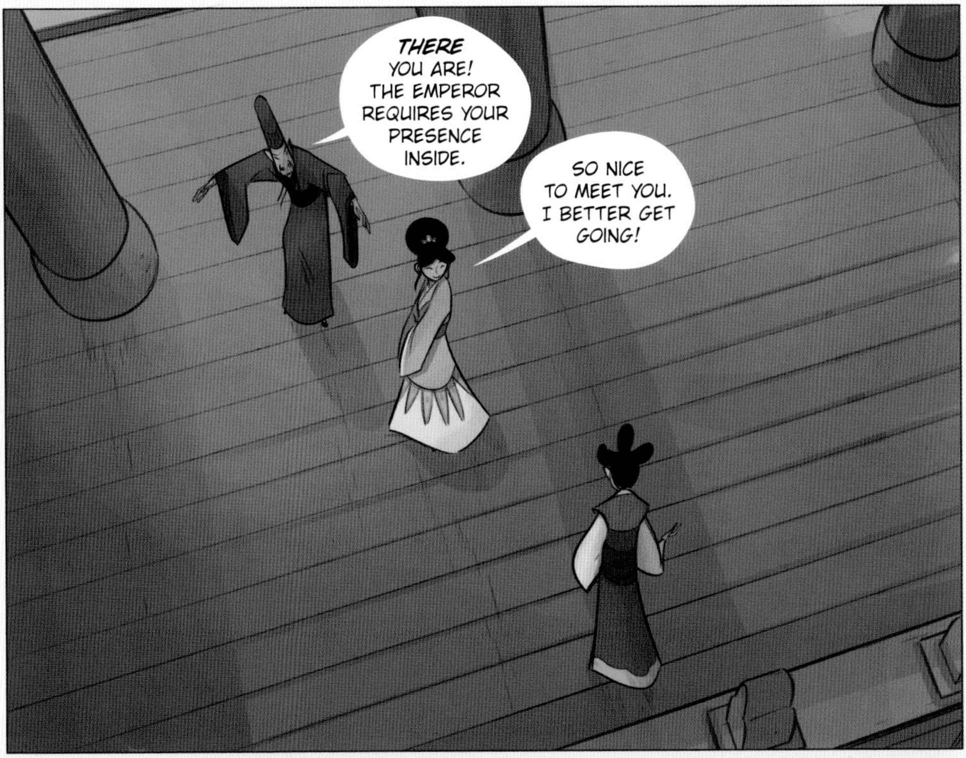
THERE YOU ARE! THE EMPEROR REQUIRES YOUR PRESENCE INSIDE.
SO NICE TO MEET YOU. I BETTER GET GOING!

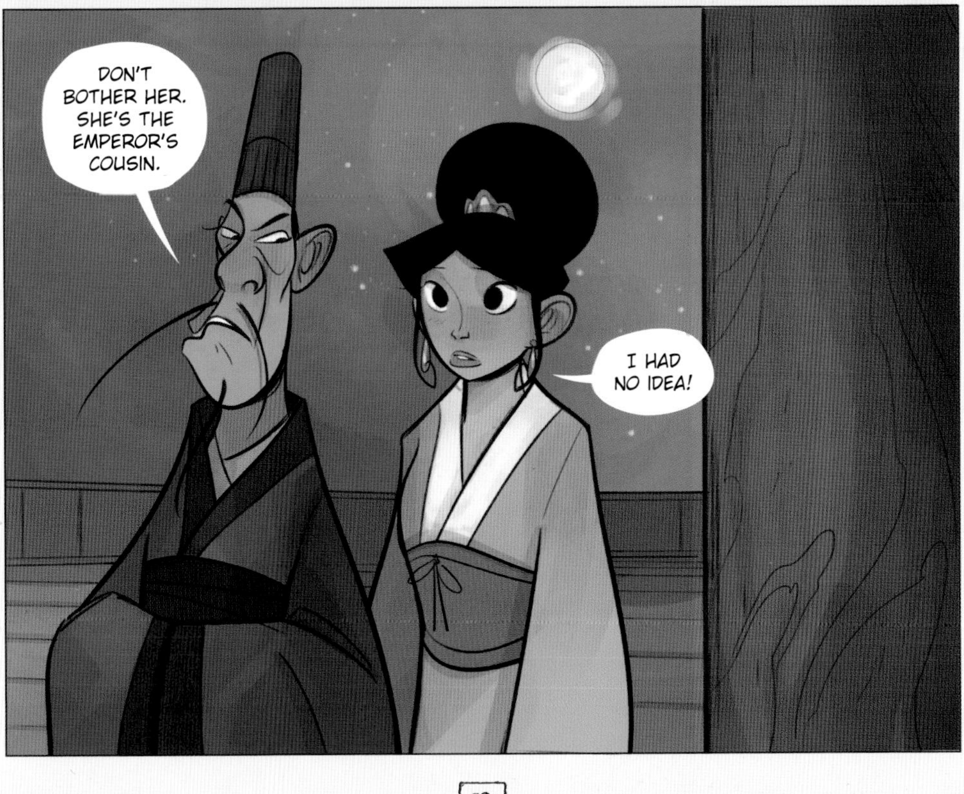
DON'T BOTHER HER. SHE'S THE EMPEROR'S COUSIN.
I HAD NO IDEA!

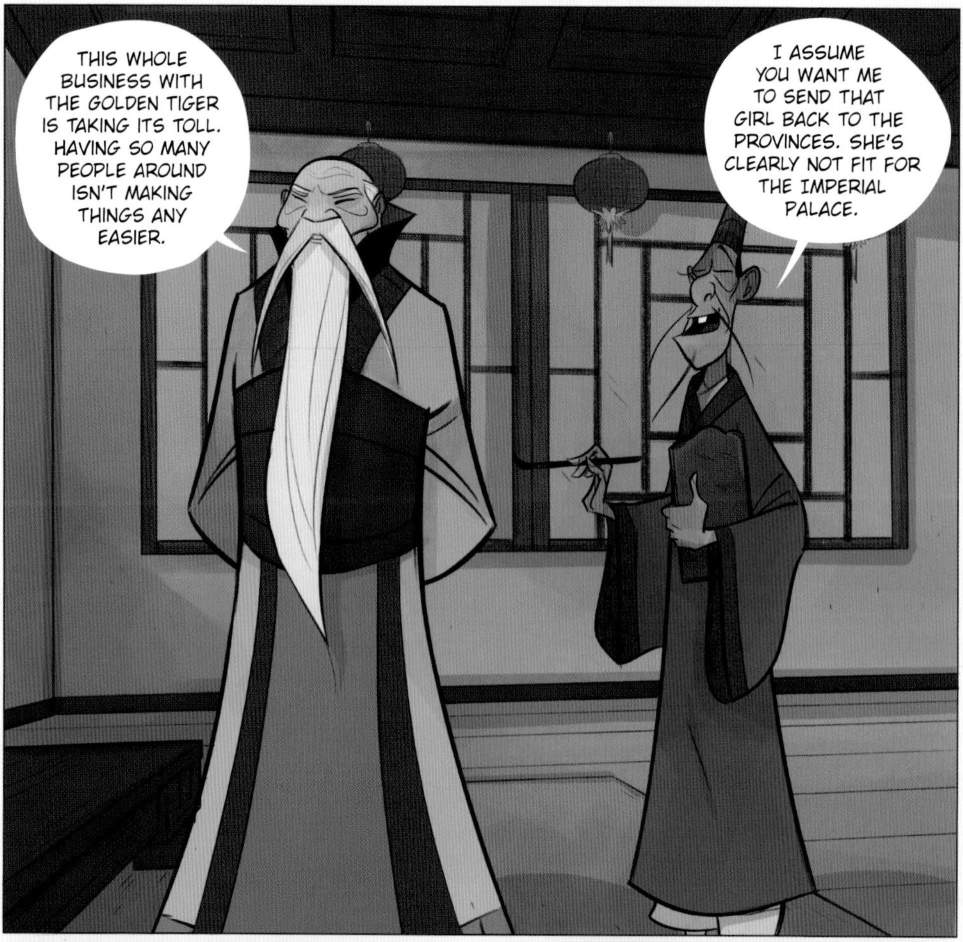
THIS WHOLE BUSINESS WITH THE GOLDEN TIGER IS TAKING ITS TOLL. HAVING SO MANY PEOPLE AROUND ISN'T MAKING THINGS ANY EASIER.
I ASSUME YOU WANT ME TO SEND THAT GIRL BACK TO THE PROVINCES. SHE'S CLEARLY NOT FIT FOR THE IMPERIAL PALACE.

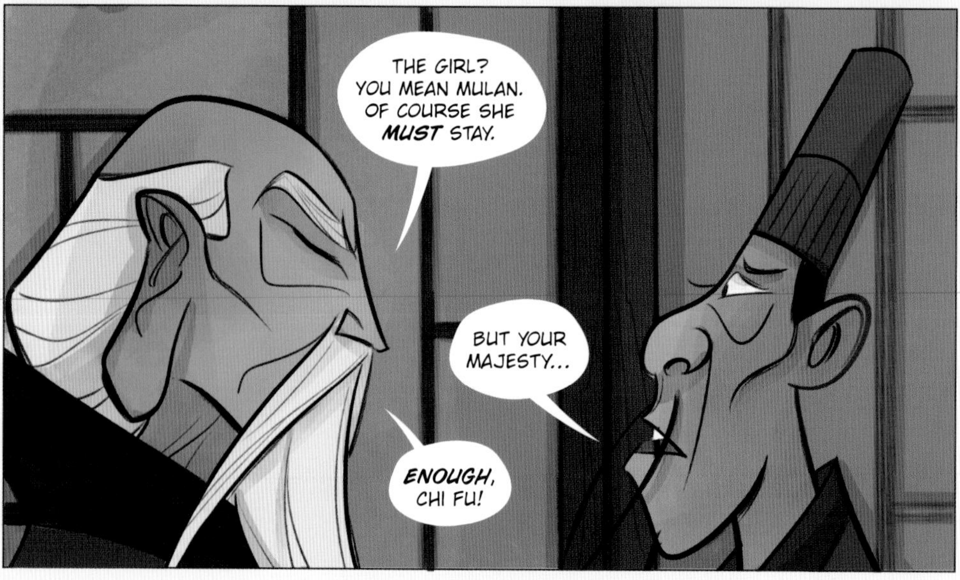
THE GIRL? YOU MEAN MULAN. OF COURSE SHE **MUST** STAY.
BUT YOUR MAJESTY...
ENOUGH, CHI FU!

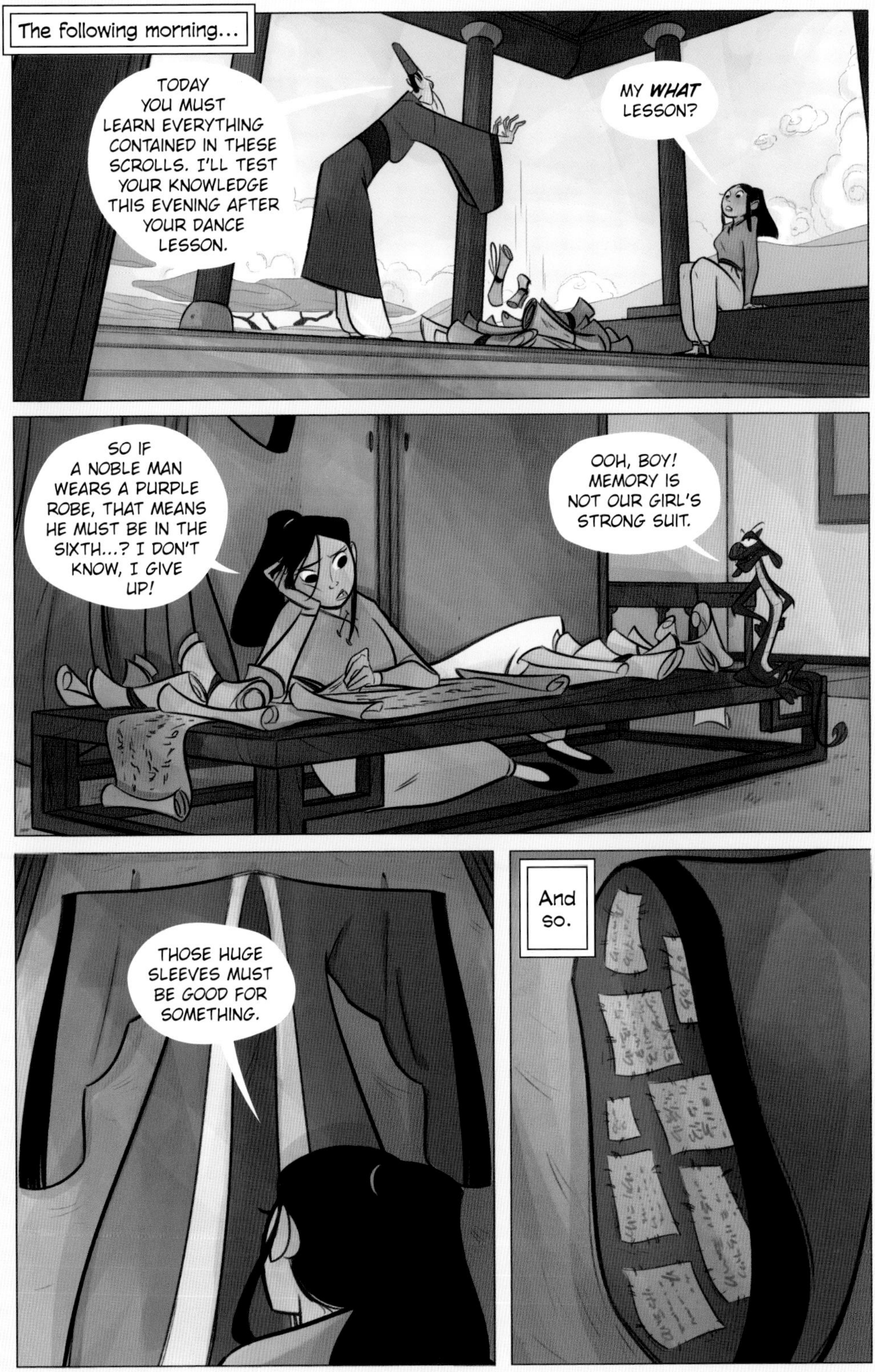
The following morning...
TODAY YOU MUST LEARN EVERYTHING CONTAINED IN THESE SCROLLS. I'LL TEST YOUR KNOWLEDGE THIS EVENING AFTER YOUR DANCE LESSON.
MY WHAT LESSON?
SO IF A NOBLE MAN WEARS A PURPLE ROBE, THAT MEANS HE MUST BE IN THE SIXTH...? I DON'T KNOW, I GIVE UP!
OOH, BOY! MEMORY IS NOT OUR GIRL'S STRONG SUIT.
THOSE HUGE SLEEVES MUST BE GOOD FOR SOMETHING.
And so.

Court Regulation Attire System

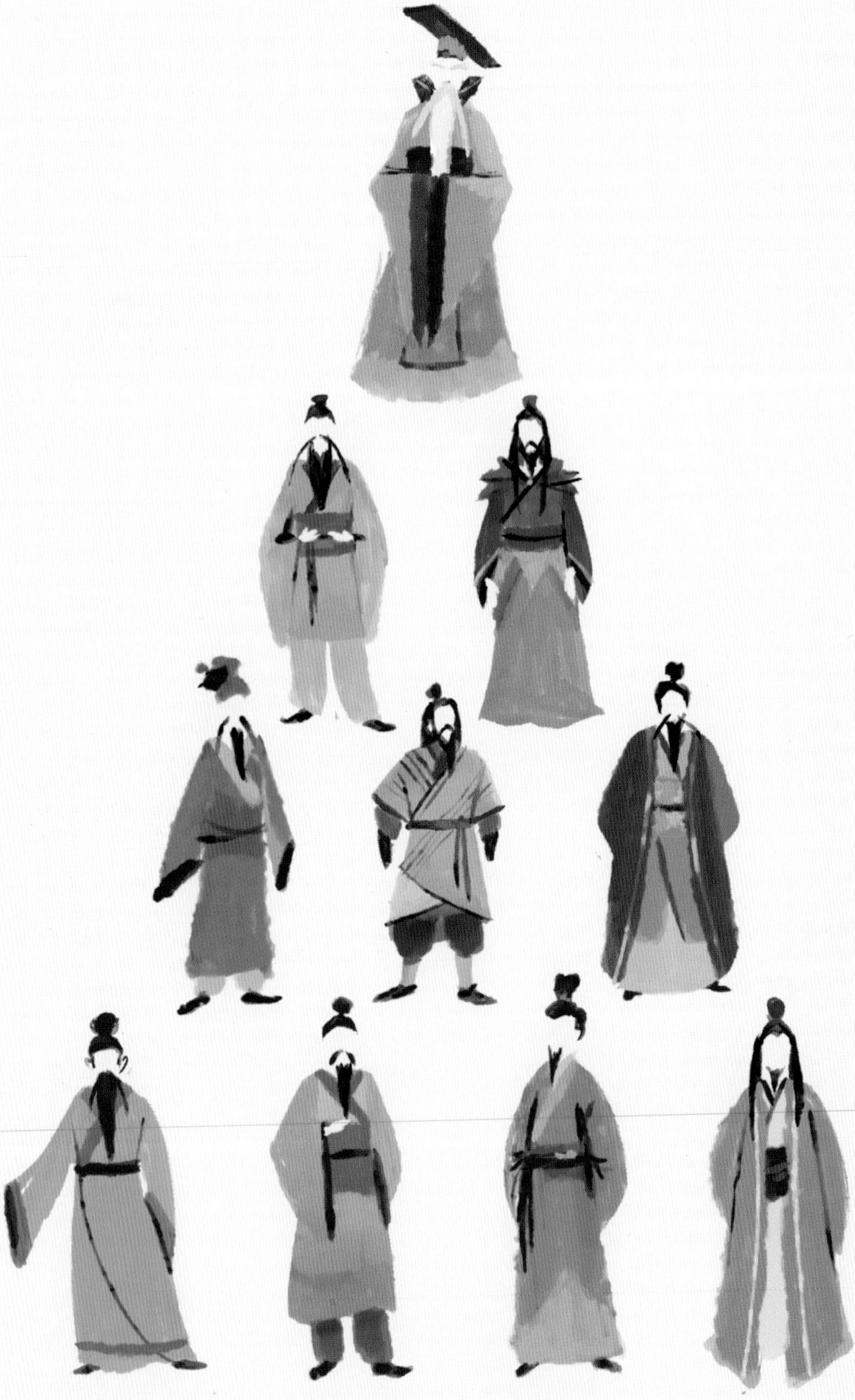

I'm so grateful for the Emperor's hospitality and I'm honored to be here for the Spring Festival, but this trip is already shaping up to be exhausting. I spent all day reading texts about court rankings, honorifics, and who knows what else. Chi Fu will be testing me, so I better have it all learned.

I think I made a fool of myself at the reception last night. There were so many high-ranking people there, I was overwhelmed. And then, at the back of my mind, I can't help but be a little suspicious of every single one of them. As I was doing my best to politely smile and bow to every new person, I was questioning if they were one of the members of the Golden Tiger... It's hard to look at those people without wondering who among them is plotting against the Emperor's life.

I'm definitely better suited to the life of a soldier on the battlefield than a noblewoman in court. Early morning training drills sound like a breeze compared to everything I'm learning here at the palace.

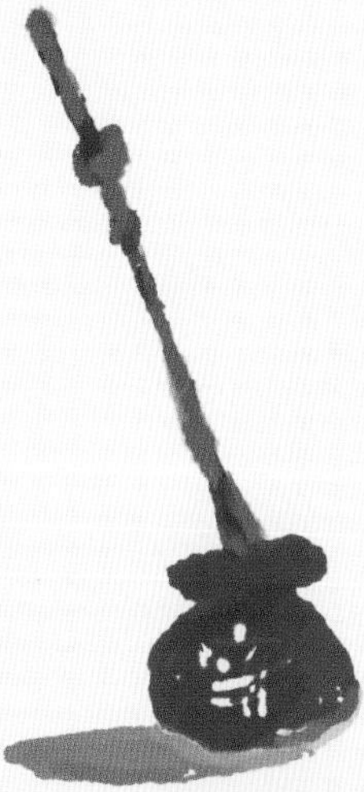

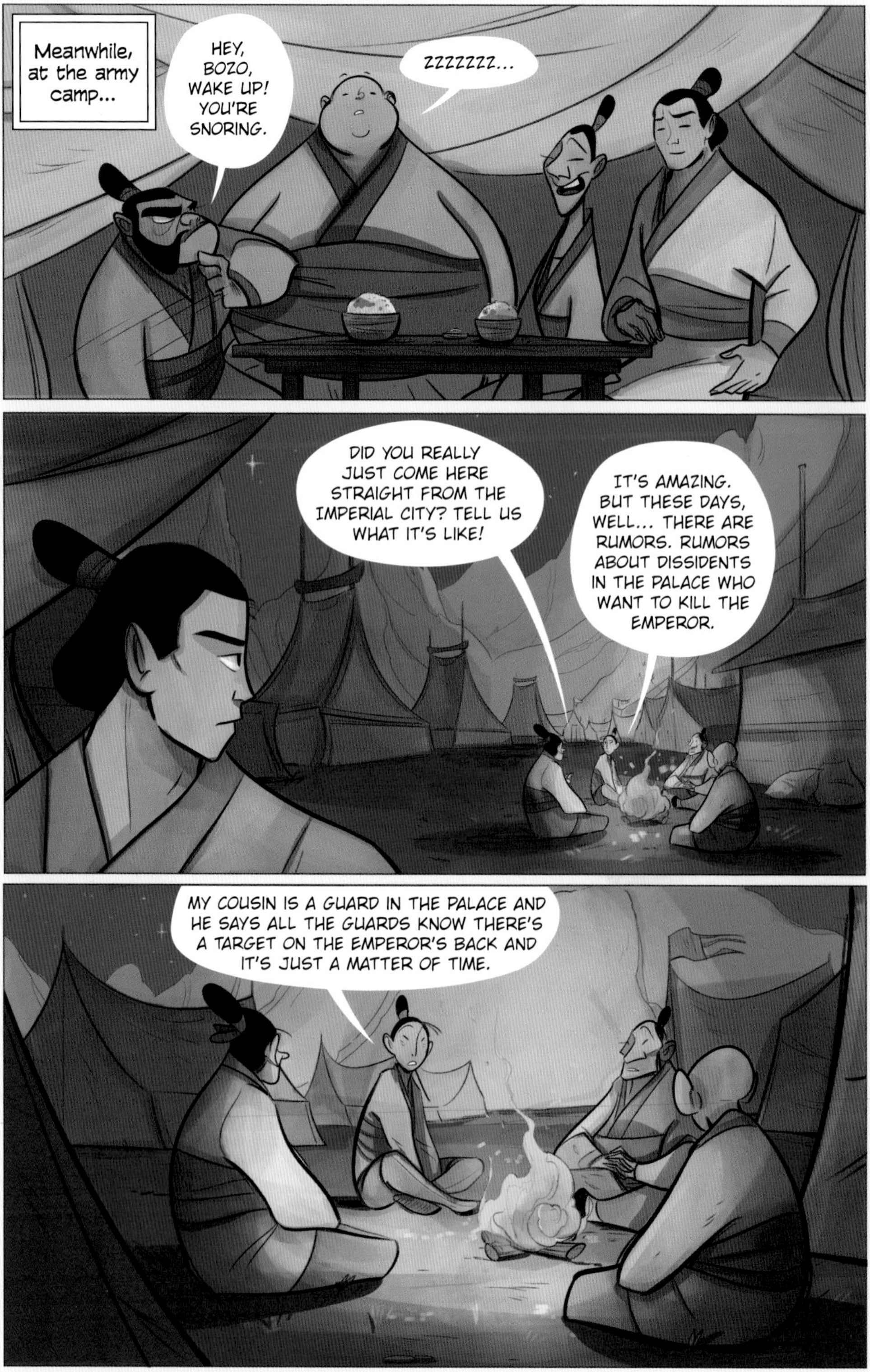
Meanwhile, at the army camp...
HEY, BOZO, WAKE UP! YOU'RE SNORING.
ZZZZZZZ...
DID YOU REALLY JUST COME HERE STRAIGHT FROM THE IMPERIAL CITY? TELL US WHAT IT'S LIKE!
IT'S AMAZING. BUT THESE DAYS, WELL... THERE ARE RUMORS. RUMORS ABOUT DISSIDENTS IN THE PALACE WHO WANT TO KILL THE EMPEROR.
MY COUSIN IS A GUARD IN THE PALACE AND HE SAYS ALL THE GUARDS KNOW THERE'S A TARGET ON THE EMPEROR'S BACK AND IT'S JUST A MATTER OF TIME.

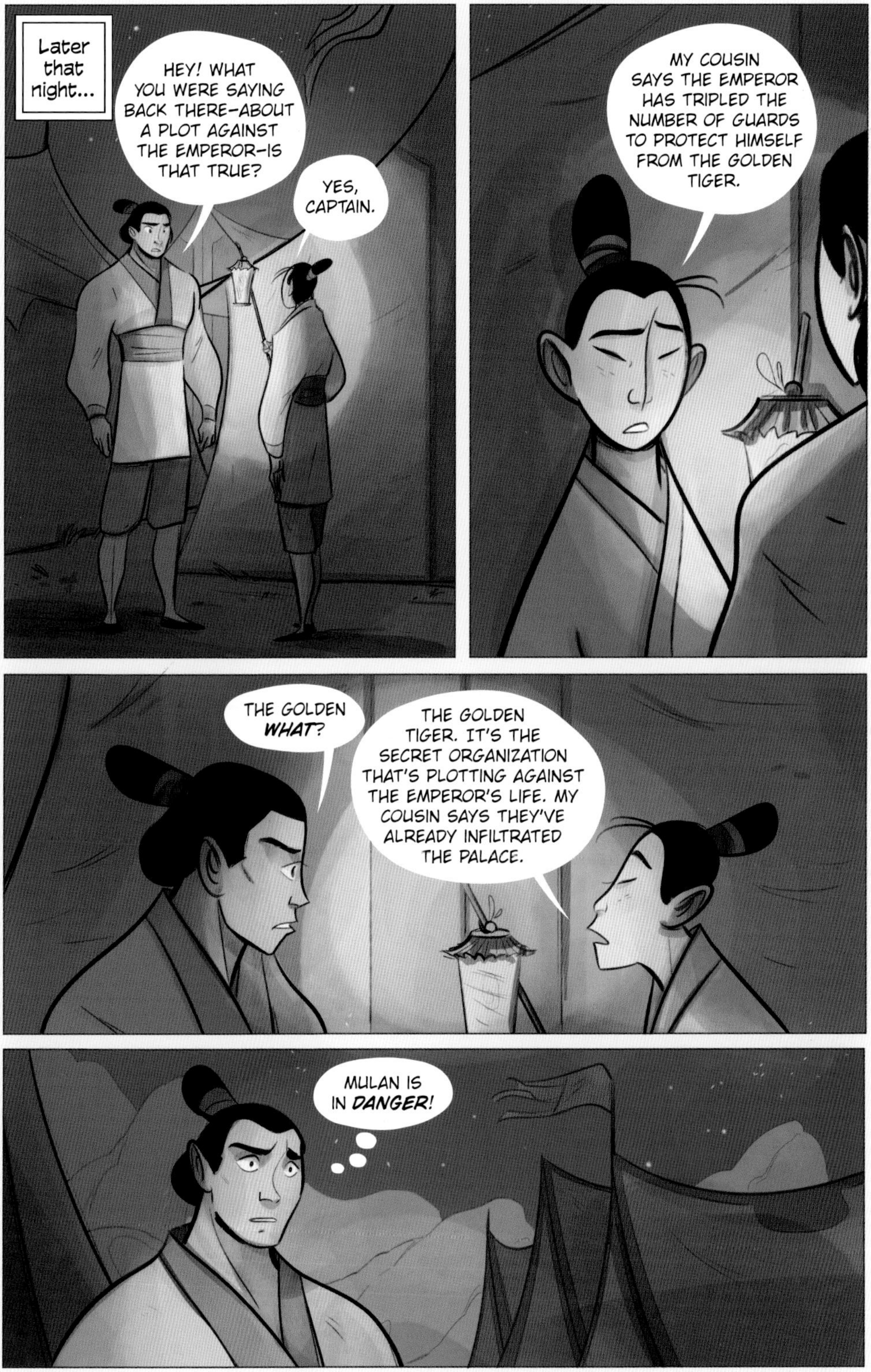
Later that night...
HEY! WHAT YOU WERE SAYING BACK THERE–ABOUT A PLOT AGAINST THE EMPEROR–IS THAT TRUE?
YES, CAPTAIN.
MY COUSIN SAYS THE EMPEROR HAS TRIPLED THE NUMBER OF GUARDS TO PROTECT HIMSELF FROM THE GOLDEN TIGER.
THE GOLDEN *WHAT*?
THE GOLDEN TIGER. IT'S THE SECRET ORGANIZATION THAT'S PLOTTING AGAINST THE EMPEROR'S LIFE. MY COUSIN SAYS THEY'VE ALREADY INFILTRATED THE PALACE.
MULAN IS IN *DANGER*!

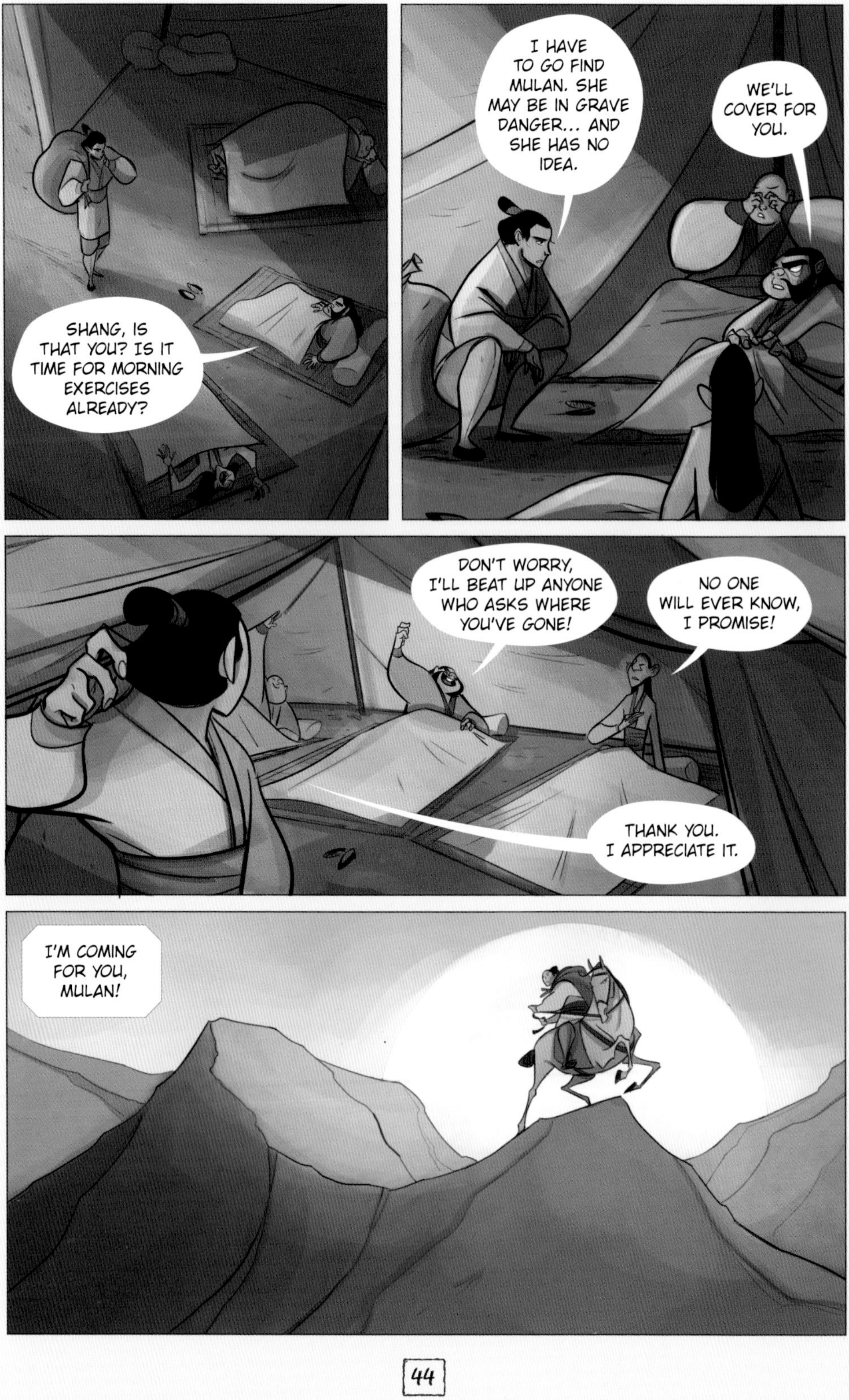
SHANG, IS THAT YOU? IS IT TIME FOR MORNING EXERCISES ALREADY?
I HAVE TO GO FIND MULAN. SHE MAY BE IN GRAVE DANGER... AND SHE HAS NO IDEA.
WE'LL COVER FOR YOU.
DON'T WORRY, I'LL BEAT UP ANYONE WHO ASKS WHERE YOU'VE GONE!
NO ONE WILL EVER KNOW, I PROMISE!
THANK YOU. I APPRECIATE IT.
I'M COMING FOR YOU, MULAN!

I'm so embarrassed! Yesterday I was going to the tea room when I accidentally interrupted a private meeting of some court officials... The palace is so full of doors and rooms within rooms, it's a like a maze! I explained that it was a mistake and everyone seemed to understand, but I did get an earful from Counselor Chi Fu afterwards. At least I'm learning from my mistakes... I think.

One of the few people in court that I feel at ease with is Princess Lian Mei. I'm so impressed by the way she seems to manage to live within the court rules and yet retain her strong spirit.

I've noticed that others seem to act nervous in her presence (she is the Emperor's cousin, after all), but luckily for me, I think she likes me. Sure, she can seem a bit distant sometimes, but I think that's probably a natural need for control that comes with living the life of an Imperial family member. I don't envy them.

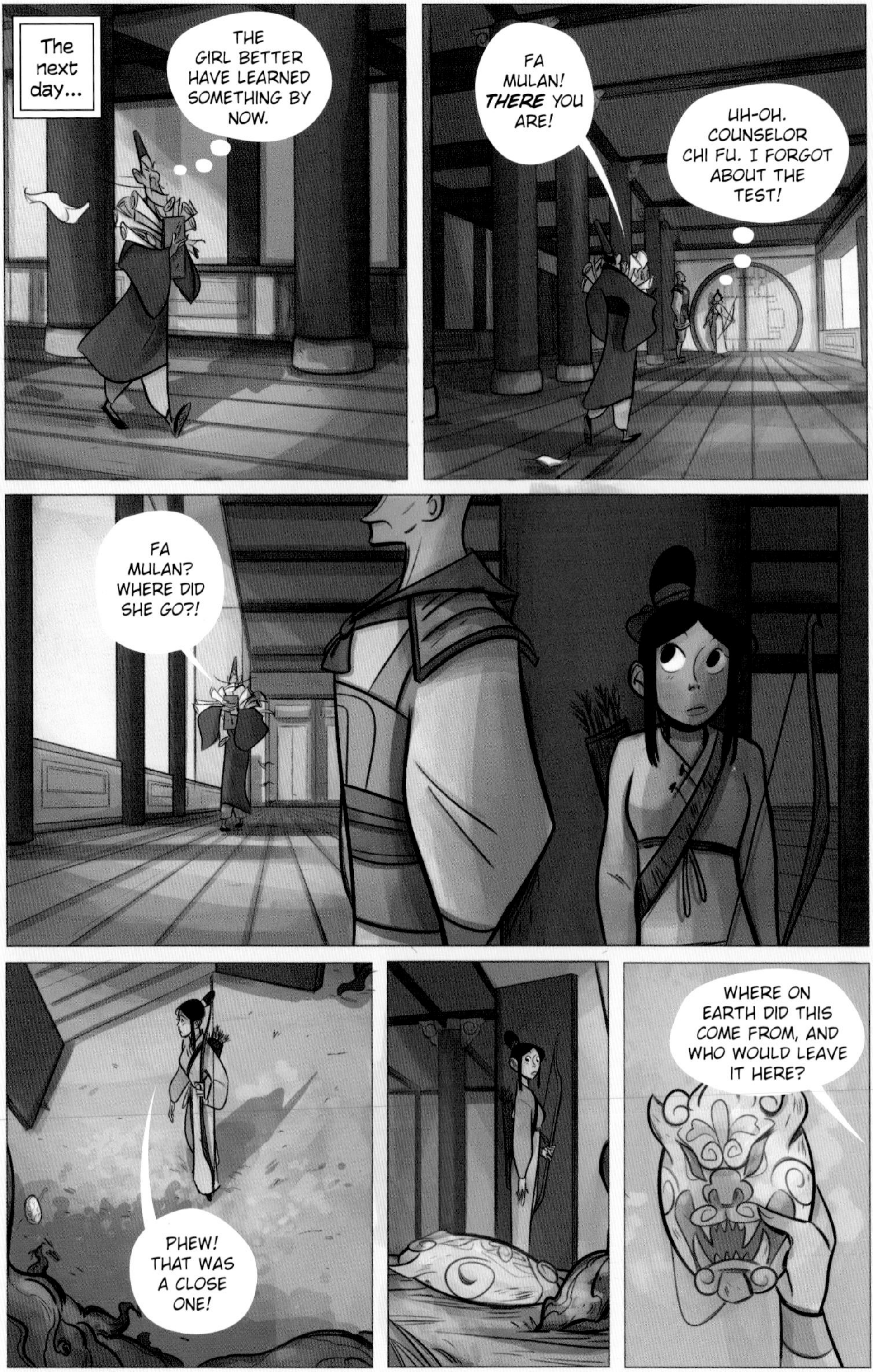
The next day...
THE GIRL BETTER HAVE LEARNED SOMETHING BY NOW.
FA MULAN! THERE YOU ARE!
UH-OH. COUNSELOR CHI FU. I FORGOT ABOUT THE TEST!
FA MULAN? WHERE DID SHE GO?!
PHEW! THAT WAS A CLOSE ONE!
WHERE ON EARTH DID THIS COME FROM, AND WHO WOULD LEAVE IT HERE?

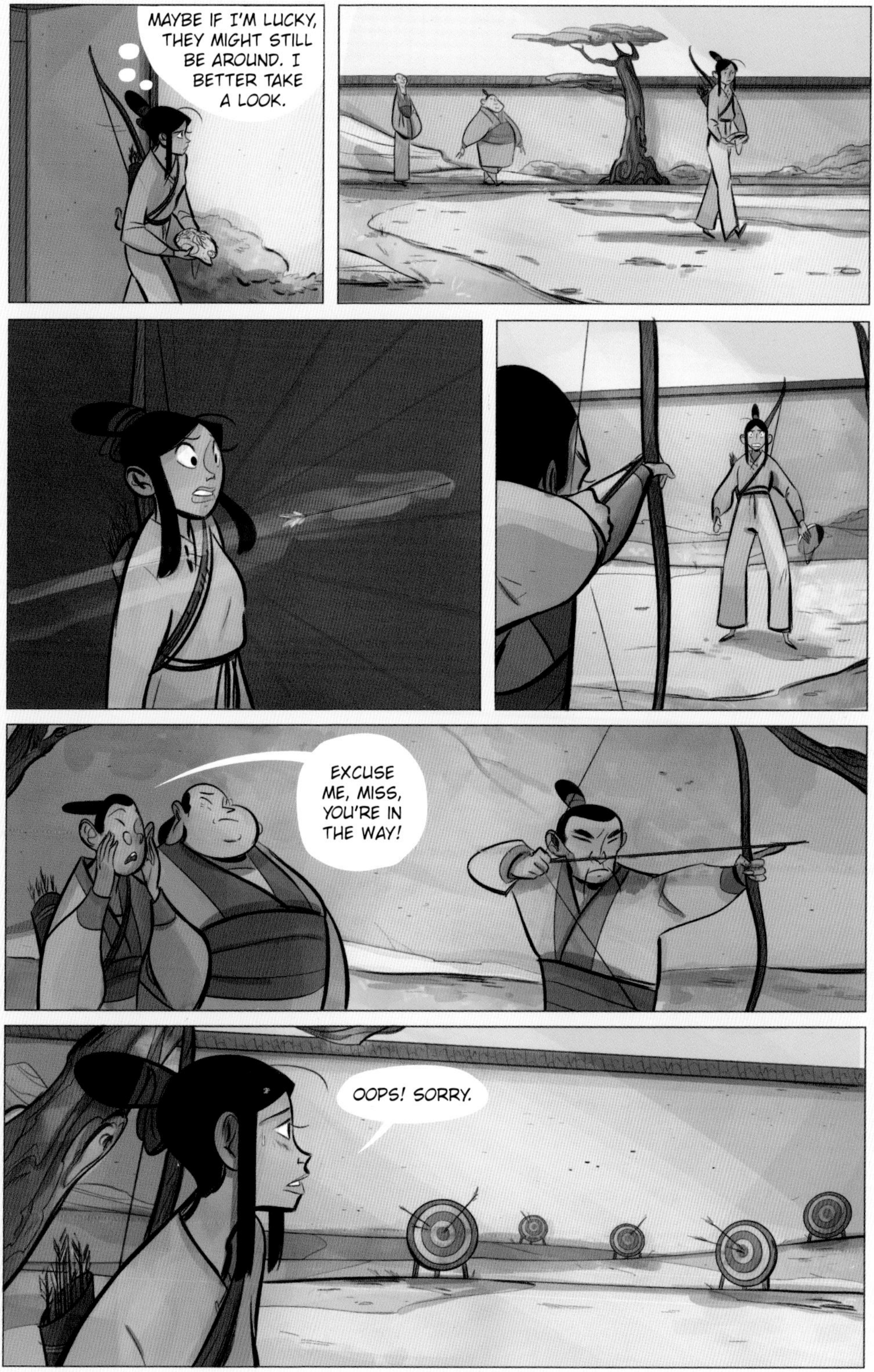
MAYBE IF I'M LUCKY, THEY MIGHT STILL BE AROUND. I BETTER TAKE A LOOK.
EXCUSE ME, MISS, YOU'RE IN THE WAY!
OOPS! SORRY.

It feels like I've been in the Imperial City forever, but I'm no closer to infiltrating the Golden Tiger than when I arrived.

I must have been to twenty state dinners, ten dance performances, and I've lost count of how many concerts. I'm honored to be able to participate, but I worry I'm not doing enough to help the Emperor.

There just has to be something I'm missing, some clue that would unlock the whole mystery and help me save the Emperor.

The question is: Who or what is the secret hiding in plain sight?

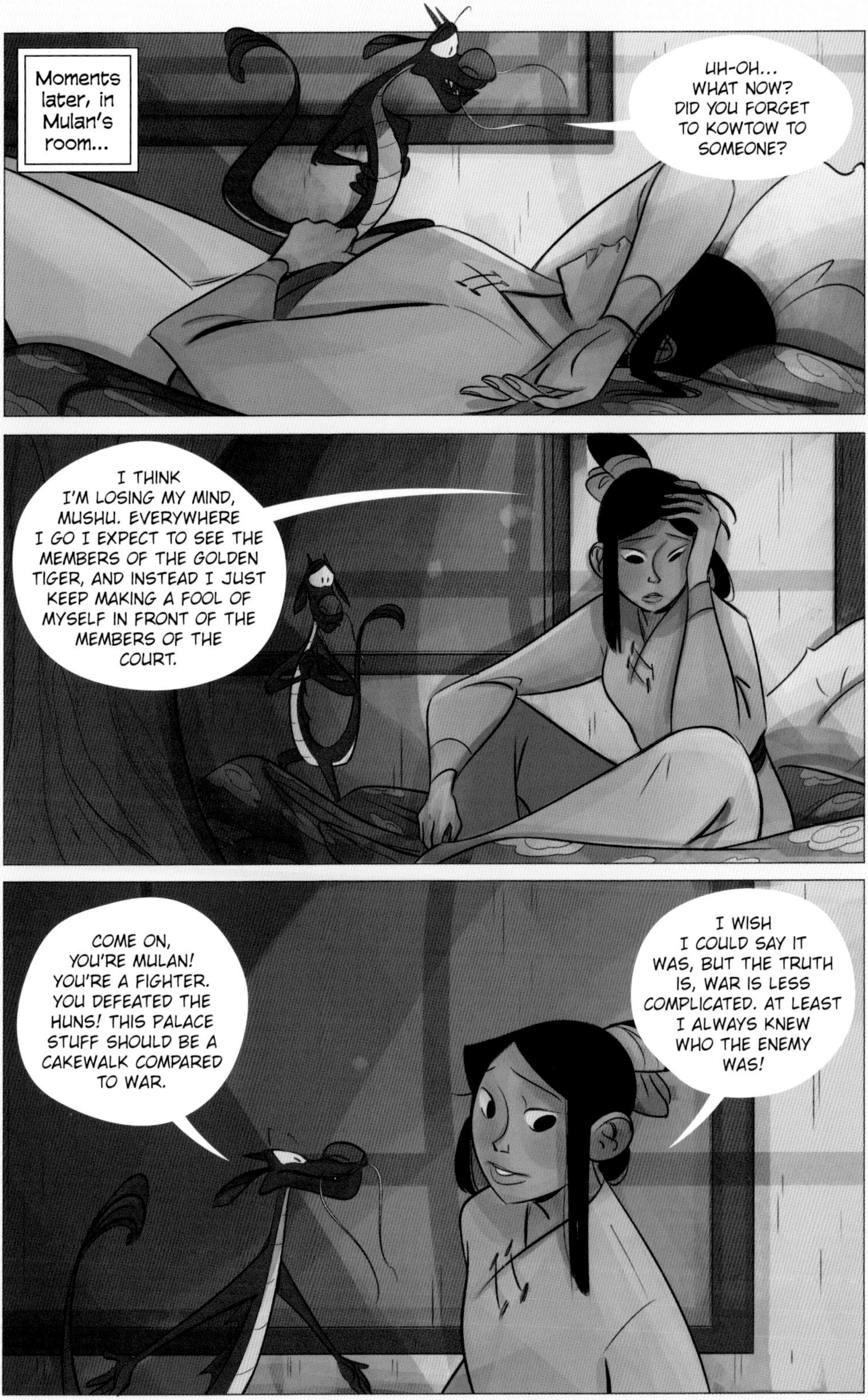
Moments later, in Mulan's room...
UH-OH... WHAT NOW? DID YOU FORGET TO KOWTOW TO SOMEONE?
I THINK I'M LOSING MY MIND, MUSHU. EVERYWHERE I GO I EXPECT TO SEE THE MEMBERS OF THE GOLDEN TIGER, AND INSTEAD I JUST KEEP MAKING A FOOL OF MYSELF IN FRONT OF THE MEMBERS OF THE COURT.
COME ON, YOU'RE MULAN! YOU'RE A FIGHTER. YOU DEFEATED THE HUNS! THIS PALACE STUFF SHOULD BE A CAKEWALK COMPARED TO WAR.
I WISH I COULD SAY IT WAS, BUT THE TRUTH IS, WAR IS LESS COMPLICATED. AT LEAST I ALWAYS KNEW WHO THE ENEMY WAS!

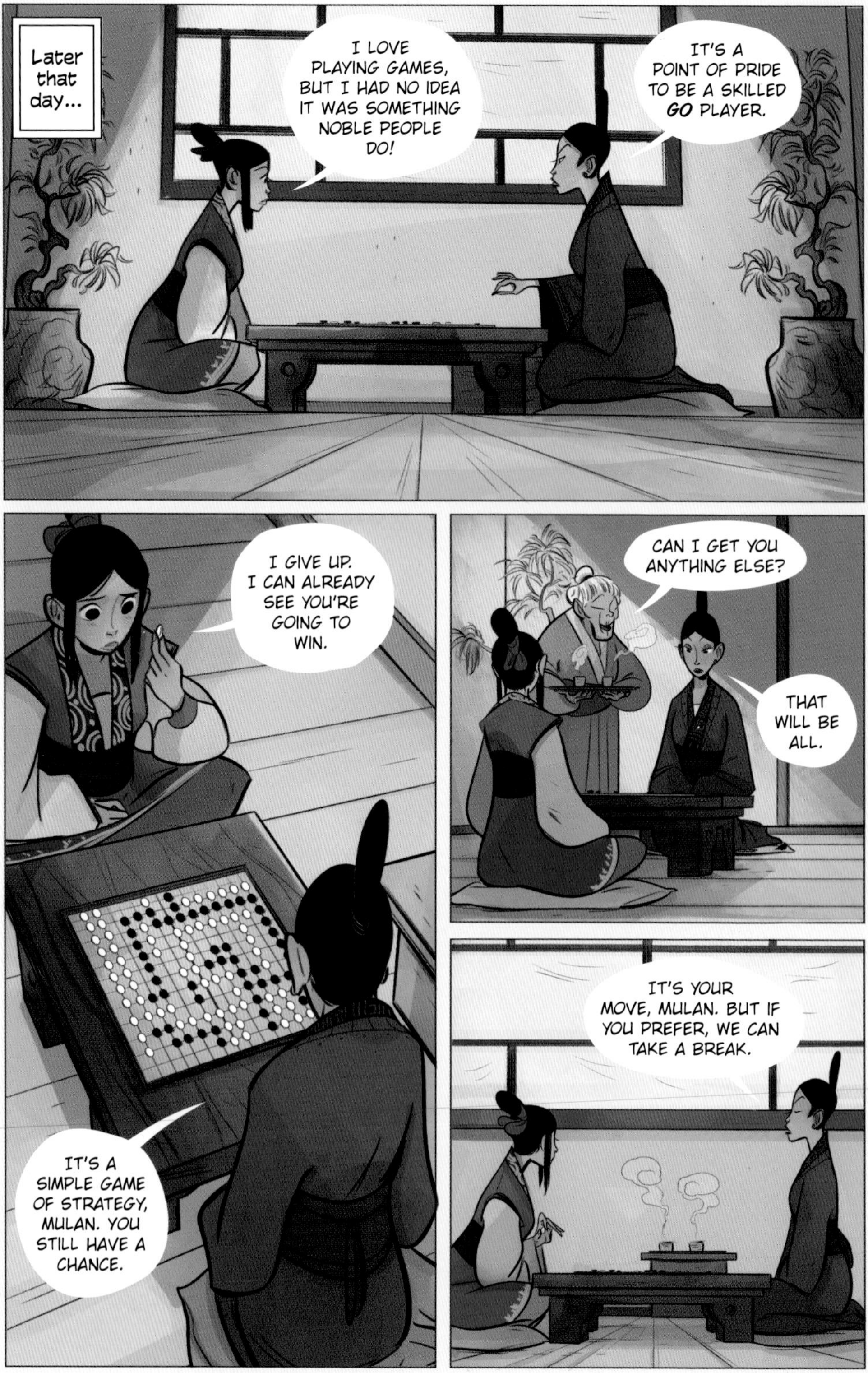
Later that day...
I LOVE PLAYING GAMES, BUT I HAD NO IDEA IT WAS SOMETHING NOBLE PEOPLE DO!
IT'S A POINT OF PRIDE TO BE A SKILLED GO PLAYER.
I GIVE UP. I CAN ALREADY SEE YOU'RE GOING TO WIN.
IT'S A SIMPLE GAME OF STRATEGY, MULAN. YOU STILL HAVE A CHANCE.
CAN I GET YOU ANYTHING ELSE?
THAT WILL BE ALL.
IT'S YOUR MOVE, MULAN. BUT IF YOU PREFER, WE CAN TAKE A BREAK.

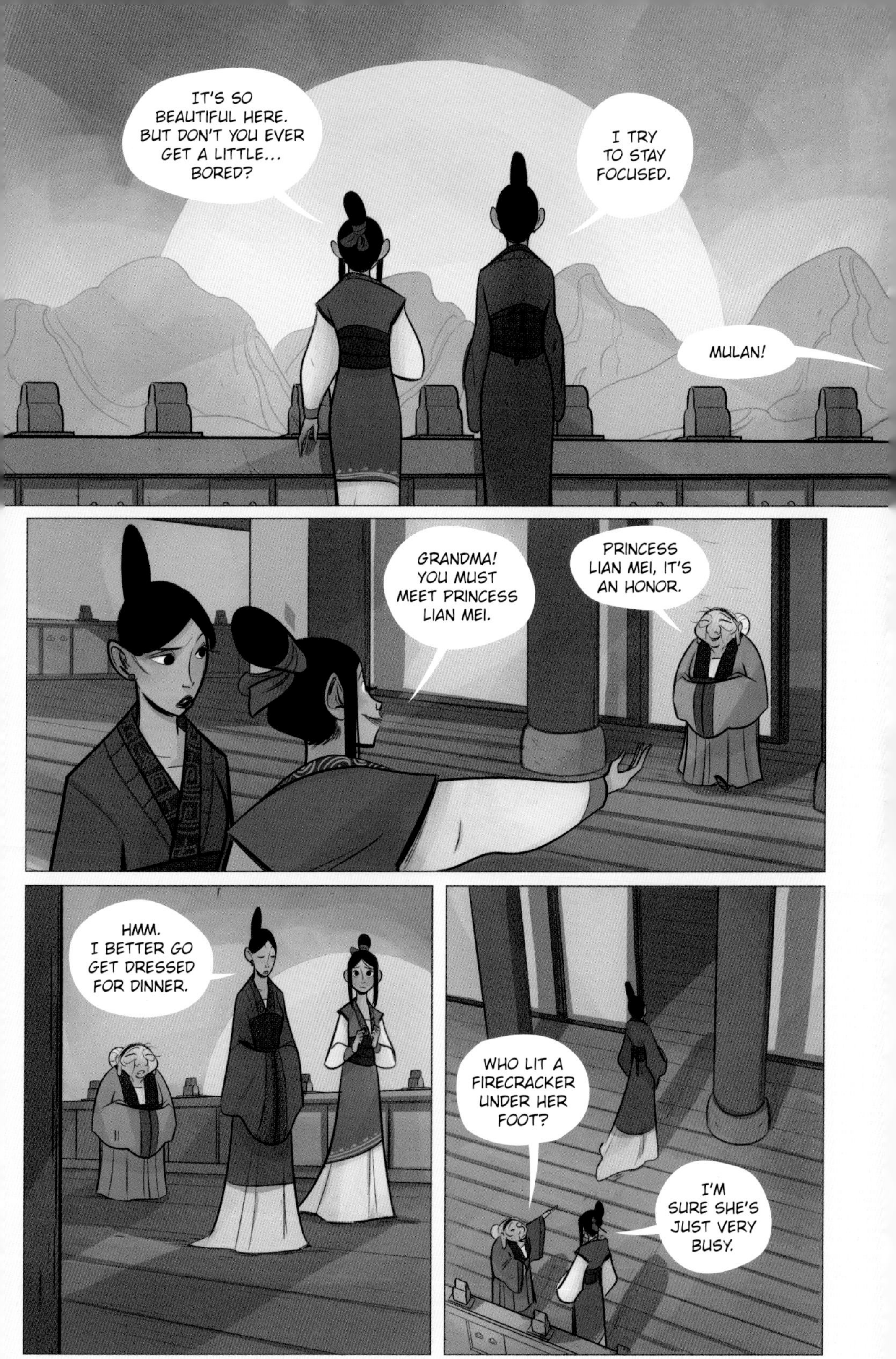
IT'S SO BEAUTIFUL HERE. BUT DON'T YOU EVER GET A LITTLE... BORED?
I TRY TO STAY FOCUSED.
MULAN!
GRANDMA! YOU MUST MEET PRINCESS LIAN MEI.
PRINCESS LIAN MEI, IT'S AN HONOR.
HMM. I BETTER GO GET DRESSED FOR DINNER.
WHO LIT A FIRECRACKER UNDER HER FOOT?
I'M SURE SHE'S JUST VERY BUSY.

I realized the strangest thing: Princess Lian Mei and Grandma don't get along! Grandma usually manages to charm everyone, but I've noticed that Princess Lian Mei grows withdrawn and distracted whenever Grandma is around.

Grandma has reacted by making cutting comments to me about Princess Lian Mei's haughtiness. It makes me uncomfortable to see them acting so strangely in each other's company.

Grandma is my family, but I like and respect Princess Lian Mei, too. She took me on a ride around the palace grounds yesterday. It was breathtakingly beautiful, but I feel a little sorry for her, being stuck inside the palace walls all the time.

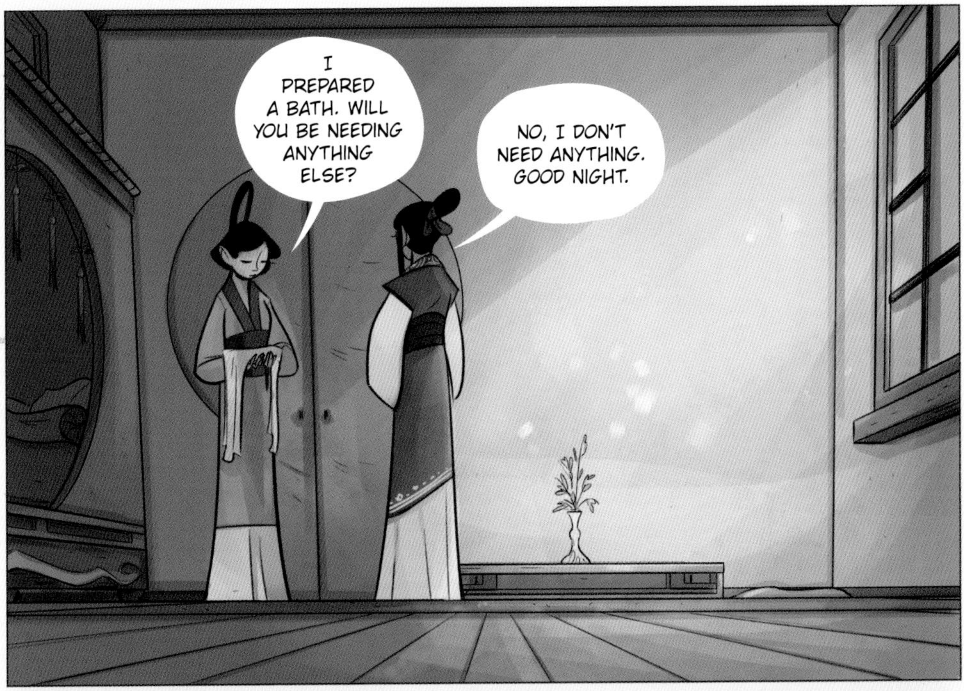
I PREPARED A BATH. WILL YOU BE NEEDING ANYTHING ELSE?
NO, I DON'T NEED ANYTHING. GOOD NIGHT.

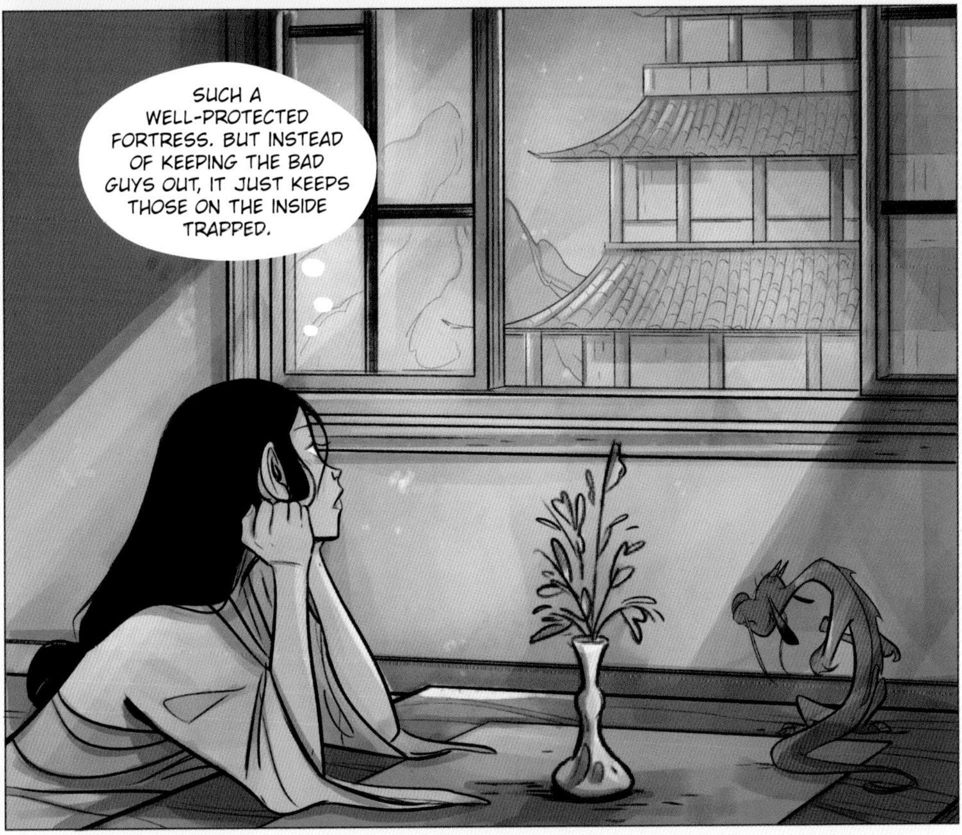
SUCH A WELL-PROTECTED FORTRESS. BUT INSTEAD OF KEEPING THE BAD GUYS OUT, IT JUST KEEPS THOSE ON THE INSIDE TRAPPED.

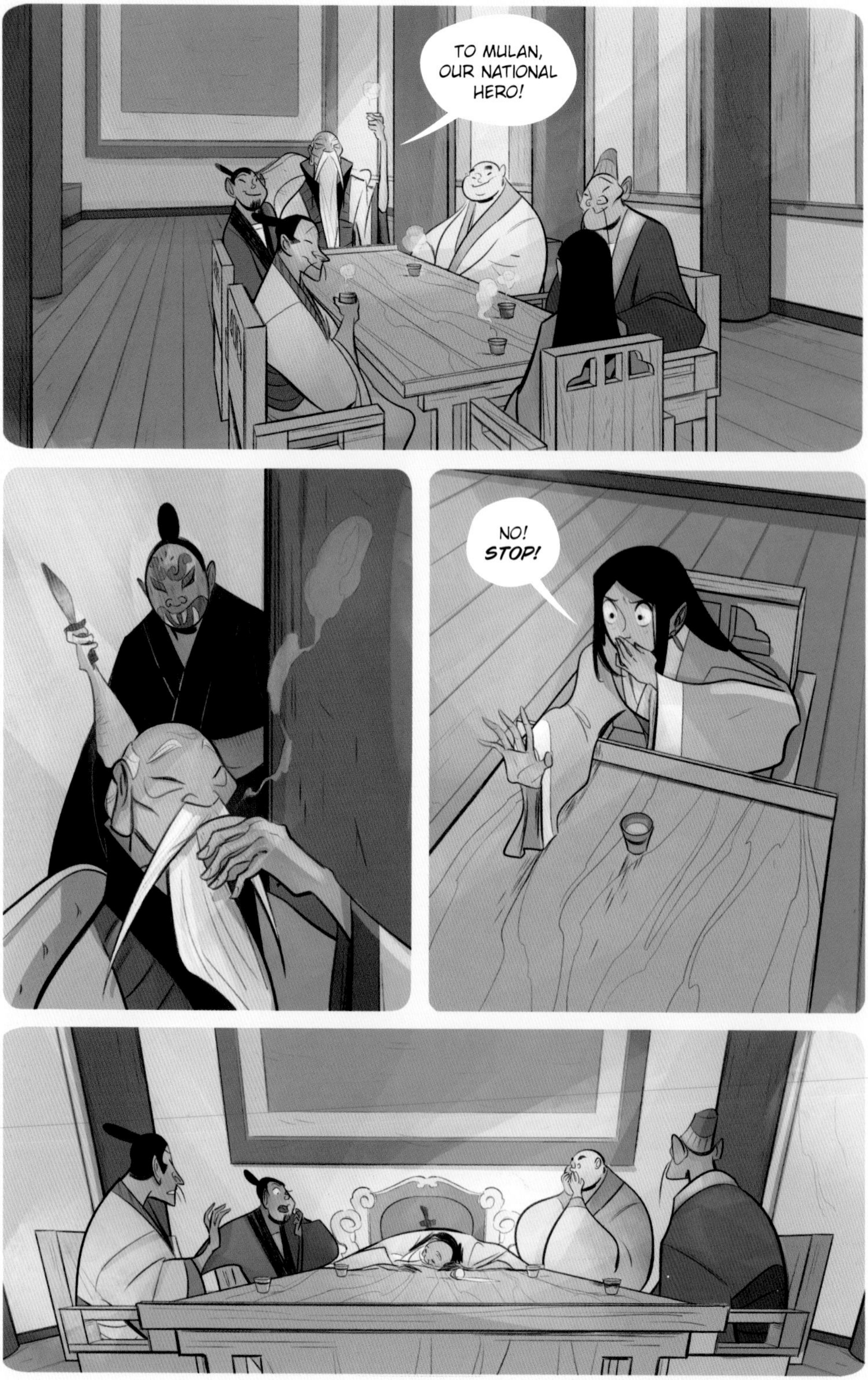
TO MULAN, OUR NATIONAL HERO!
NO! STOP!

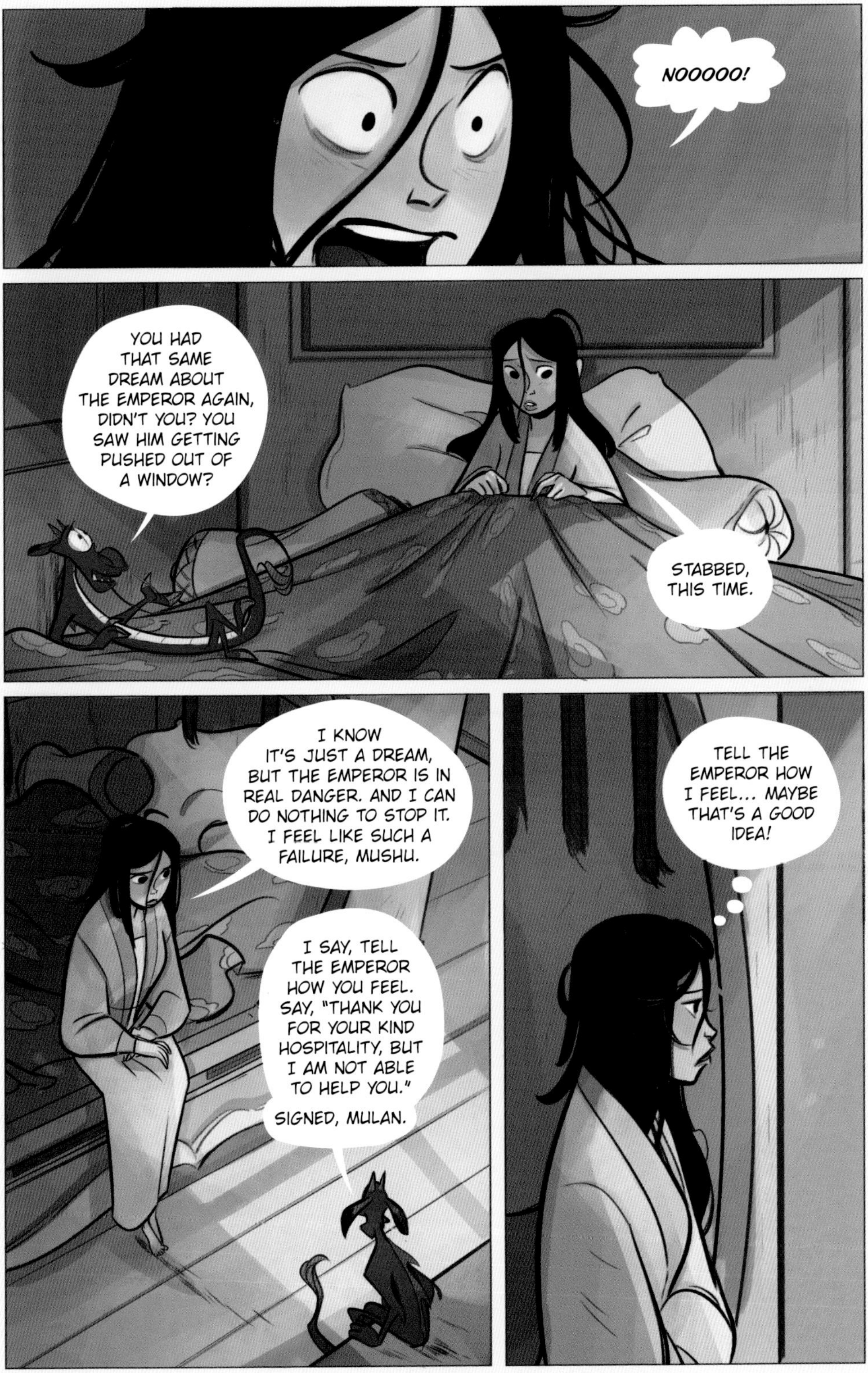
NOOOOO!
YOU HAD THAT SAME DREAM ABOUT THE EMPEROR AGAIN, DIDN'T YOU? YOU SAW HIM GETTING PUSHED OUT OF A WINDOW?
STABBED, THIS TIME.
I KNOW IT'S JUST A DREAM, BUT THE EMPEROR IS IN REAL DANGER. AND I CAN DO NOTHING TO STOP IT. I FEEL LIKE SUCH A FAILURE, MUSHU.
I SAY, TELL THE EMPEROR HOW YOU FEEL. SAY, "THANK YOU FOR YOUR KIND HOSPITALITY, BUT I AM NOT ABLE TO HELP YOU."
SIGNED, MULAN.
TELL THE EMPEROR HOW I FEEL... MAYBE THAT'S A GOOD IDEA!

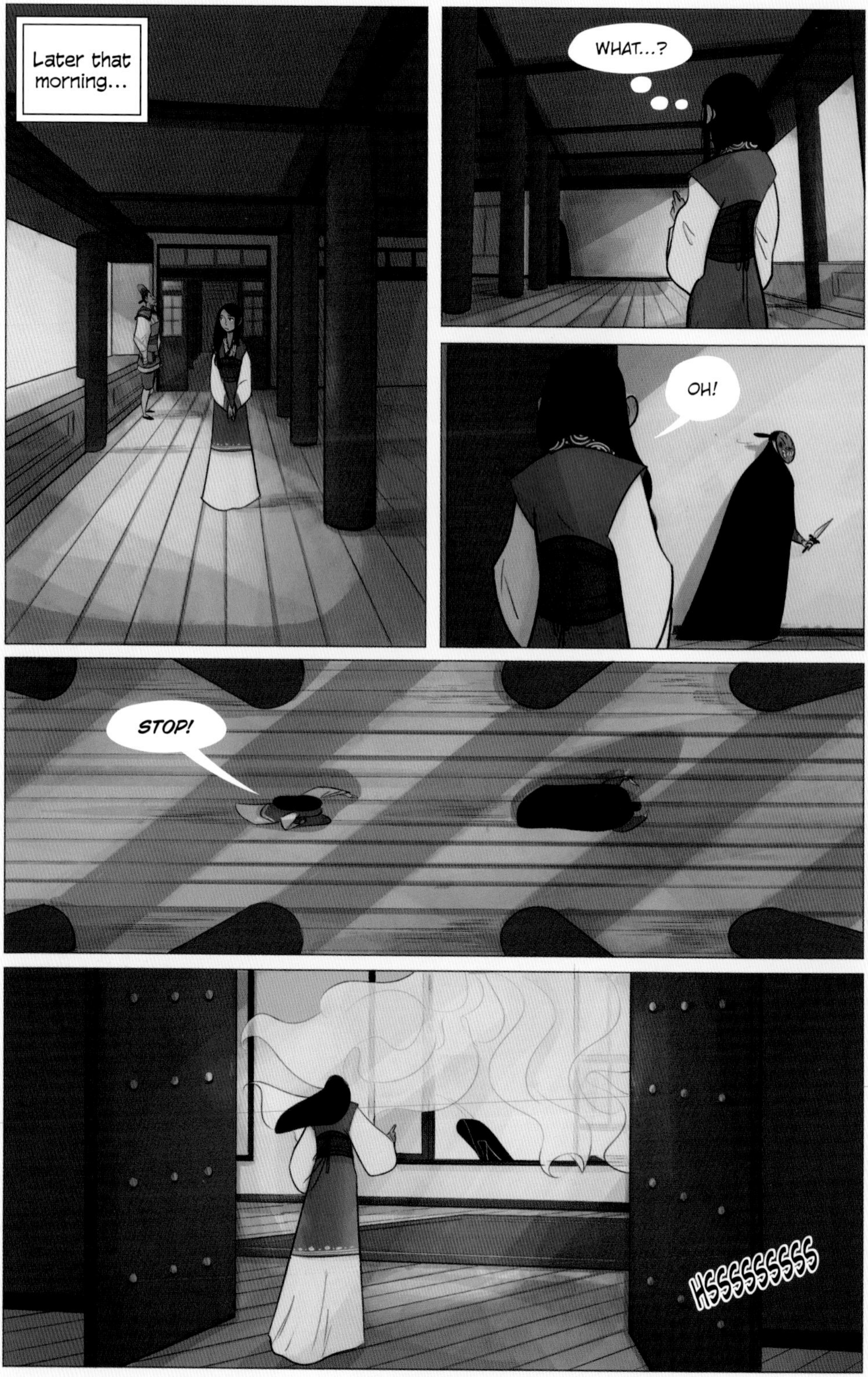
Later that morning...
WHAT...?
OH!
STOP!
HSSSSSSSSS

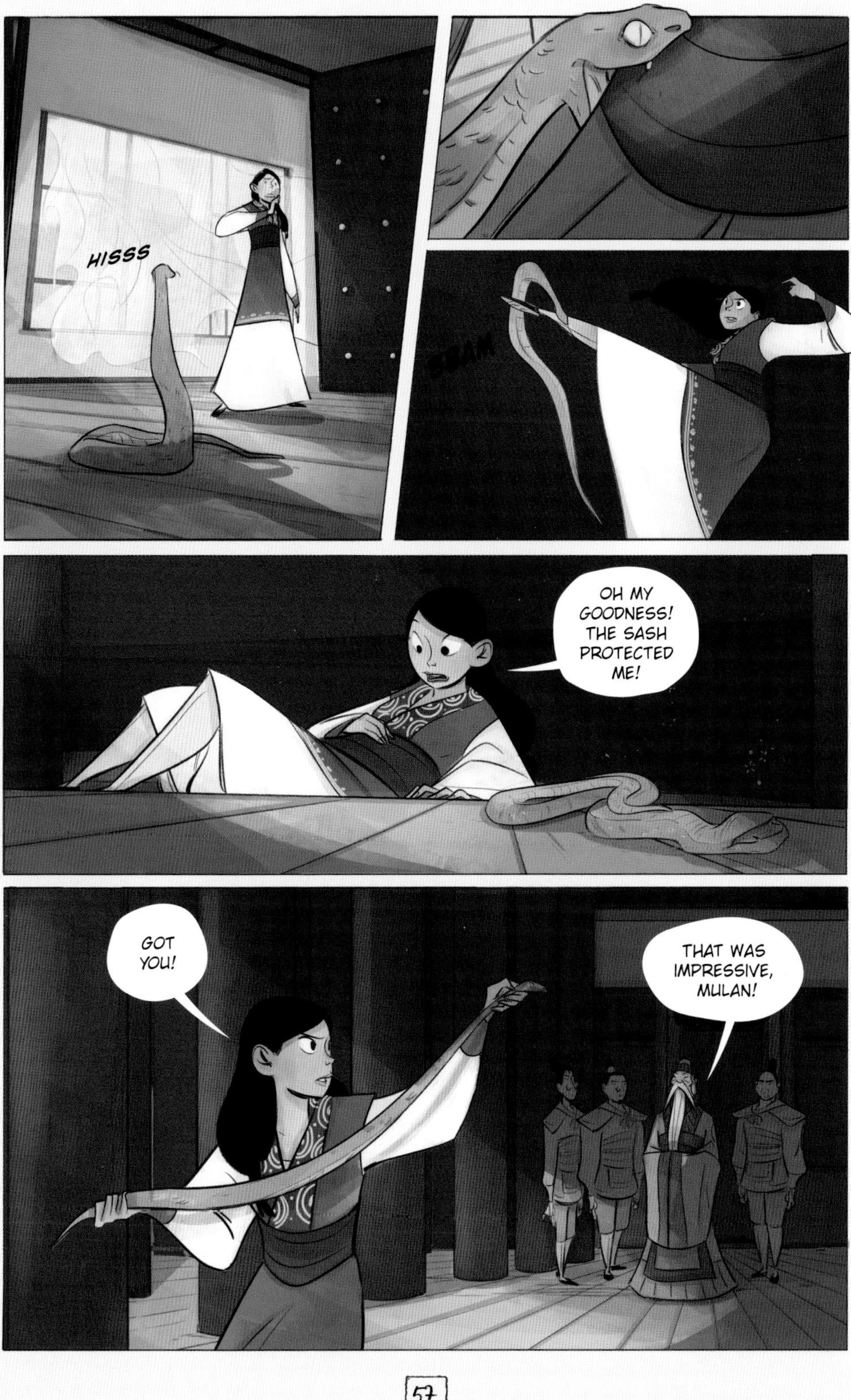
HISSS
OH MY GOODNESS! THE SASH PROTECTED ME!
GOT YOU!
THAT WAS IMPRESSIVE, MULAN!

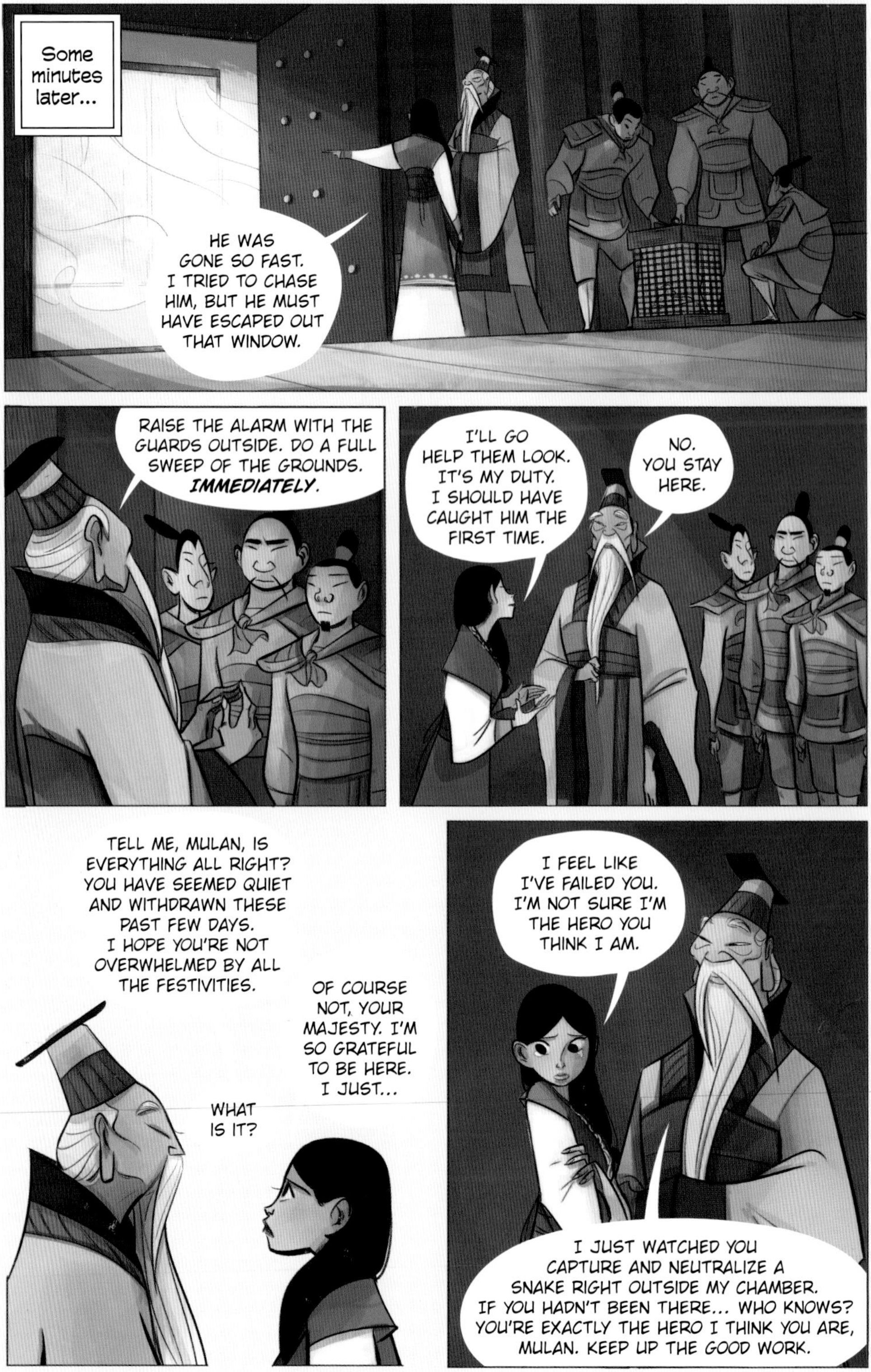
Some minutes later...
HE WAS GONE SO FAST. I TRIED TO CHASE HIM, BUT HE MUST HAVE ESCAPED OUT THAT WINDOW.
RAISE THE ALARM WITH THE GUARDS OUTSIDE. DO A FULL SWEEP OF THE GROUNDS. IMMEDIATELY.
I'LL GO HELP THEM LOOK. IT'S MY DUTY. I SHOULD HAVE CAUGHT HIM THE FIRST TIME.
NO. YOU STAY HERE.
TELL ME, MULAN, IS EVERYTHING ALL RIGHT? YOU HAVE SEEMED QUIET AND WITHDRAWN THESE PAST FEW DAYS. I HOPE YOU'RE NOT OVERWHELMED BY ALL THE FESTIVITIES.
OF COURSE NOT, YOUR MAJESTY. I'M SO GRATEFUL TO BE HERE. I JUST...
WHAT IS IT?
I FEEL LIKE I'VE FAILED YOU. I'M NOT SURE I'M THE HERO YOU THINK I AM.
I JUST WATCHED YOU CAPTURE AND NEUTRALIZE A SNAKE RIGHT OUTSIDE MY CHAMBER. IF YOU HADN'T BEEN THERE... WHO KNOWS? YOU'RE EXACTLY THE HERO I THINK YOU ARE, MULAN. KEEP UP THE GOOD WORK.

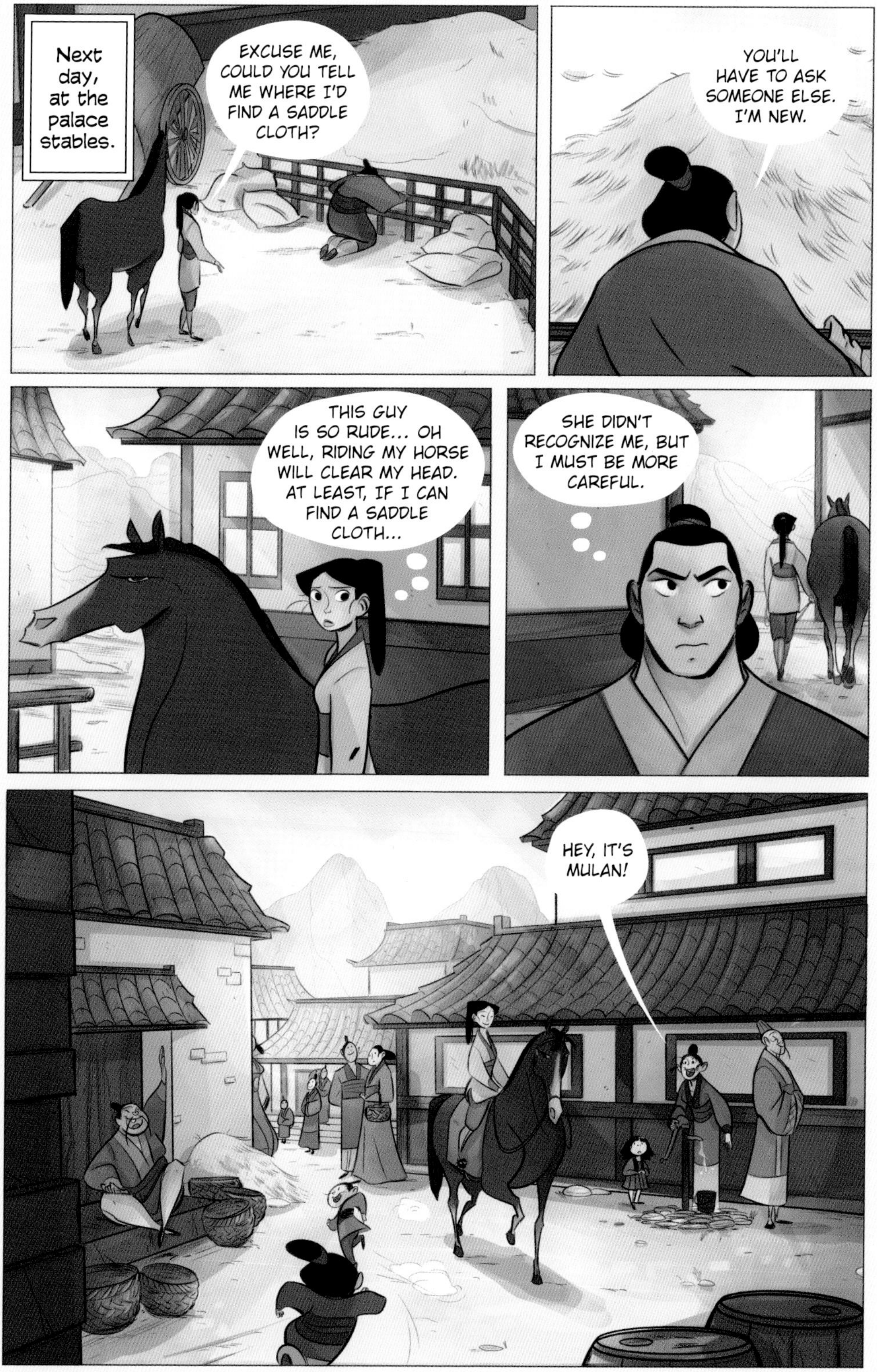
Next day, at the palace stables.
EXCUSE ME, COULD YOU TELL ME WHERE I'D FIND A SADDLE CLOTH?
YOU'LL HAVE TO ASK SOMEONE ELSE. I'M NEW.
THIS GUY IS SO RUDE... OH WELL, RIDING MY HORSE WILL CLEAR MY HEAD. AT LEAST, IF I CAN FIND A SADDLE CLOTH...
SHE DIDN'T RECOGNIZE ME, BUT I MUST BE MORE CAREFUL.
HEY, IT'S MULAN!

I'm so glad I was finally able to prove my value to the Emperor. The truth is, I doubted my ability to protect him, but now I can see that he really needs me. Next time there's an intruder in the palace, they won't get away so easily. I didn't train for months with the Chinese army for nothing!

Spending time outside the palace walls has helped shift my perspective. Now I know that it's not just the Emperor I'm protecting, it's the people of China.

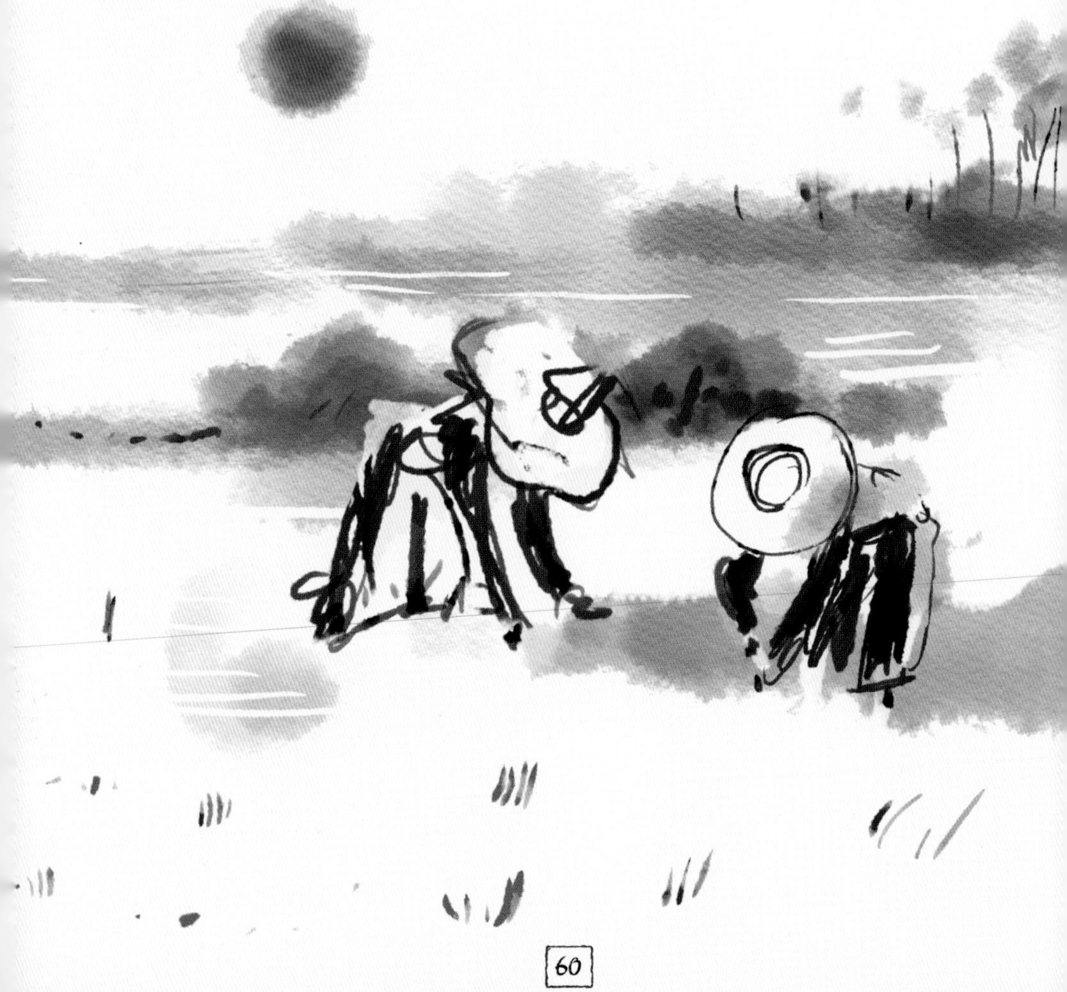

Which got me thinking: Who in the palace knows what's going on in all rooms at all times? The servants!

From now on, I'm making it my mission to learn everything that the servants know.

Besides, I'll probably have an easier time chatting with them than with all the court officials I've been meeting lately.

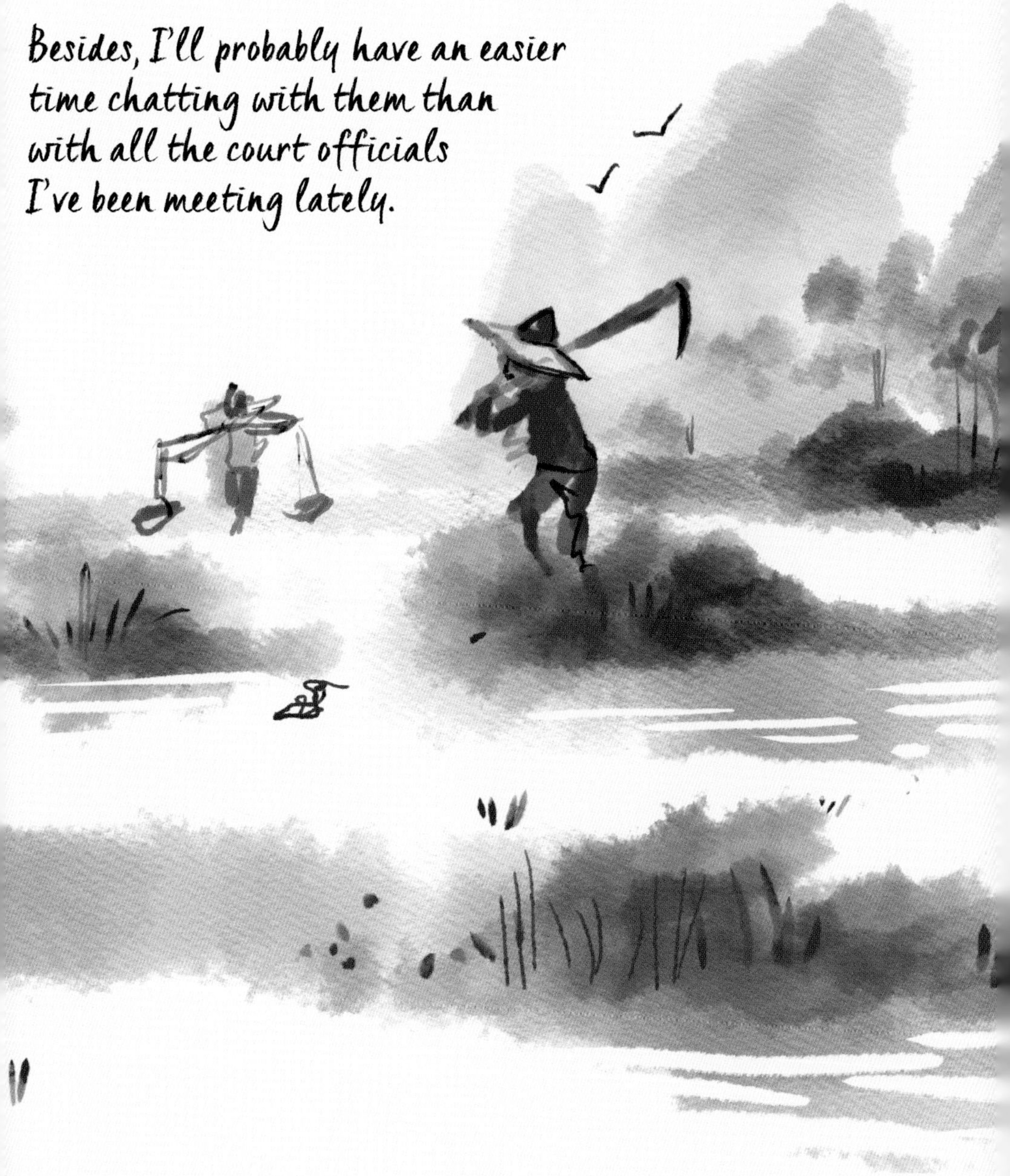

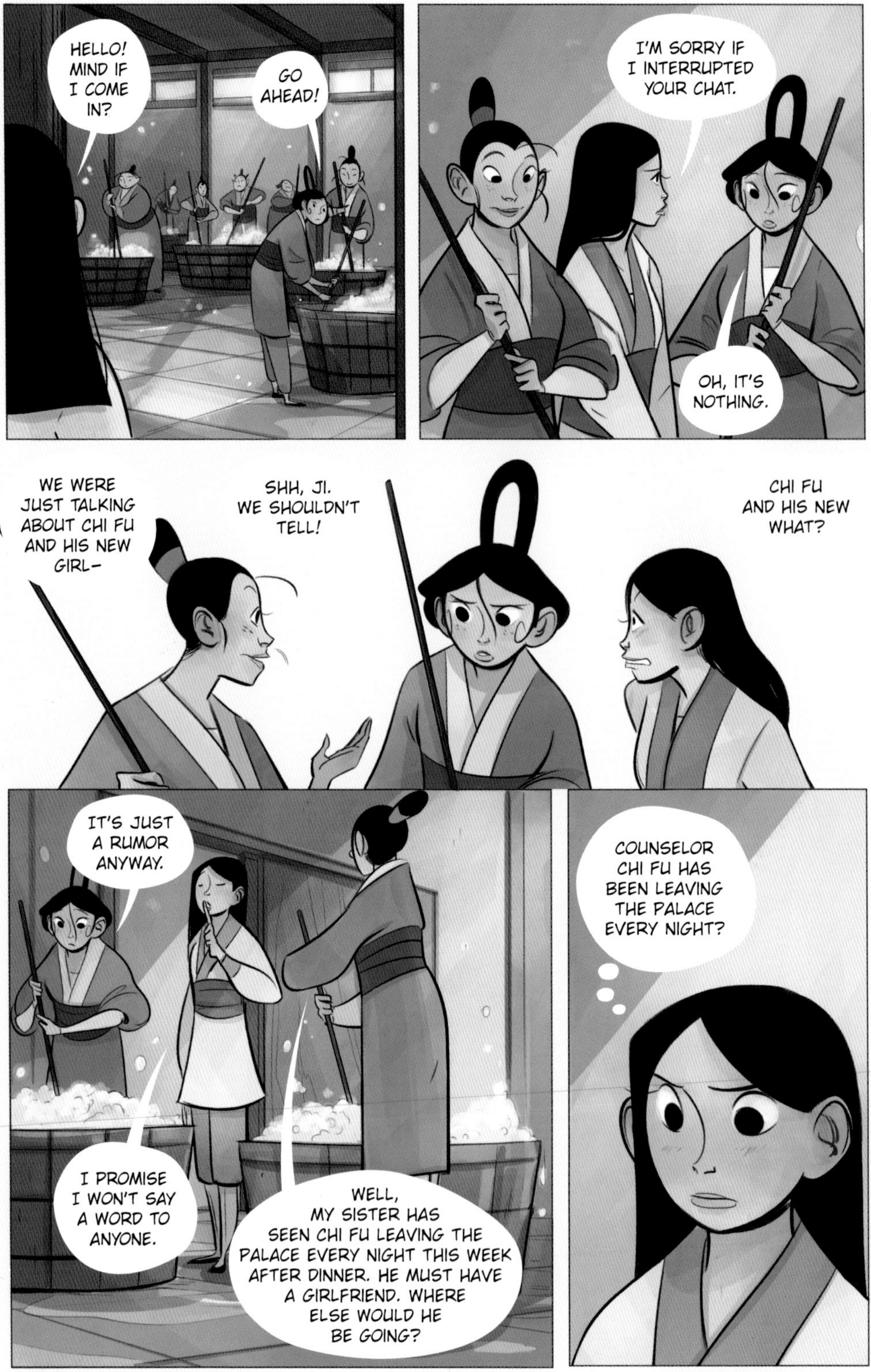
HELLO! MIND IF I COME IN?
GO AHEAD!
I'M SORRY IF I INTERRUPTED YOUR CHAT.
OH, IT'S NOTHING.
WE WERE JUST TALKING ABOUT CHI FU AND HIS NEW GIRL–
SHH, JI. WE SHOULDN'T TELL!
CHI FU AND HIS NEW WHAT?
IT'S JUST A RUMOR ANYWAY.
I PROMISE I WON'T SAY A WORD TO ANYONE.
WELL, MY SISTER HAS SEEN CHI FU LEAVING THE PALACE EVERY NIGHT THIS WEEK AFTER DINNER. HE MUST HAVE A GIRLFRIEND. WHERE ELSE WOULD HE BE GOING?
COUNSELOR CHI FU HAS BEEN LEAVING THE PALACE EVERY NIGHT?

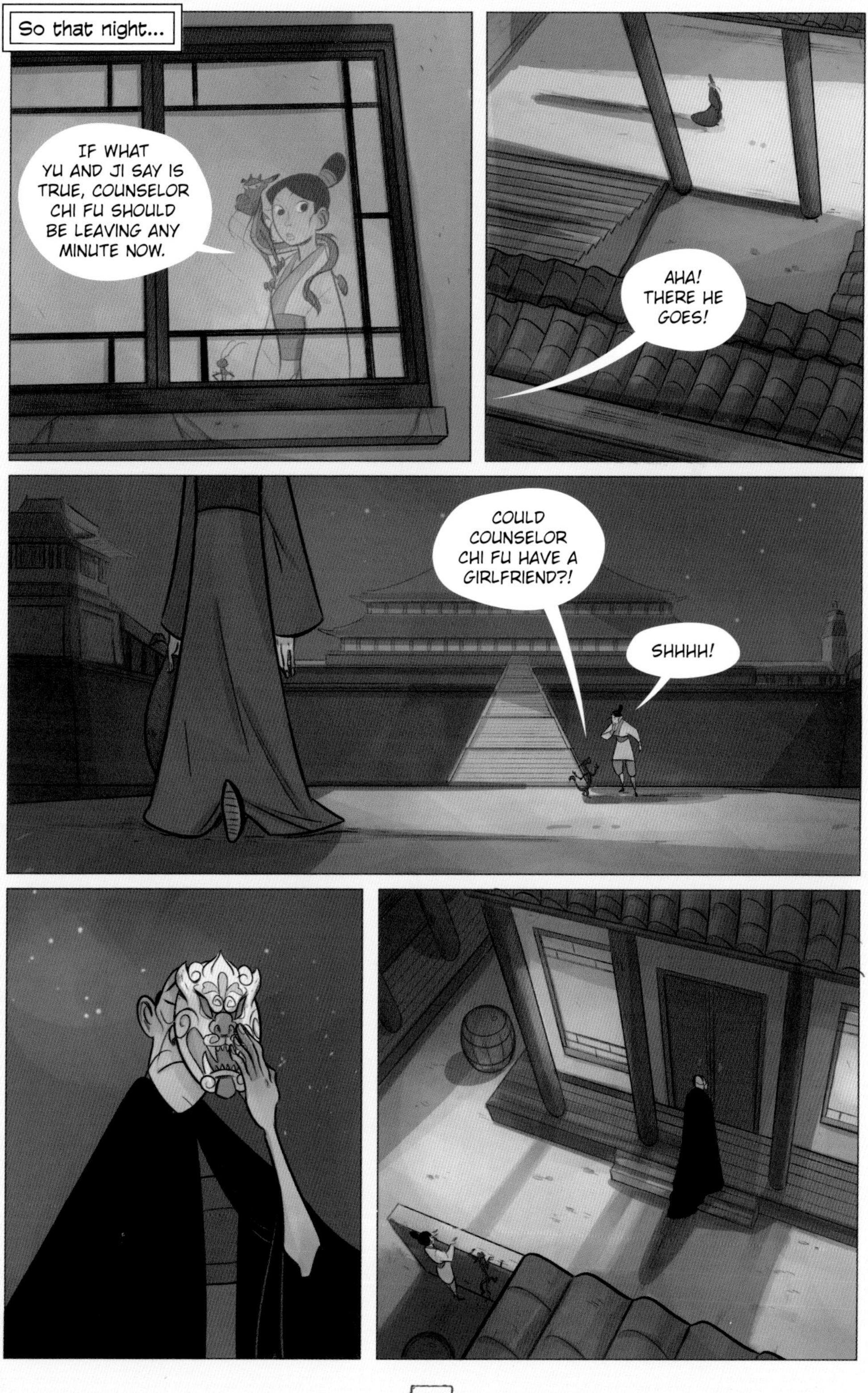
So that night...
IF WHAT YU AND JI SAY IS TRUE, COUNSELOR CHI FU SHOULD BE LEAVING ANY MINUTE NOW.
AHA! THERE HE GOES!
COULD COUNSELOR CHI FU HAVE A GIRLFRIEND?!
SHHHH!

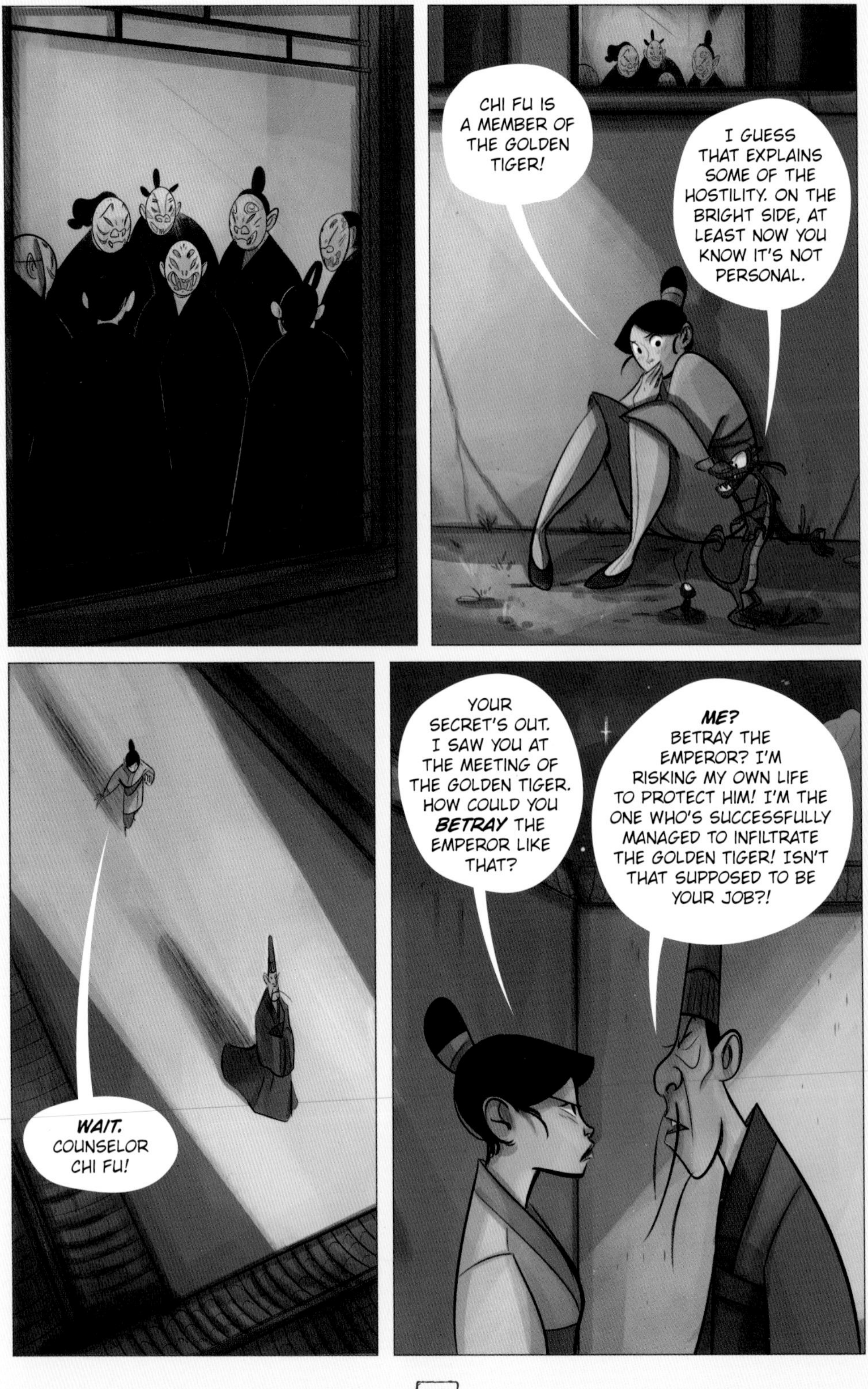

CHI FU IS A MEMBER OF THE GOLDEN TIGER!
I GUESS THAT EXPLAINS SOME OF THE HOSTILITY. ON THE BRIGHT SIDE, AT LEAST NOW YOU KNOW IT'S NOT PERSONAL.
WAIT. COUNSELOR CHI FU!
YOUR SECRET'S OUT. I SAW YOU AT THE MEETING OF THE GOLDEN TIGER. HOW COULD YOU BETRAY THE EMPEROR LIKE THAT?
ME? BETRAY THE EMPEROR? I'M RISKING MY OWN LIFE TO PROTECT HIM! I'M THE ONE WHO'S SUCCESSFULLY MANAGED TO INFILTRATE THE GOLDEN TIGER! ISN'T THAT SUPPOSED TO BE YOUR JOB?!

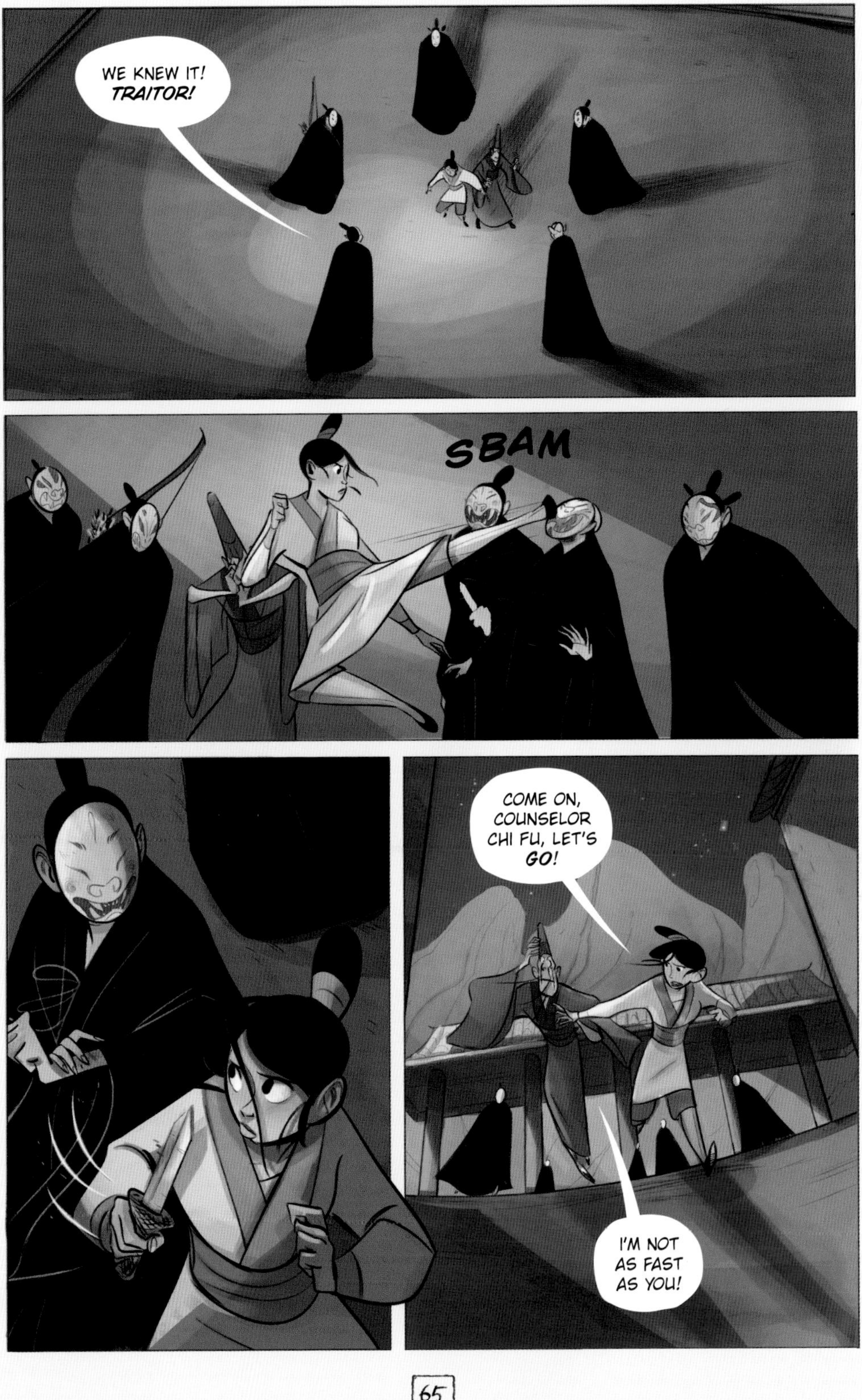
WE KNEW IT! TRAITOR!
SBAM
COME ON, COUNSELOR CHI FU, LET'S GO!
I'M NOT AS FAST AS YOU!

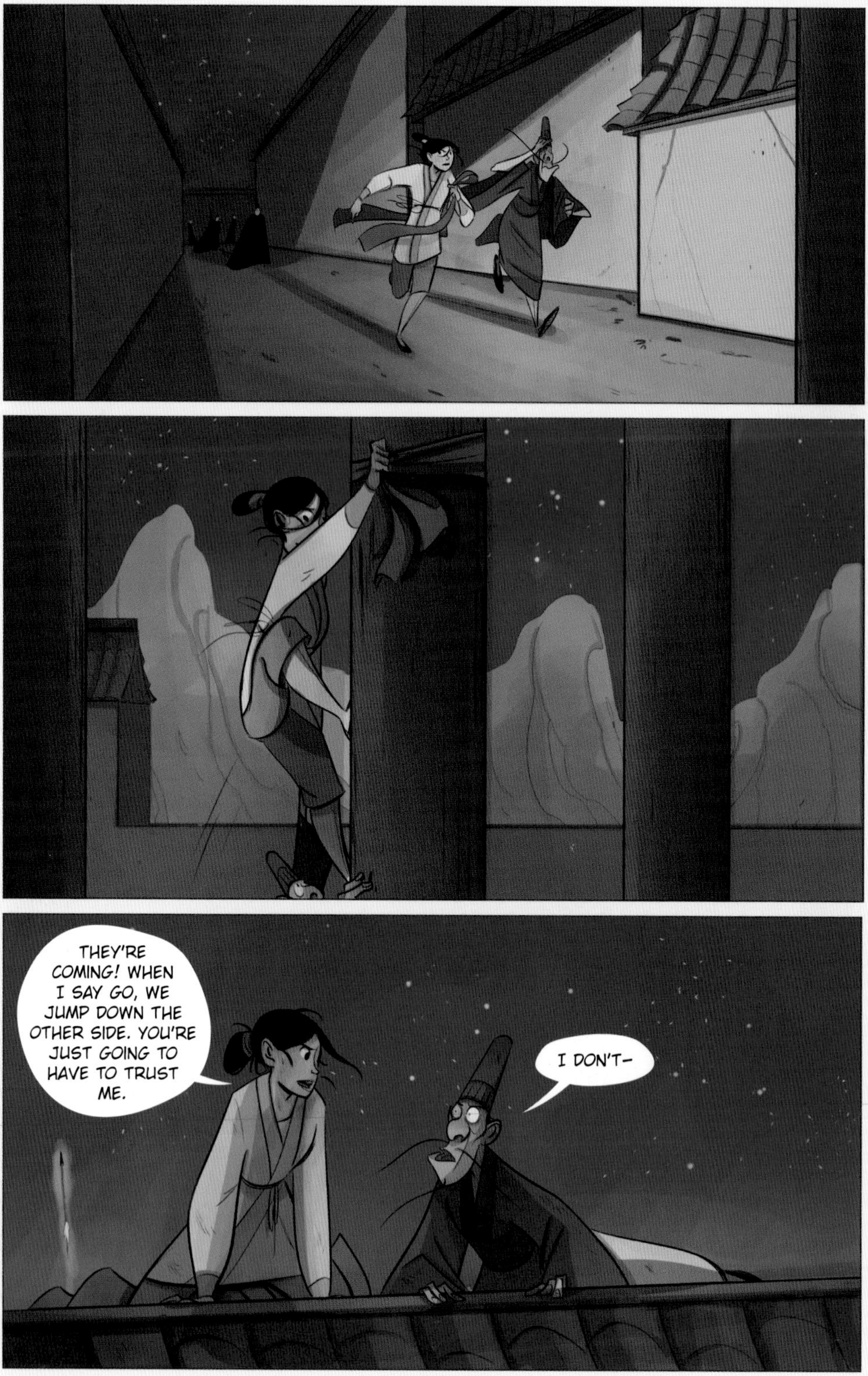
THEY'RE COMING! WHEN I SAY GO, WE JUMP DOWN THE OTHER SIDE. YOU'RE JUST GOING TO HAVE TO TRUST ME.
I DON'T-

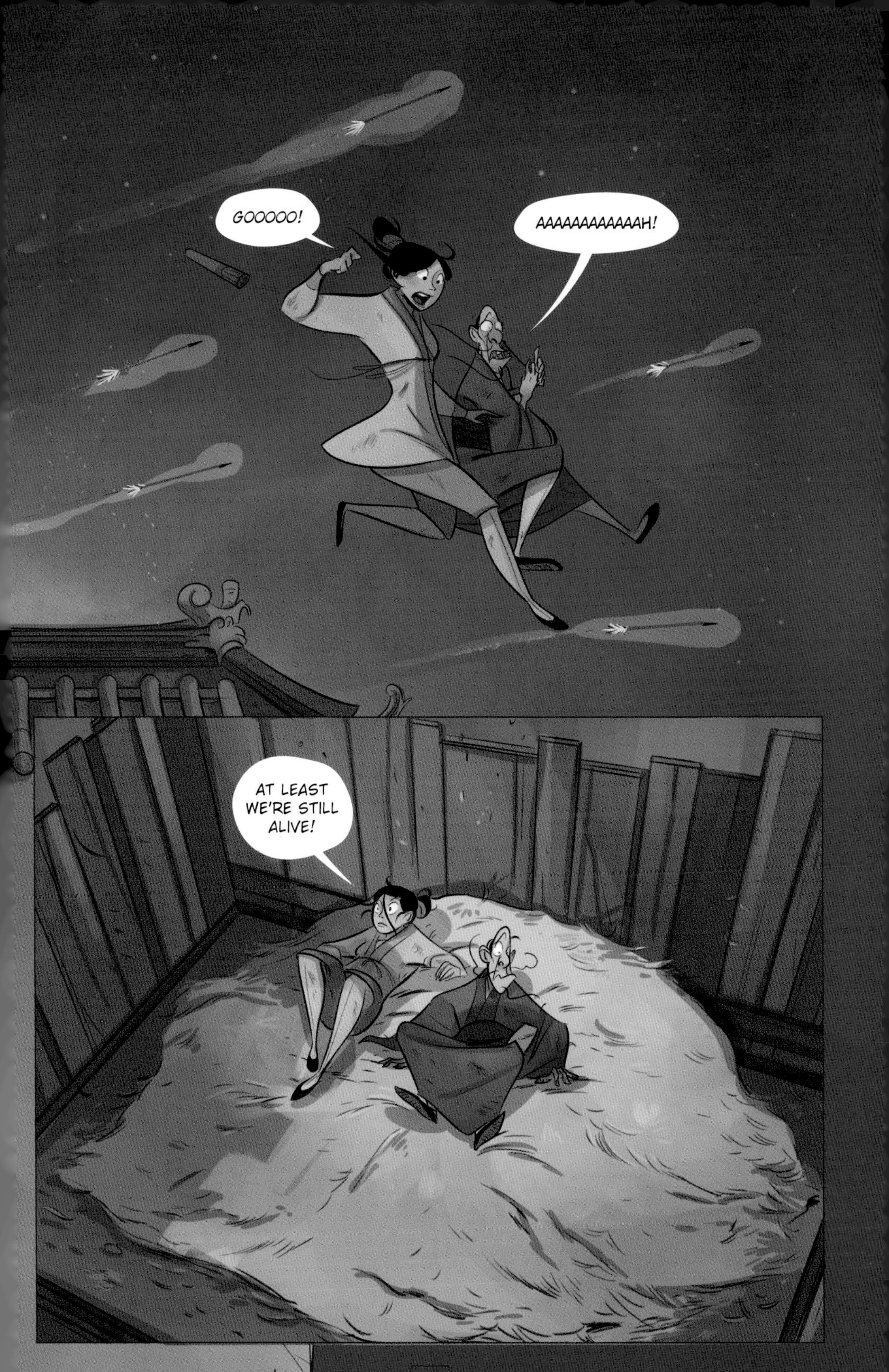
GOOOOO!
AAAAAAAAAAAAAH!
AT LEAST WE'RE STILL ALIVE!

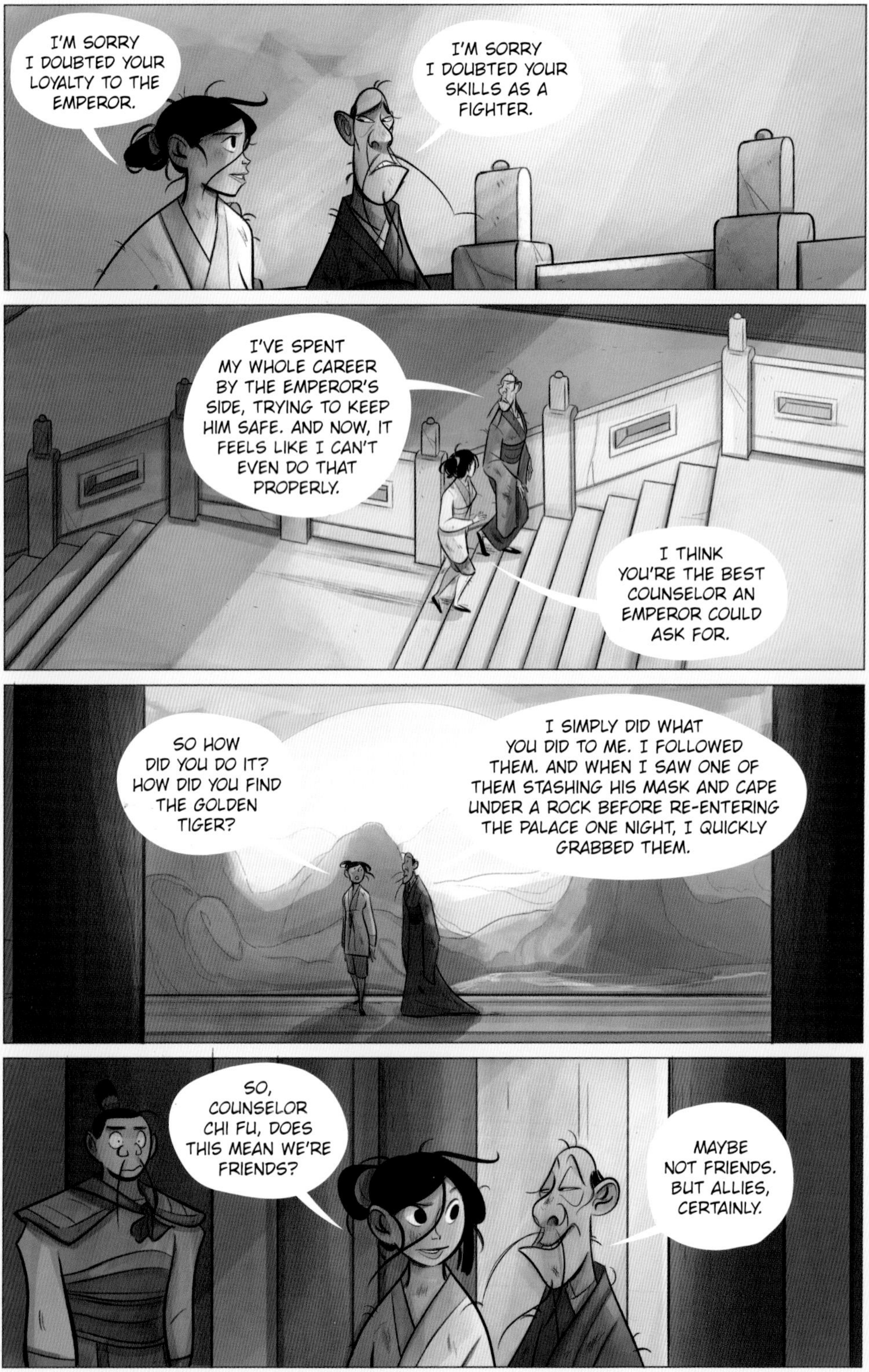
I'M SORRY I DOUBTED YOUR LOYALTY TO THE EMPEROR.
I'M SORRY I DOUBTED YOUR SKILLS AS A FIGHTER.
I'VE SPENT MY WHOLE CAREER BY THE EMPEROR'S SIDE, TRYING TO KEEP HIM SAFE. AND NOW, IT FEELS LIKE I CAN'T EVEN DO THAT PROPERLY.
I THINK YOU'RE THE BEST COUNSELOR AN EMPEROR COULD ASK FOR.
SO HOW DID YOU DO IT? HOW DID YOU FIND THE GOLDEN TIGER?
I SIMPLY DID WHAT YOU DID TO ME. I FOLLOWED THEM. AND WHEN I SAW ONE OF THEM STASHING HIS MASK AND CAPE UNDER A ROCK BEFORE RE-ENTERING THE PALACE ONE NIGHT, I QUICKLY GRABBED THEM.
SO, COUNSELOR CHI FU, DOES THIS MEAN WE'RE FRIENDS?
MAYBE NOT FRIENDS. BUT ALLIES, CERTAINLY.

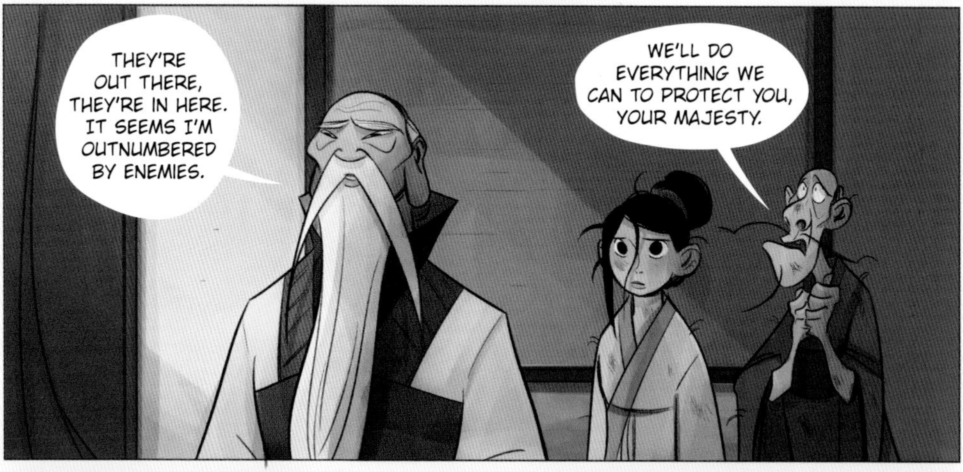
THEY'RE OUT THERE, THEY'RE IN HERE. IT SEEMS I'M OUTNUMBERED BY ENEMIES.
WE'LL DO EVERYTHING WE CAN TO PROTECT YOU, YOUR MAJESTY.

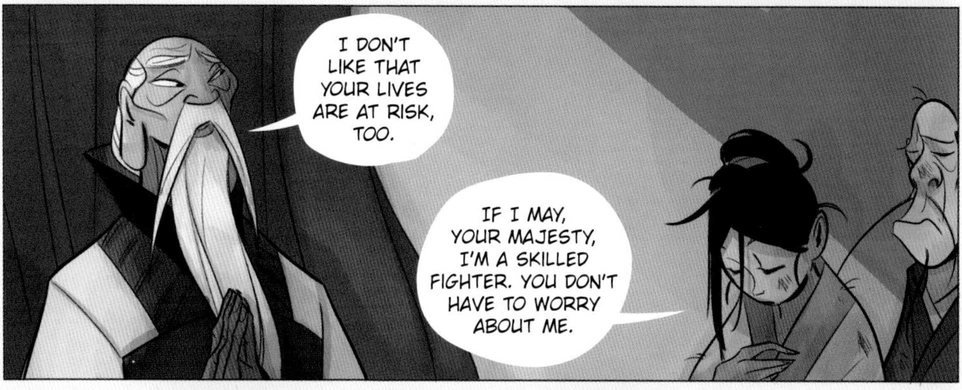
I DON'T LIKE THAT YOUR LIVES ARE AT RISK, TOO.
IF I MAY, YOUR MAJESTY, I'M A SKILLED FIGHTER. YOU DON'T HAVE TO WORRY ABOUT ME.

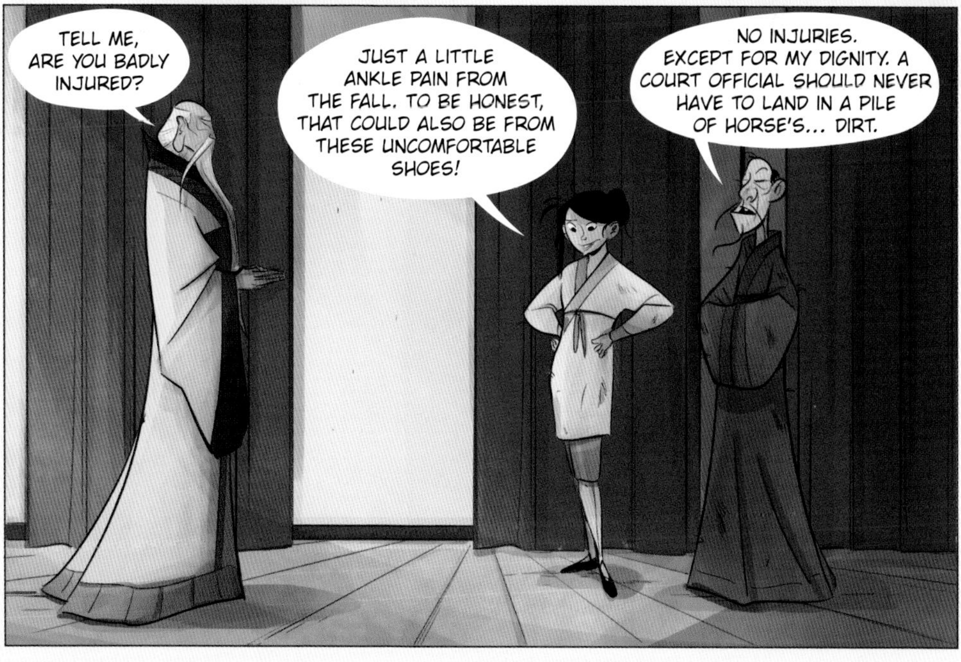
TELL ME, ARE YOU BADLY INJURED?
JUST A LITTLE ANKLE PAIN FROM THE FALL. TO BE HONEST, THAT COULD ALSO BE FROM THESE UNCOMFORTABLE SHOES!
NO INJURIES. EXCEPT FOR MY DIGNITY. A COURT OFFICIAL SHOULD NEVER HAVE TO LAND IN A PILE OF HORSE'S... DIRT.

I can't believe I have to get dressed up and go to another court performance tonight. After I got back to my room this morning, I couldn't sleep a wink.

Last night's adventure still has my adrenaline pumping. We were lucky to escape the members of the Golden Tiger. My only injury is a sore ankle, but it could have been much worse.

Yesterday when Yu was helping me dress she said that she would love to be in my position, attending all the dinners and concerts with high-ranking members of the court. I can honestly say that in this moment I would happily swap places with her.

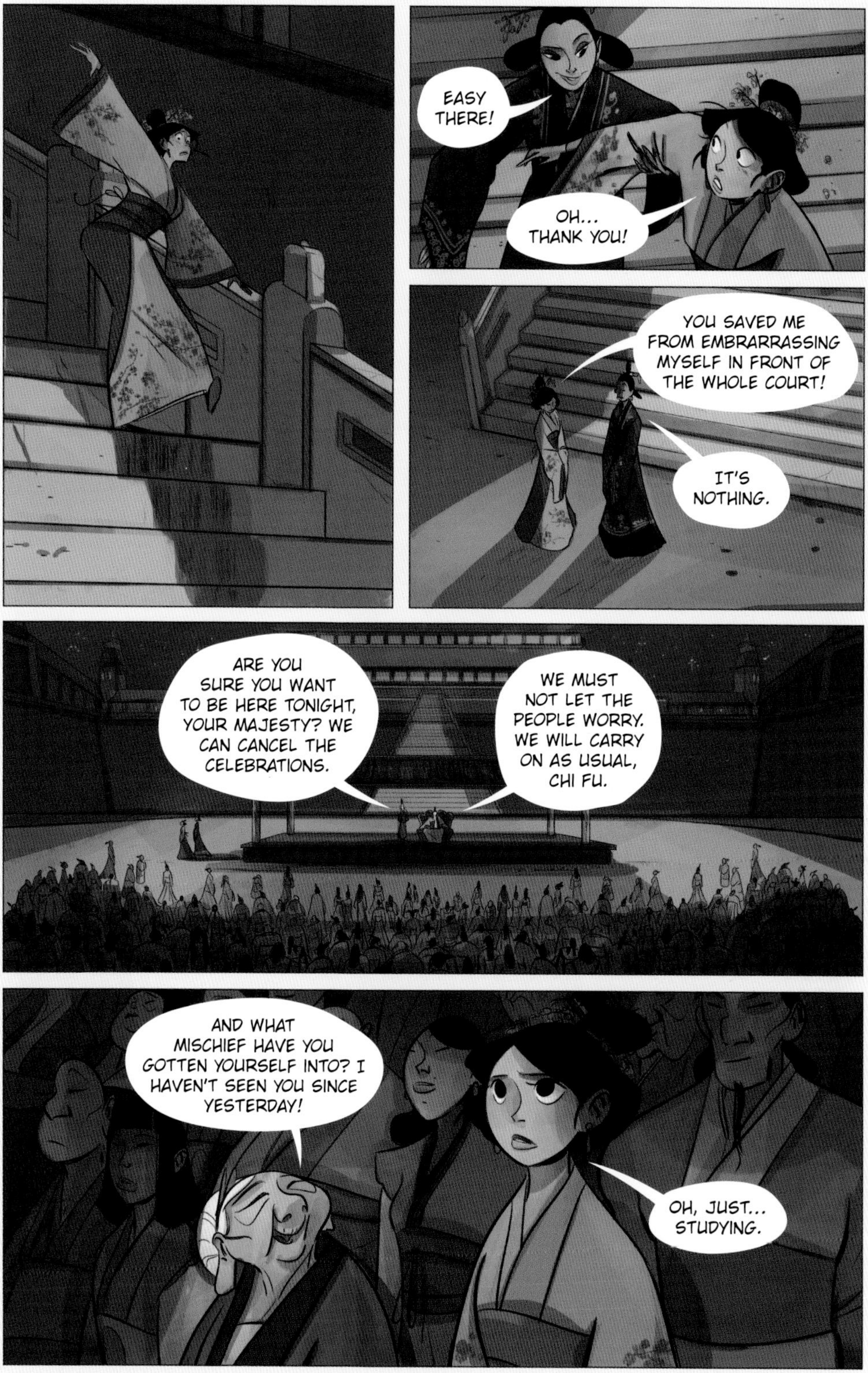
EASY THERE!
OH... THANK YOU!
YOU SAVED ME FROM EMBRARRASSING MYSELF IN FRONT OF THE WHOLE COURT!
IT'S NOTHING.
ARE YOU SURE YOU WANT TO BE HERE TONIGHT, YOUR MAJESTY? WE CAN CANCEL THE CELEBRATIONS.
WE MUST NOT LET THE PEOPLE WORRY. WE WILL CARRY ON AS USUAL, CHI FU.
AND WHAT MISCHIEF HAVE YOU GOTTEN YOURSELF INTO? I HAVEN'T SEEN YOU SINCE YESTERDAY!
OH, JUST... STUDYING.

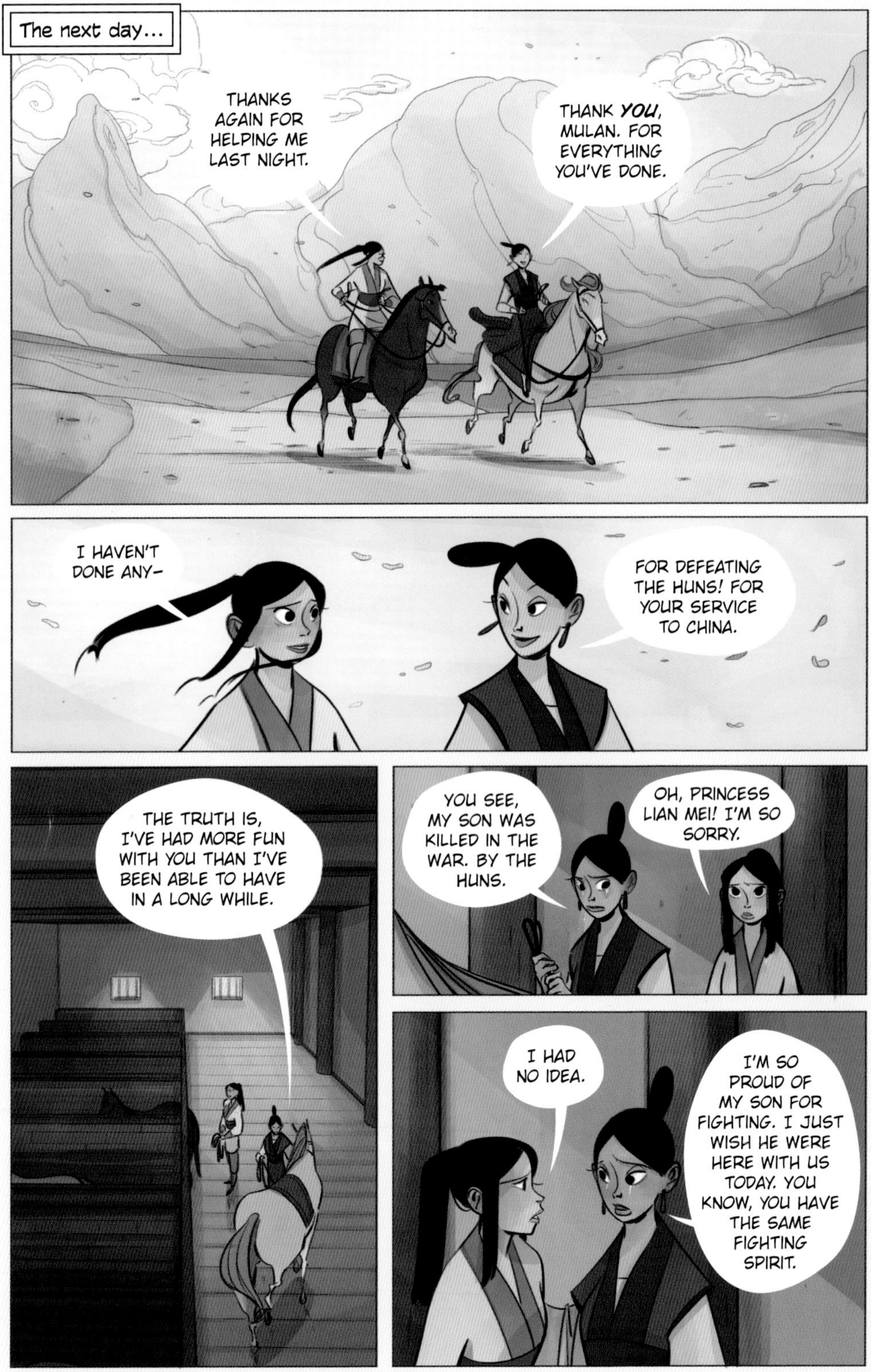

The next day...
THANKS AGAIN FOR HELPING ME LAST NIGHT.
THANK *YOU*, MULAN. FOR EVERYTHING YOU'VE DONE.
I HAVEN'T DONE ANY–
FOR DEFEATING THE HUNS! FOR YOUR SERVICE TO CHINA.
THE TRUTH IS, I'VE HAD MORE FUN WITH YOU THAN I'VE BEEN ABLE TO HAVE IN A LONG WHILE.
YOU SEE, MY SON WAS KILLED IN THE WAR. BY THE HUNS.
OH, PRINCESS LIAN MEI! I'M SO SORRY.
I HAD NO IDEA.
I'M SO PROUD OF MY SON FOR FIGHTING. I JUST WISH HE WERE HERE WITH US TODAY. YOU KNOW, YOU HAVE THE SAME FIGHTING SPIRIT.

I'm so honored that Princess Lian Mei opened up to me today. It's the first time I've felt like our friendship is balanced. She's always helping me, and I feel like I have nothing to offer. Now I finally understand why she feels close to me; she wants to feel closer to her son. I had no idea that she was suffering such a loss...

I know she and Grandma haven't been getting along, but I think that's finally changing. She sent gifts for Grandma and me to our rooms this evening, as a gesture of friendship. I hope Grandma gives Princess Lian Mei a chance now. She was so taken aback by the gesture, she almost fell off her chair!

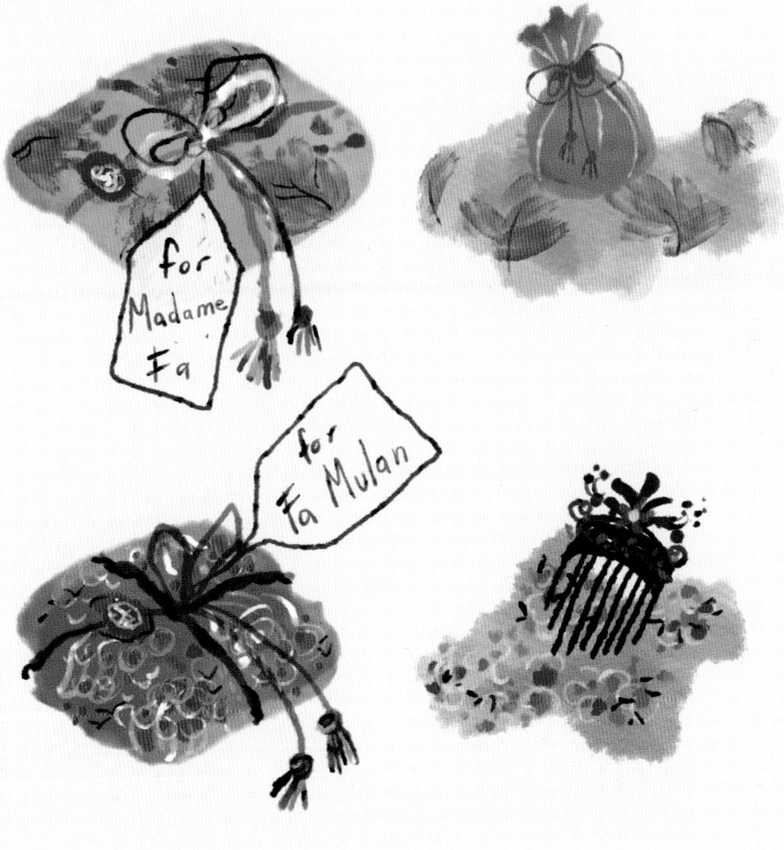
for Madame Fa
for Fa Mulan

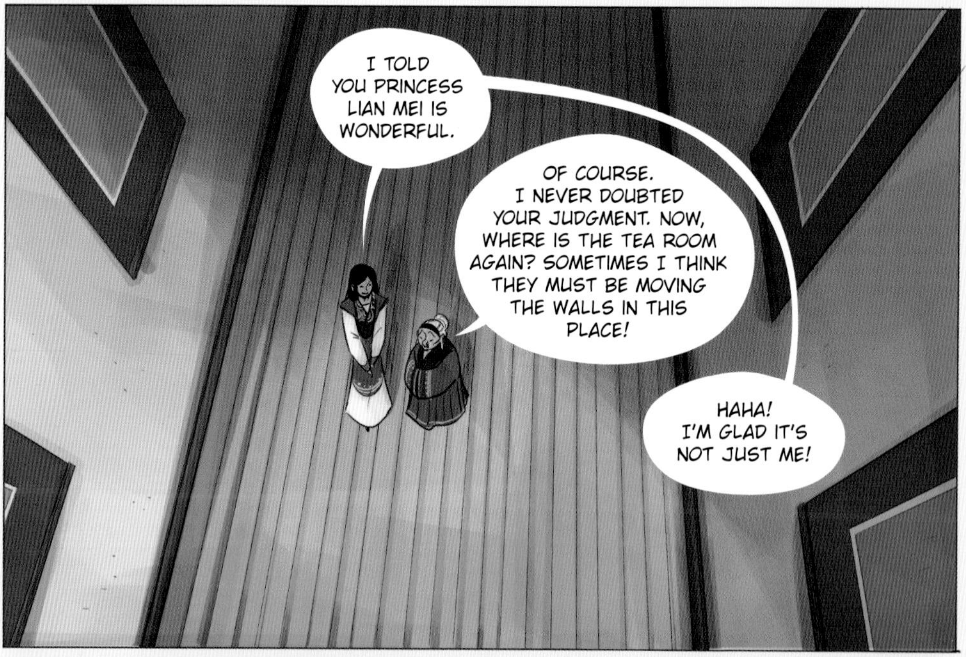
I TOLD YOU PRINCESS LIAN MEI IS WONDERFUL.
OF COURSE. I NEVER DOUBTED YOUR JUDGMENT. NOW, WHERE IS THE TEA ROOM AGAIN? SOMETIMES I THINK THEY MUST BE MOVING THE WALLS IN THIS PLACE!
HAHA! I'M GLAD IT'S NOT JUST ME!

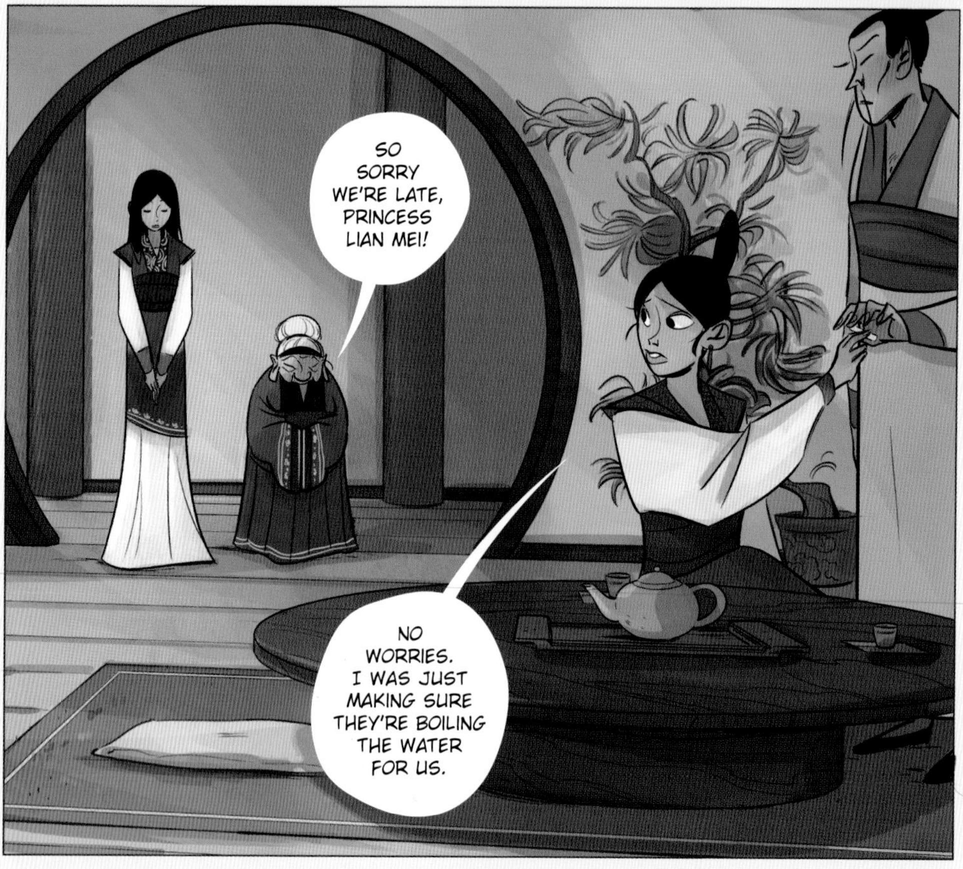
SO SORRY WE'RE LATE, PRINCESS LIAN MEI!
NO WORRIES. I WAS JUST MAKING SURE THEY'RE BOILING THE WATER FOR US.

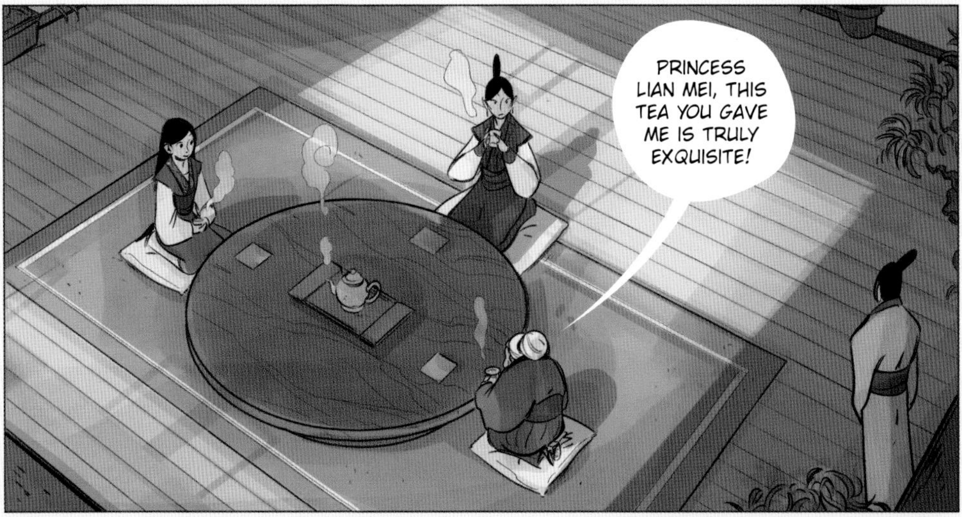
PRINCESS LIAN MEI, THIS TEA YOU GAVE ME IS TRULY EXQUISITE!

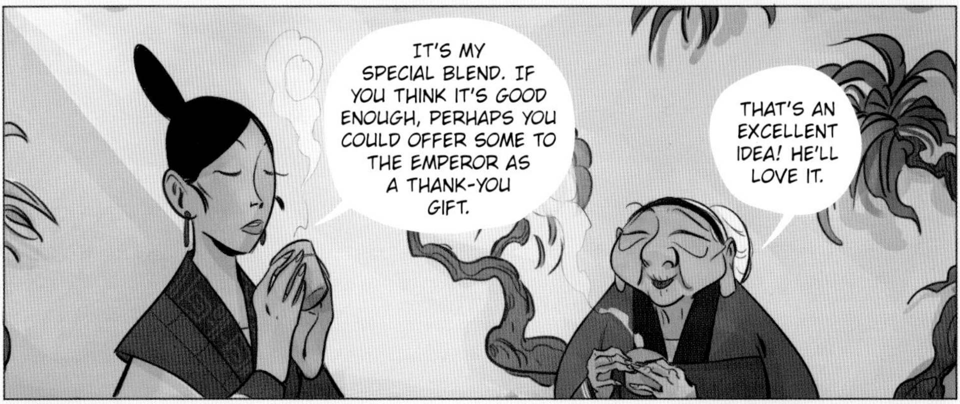
IT'S MY SPECIAL BLEND. IF YOU THINK IT'S GOOD ENOUGH, PERHAPS YOU COULD OFFER SOME TO THE EMPEROR AS A THANK-YOU GIFT.
THAT'S AN EXCELLENT IDEA! HE'LL LOVE IT.

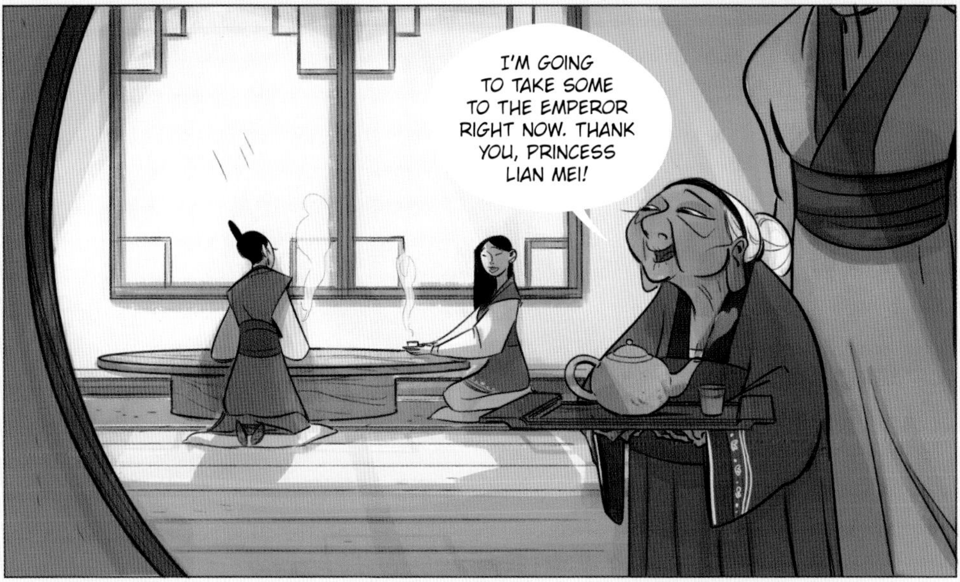
I'M GOING TO TAKE SOME TO THE EMPEROR RIGHT NOW. THANK YOU, PRINCESS LIAN MEI!

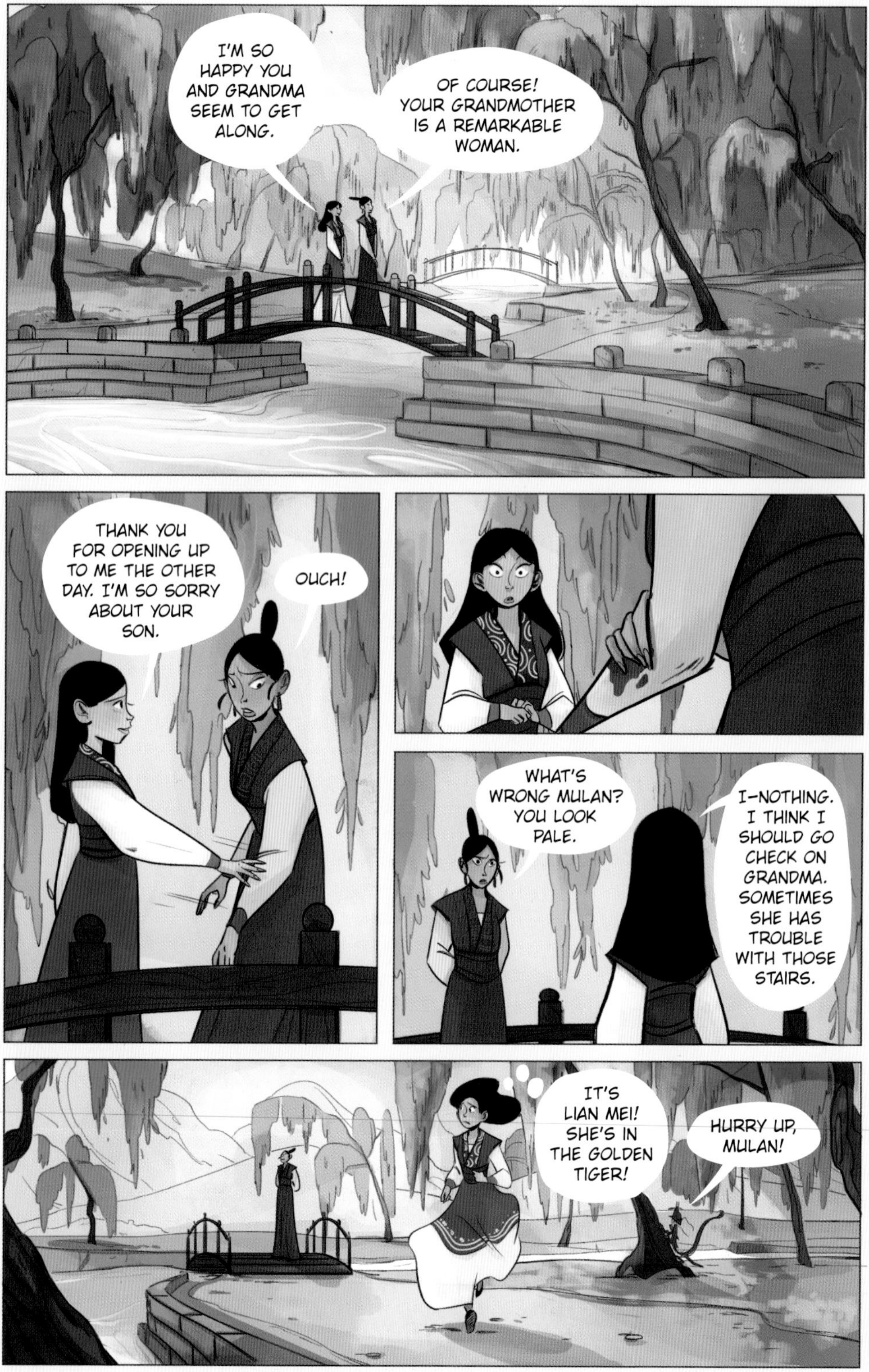
I'M SO HAPPY YOU AND GRANDMA SEEM TO GET ALONG.
OF COURSE! YOUR GRANDMOTHER IS A REMARKABLE WOMAN.
THANK YOU FOR OPENING UP TO ME THE OTHER DAY. I'M SO SORRY ABOUT YOUR SON.
OUCH!
WHAT'S WRONG MULAN? YOU LOOK PALE.
I-NOTHING. I THINK I SHOULD GO CHECK ON GRANDMA. SOMETIMES SHE HAS TROUBLE WITH THOSE STAIRS.
IT'S LIAN MEI! SHE'S IN THE GOLDEN TIGER!
HURRY UP, MULAN!

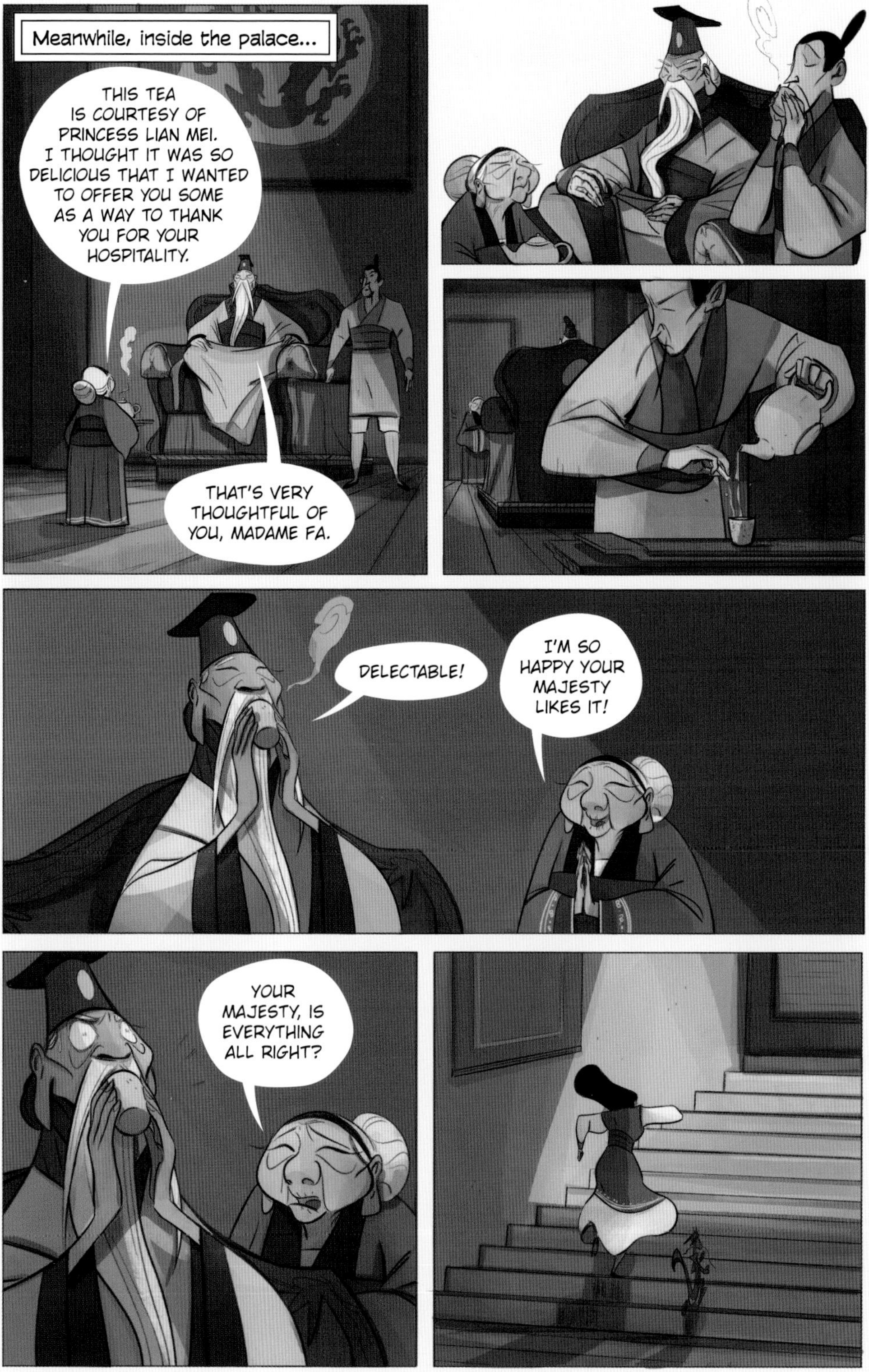
Meanwhile, inside the palace...
THIS TEA IS COURTESY OF PRINCESS LIAN MEI. I THOUGHT IT WAS SO DELICIOUS THAT I WANTED TO OFFER YOU SOME AS A WAY TO THANK YOU FOR YOUR HOSPITALITY.
THAT'S VERY THOUGHTFUL OF YOU, MADAME FA.
DELECTABLE!
I'M SO HAPPY YOUR MAJESTY LIKES IT!
YOUR MAJESTY, IS EVERYTHING ALL RIGHT?

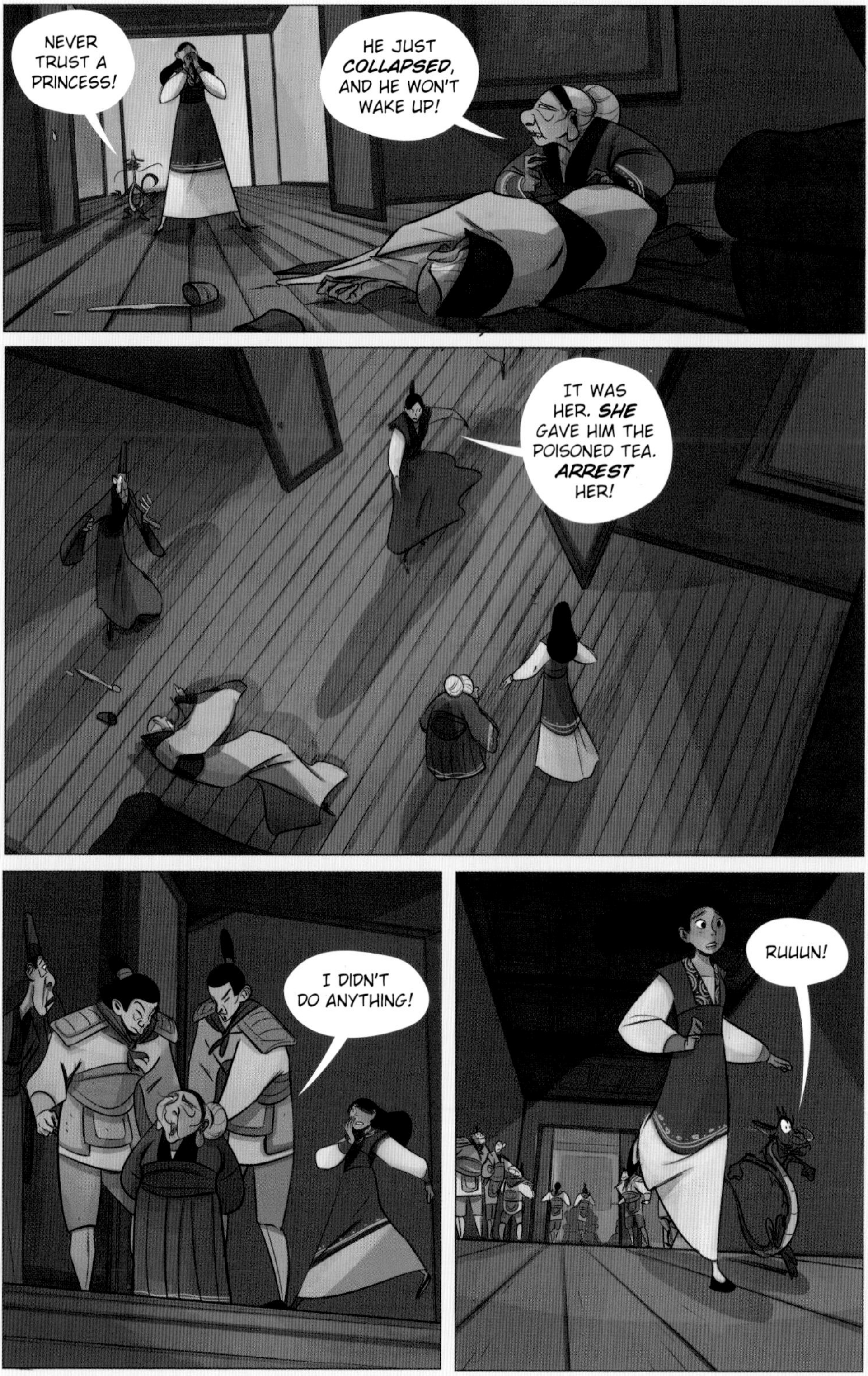
NEVER TRUST A PRINCESS!
HE JUST COLLAPSED, AND HE WON'T WAKE UP!
IT WAS HER. SHE GAVE HIM THE POISONED TEA. ARREST HER!
I DIDN'T DO ANYTHING!
RUUUN!

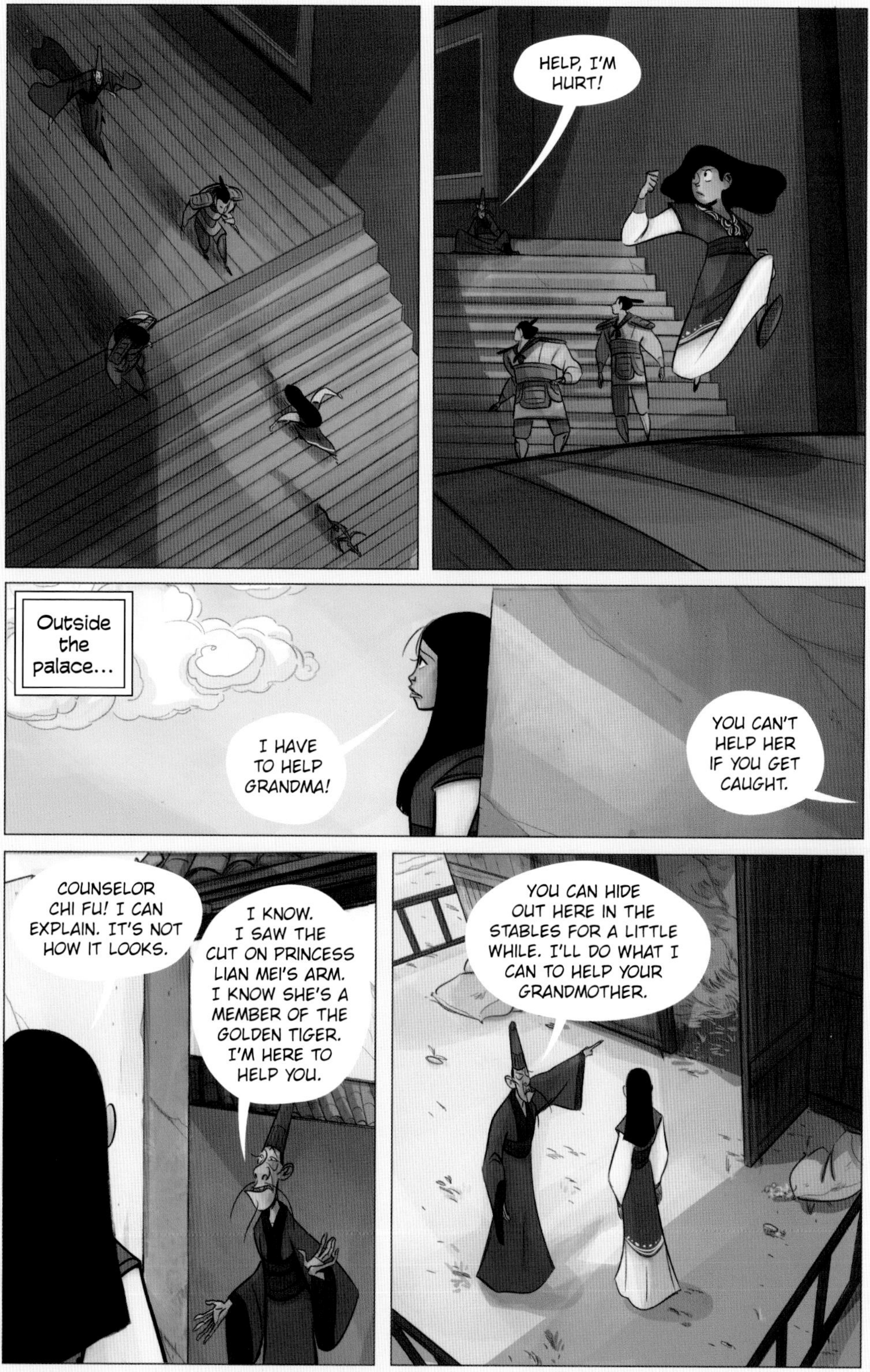
HELP, I'M HURT!
Outside the palace...
I HAVE TO HELP GRANDMA!
YOU CAN'T HELP HER IF YOU GET CAUGHT.
COUNSELOR CHI FU! I CAN EXPLAIN. IT'S NOT HOW IT LOOKS.
I KNOW. I SAW THE CUT ON PRINCESS LIAN MEI'S ARM. I KNOW SHE'S A MEMBER OF THE GOLDEN TIGER. I'M HERE TO HELP YOU.
YOU CAN HIDE OUT HERE IN THE STABLES FOR A LITTLE WHILE. I'LL DO WHAT I CAN TO HELP YOUR GRANDMOTHER.

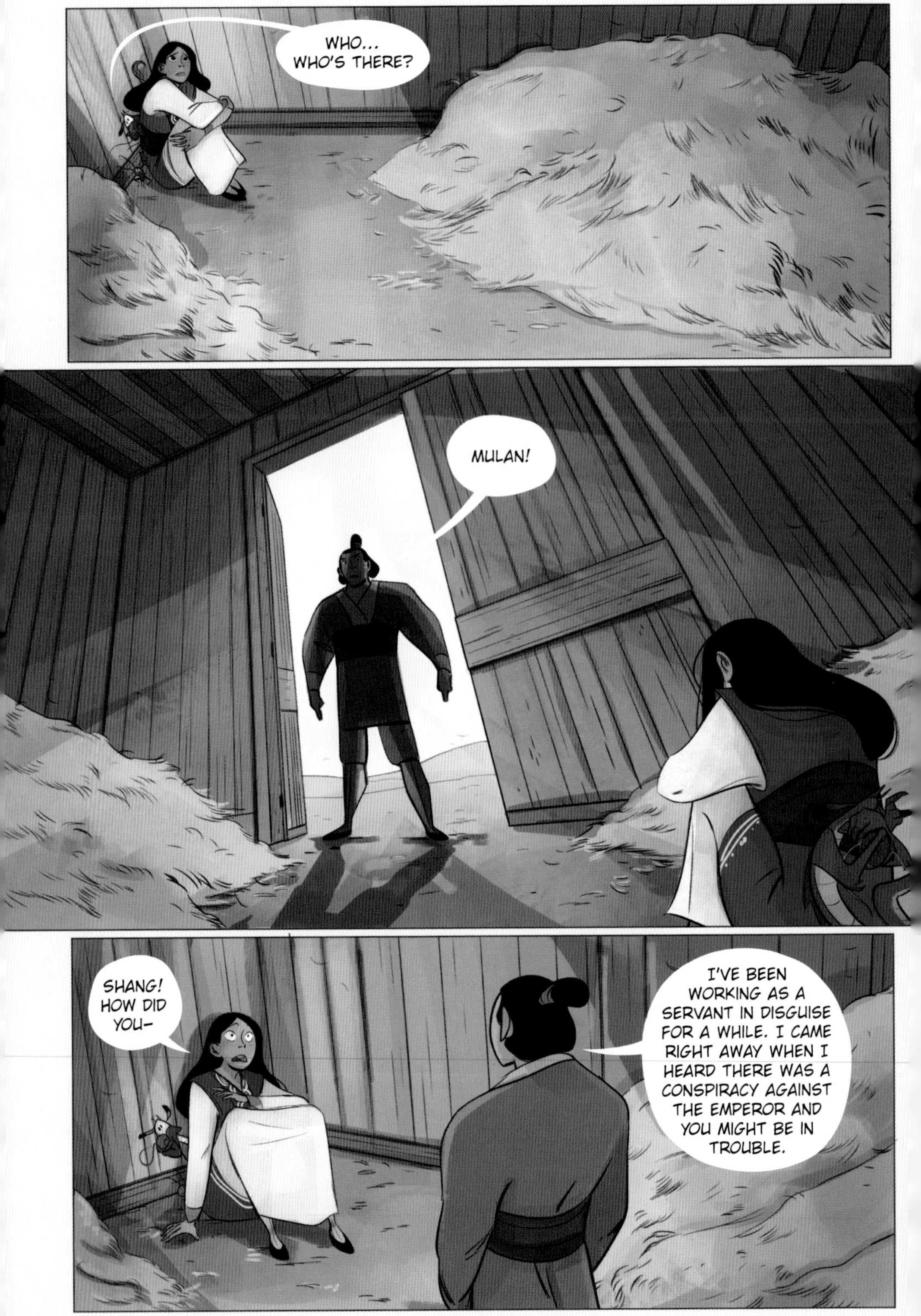
WHO... WHO'S THERE?
MULAN!
SHANG! HOW DID YOU-
I'VE BEEN WORKING AS A SERVANT IN DISGUISE FOR A WHILE. I CAME RIGHT AWAY WHEN I HEARD THERE WAS A CONSPIRACY AGAINST THE EMPEROR AND YOU MIGHT BE IN TROUBLE.

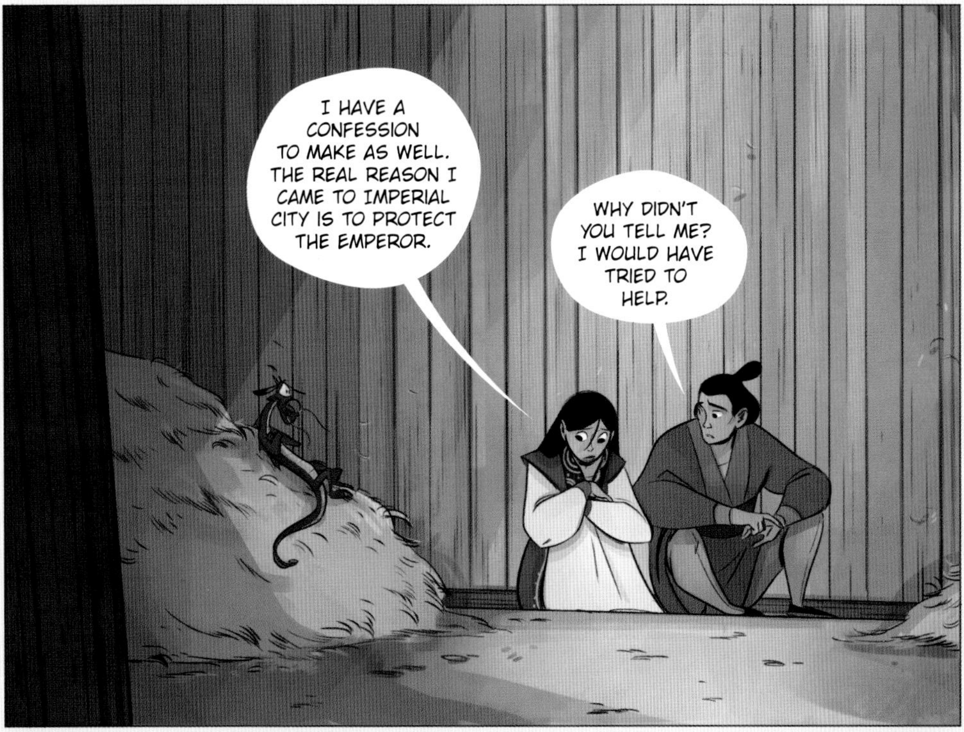
I HAVE A CONFESSION TO MAKE AS WELL. THE REAL REASON I CAME TO IMPERIAL CITY IS TO PROTECT THE EMPEROR.
WHY DIDN'T YOU TELL ME? I WOULD HAVE TRIED TO HELP.

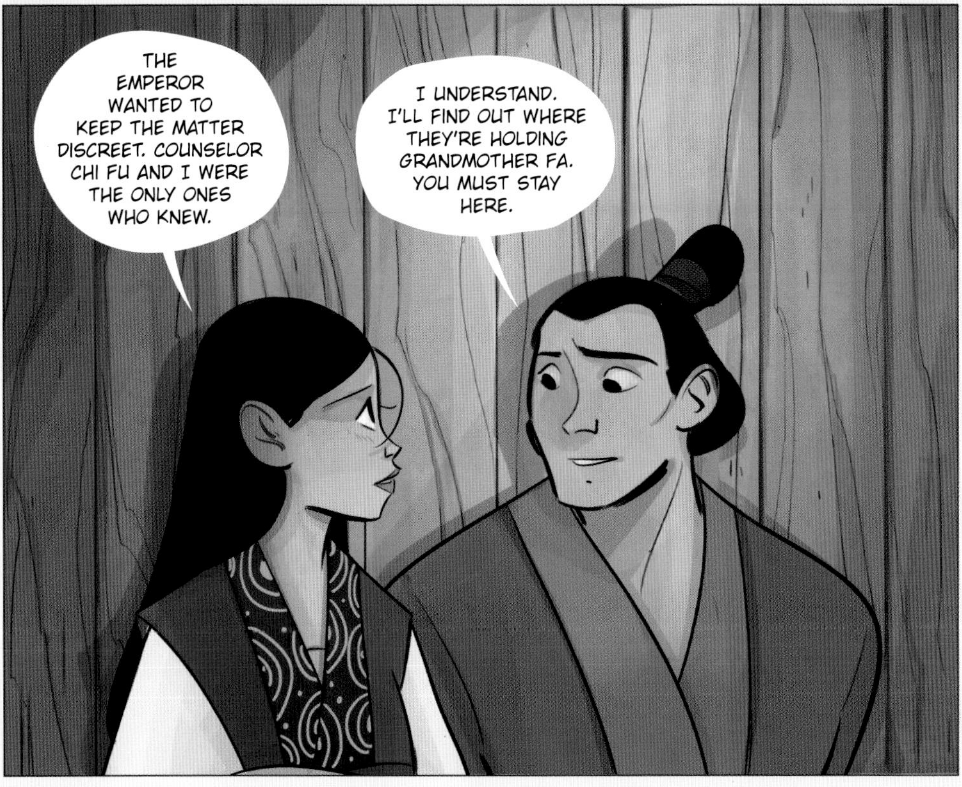
THE EMPEROR WANTED TO KEEP THE MATTER DISCREET. COUNSELOR CHI FU AND I WERE THE ONLY ONES WHO KNEW.
I UNDERSTAND. I'LL FIND OUT WHERE THEY'RE HOLDING GRANDMOTHER FA. YOU MUST STAY HERE.

It's getting dark outside, but I'm afraid to move in case there are any guards standing nearby. I'm so worried about Grandma. I know she's still strong, even though she must be scared. But I would be of even less help if I were stuck in prison with her, so I had to escape quickly.

I'm still reeling from the realization that Princess Lian Mei is a member of the Golden Tiger. She must have been carrying so much anger about her son dying in battle against the Huns. I know she blames the Emperor for not going to war.

I feel so naive for not seeing that her friendliness was all an act. I can't believe she would do that to her own cousin. It's devastating to think about!

I hope I don't have to stay in here too long. I'm glad to be safe for now, but I can't stay in hiding while the members of the Golden Tiger still roam free and the Emperor is on his deathbed. Also, I don't think I can stand the smell of horses for much longer.

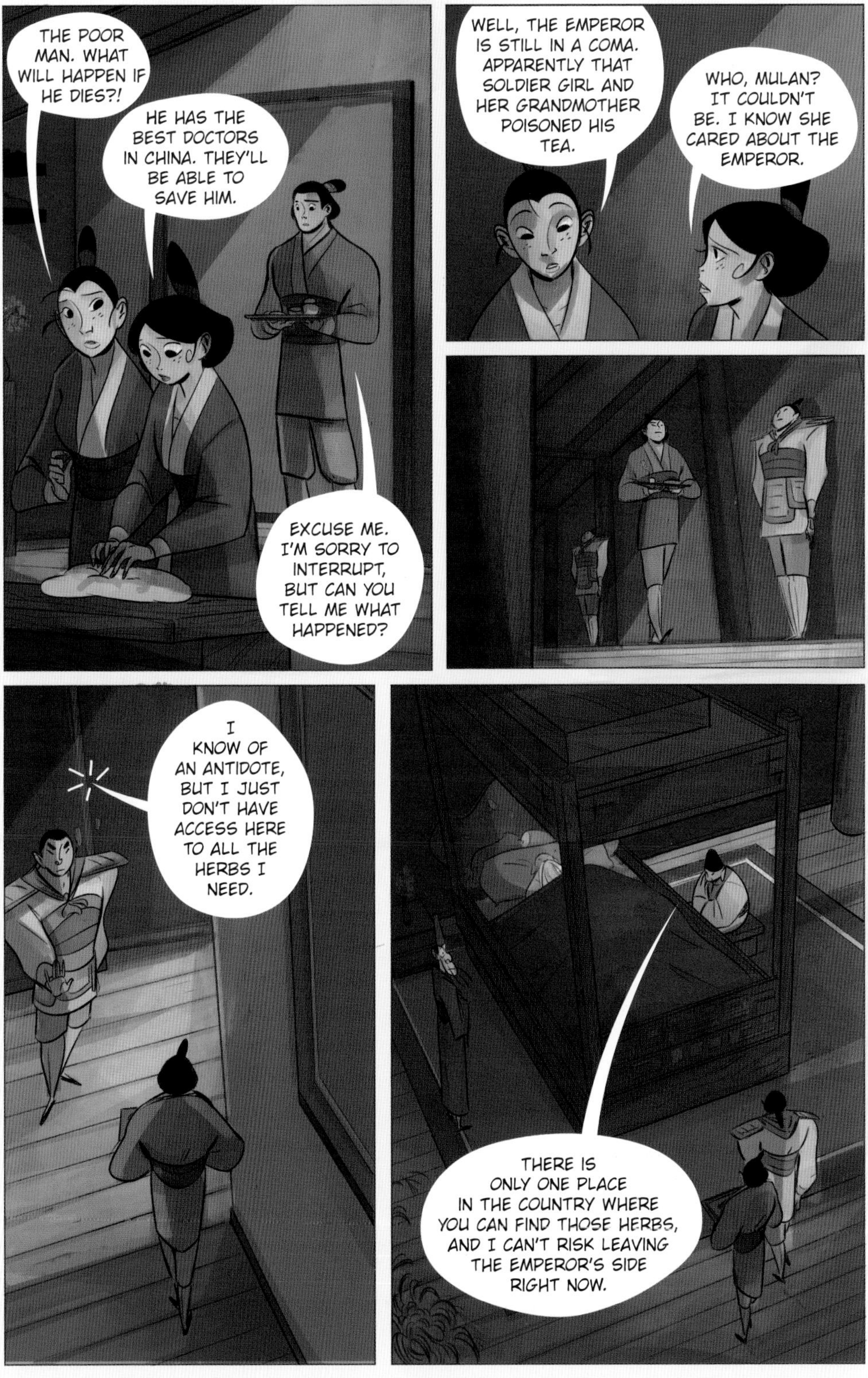
THE POOR MAN. WHAT WILL HAPPEN IF HE DIES?!
HE HAS THE BEST DOCTORS IN CHINA. THEY'LL BE ABLE TO SAVE HIM.
EXCUSE ME. I'M SORRY TO INTERRUPT, BUT CAN YOU TELL ME WHAT HAPPENED?
WELL, THE EMPEROR IS STILL IN A COMA. APPARENTLY THAT SOLDIER GIRL AND HER GRANDMOTHER POISONED HIS TEA.
WHO, MULAN? IT COULDN'T BE. I KNOW SHE CARED ABOUT THE EMPEROR.
I KNOW OF AN ANTIDOTE, BUT I JUST DON'T HAVE ACCESS HERE TO ALL THE HERBS I NEED.
THERE IS ONLY ONE PLACE IN THE COUNTRY WHERE YOU CAN FIND THOSE HERBS, AND I CAN'T RISK LEAVING THE EMPEROR'S SIDE RIGHT NOW.

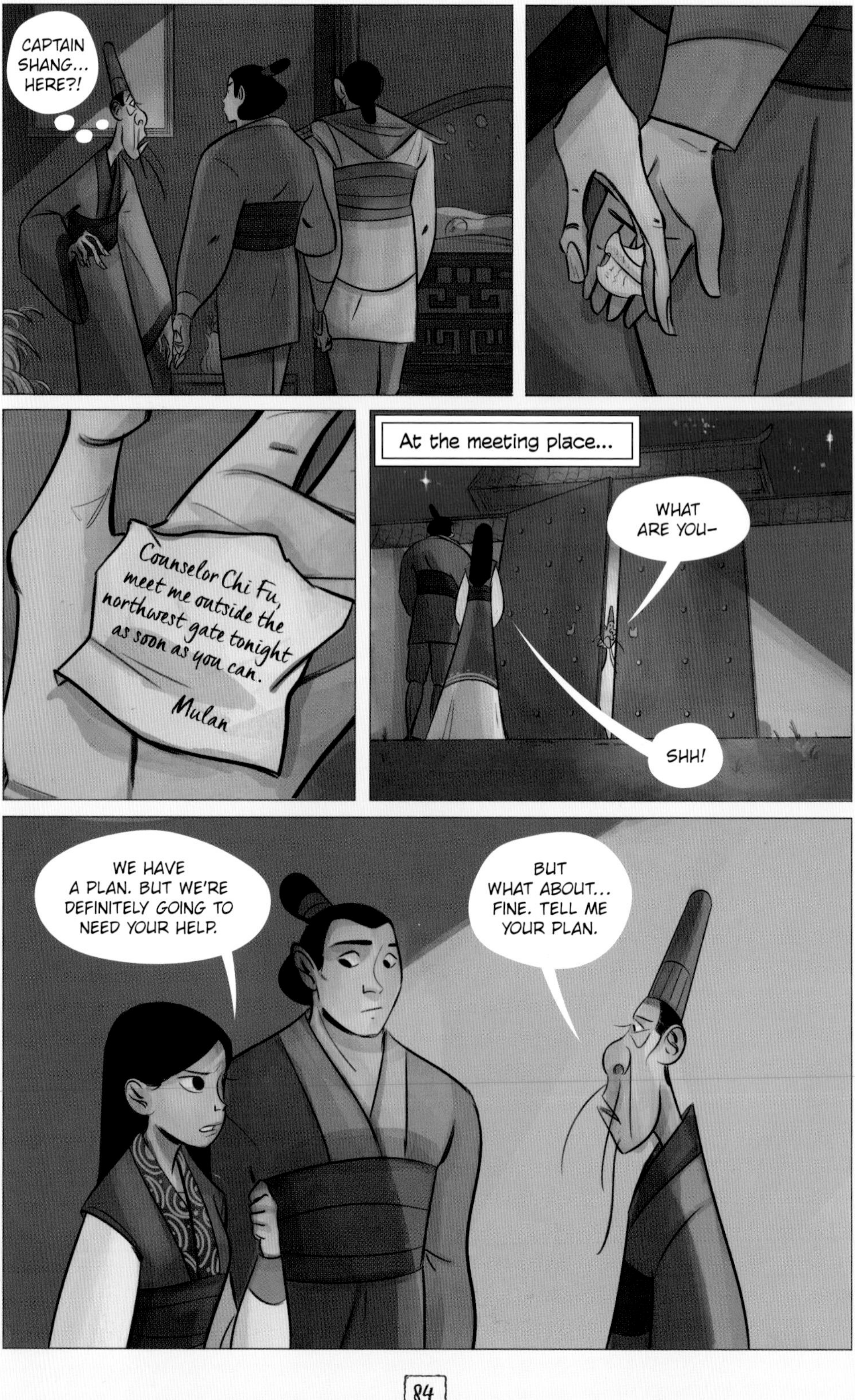

CAPTAIN SHANG... HERE?!
Counselor Chi Fu, meet me outside the northwest gate tonight as soon as you can. Mulan
At the meeting place...
WHAT ARE YOU-
SHH!
WE HAVE A PLAN. BUT WE'RE DEFINITELY GOING TO NEED YOUR HELP.
BUT WHAT ABOUT... FINE. TELL ME YOUR PLAN.

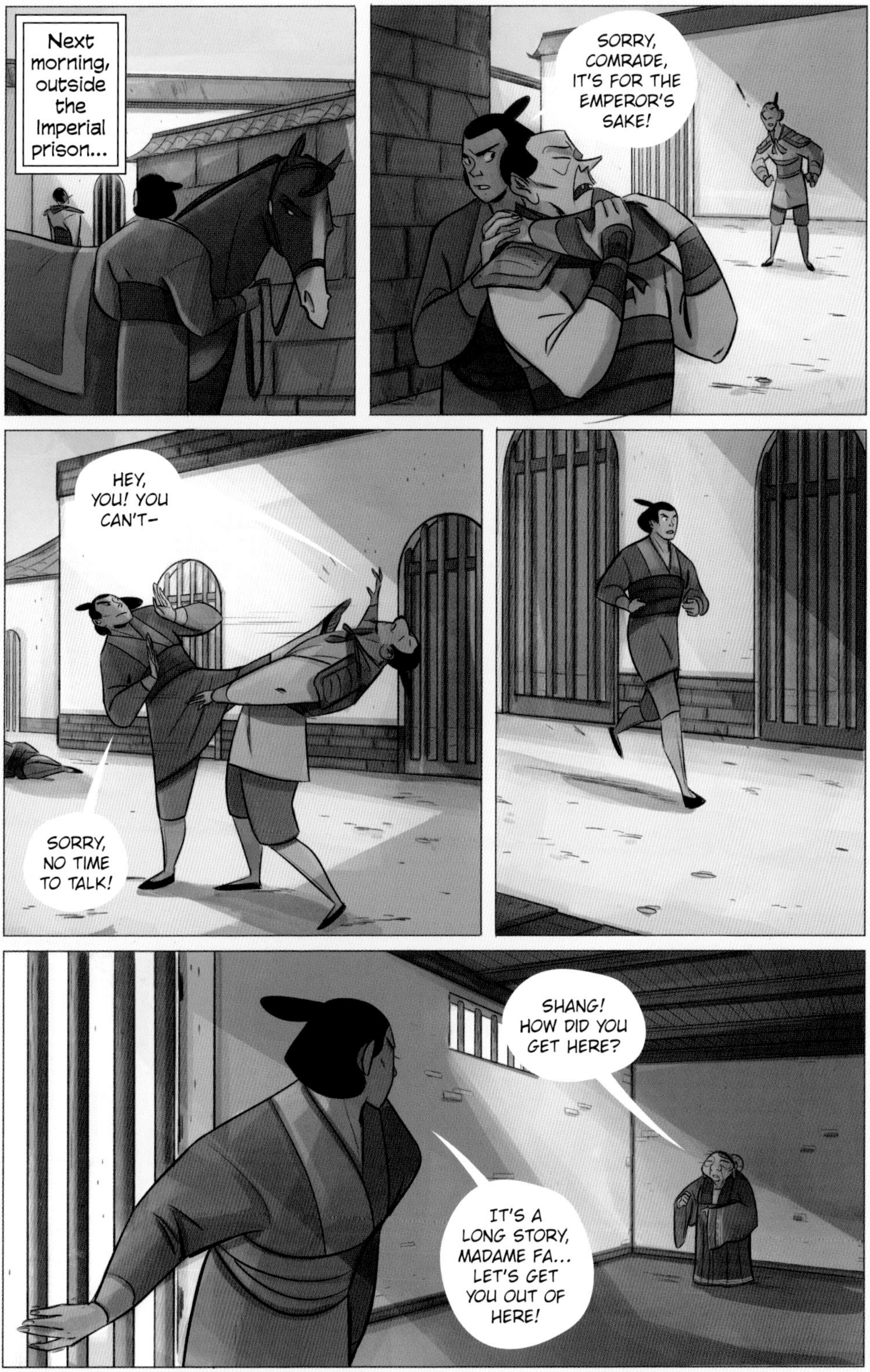
Next morning, outside the Imperial prison...
SORRY, COMRADE, IT'S FOR THE EMPEROR'S SAKE!
HEY, YOU! YOU CAN'T-
SORRY, NO TIME TO TALK!
SHANG! HOW DID YOU GET HERE?
IT'S A LONG STORY, MADAME FA... LET'S GET YOU OUT OF HERE!

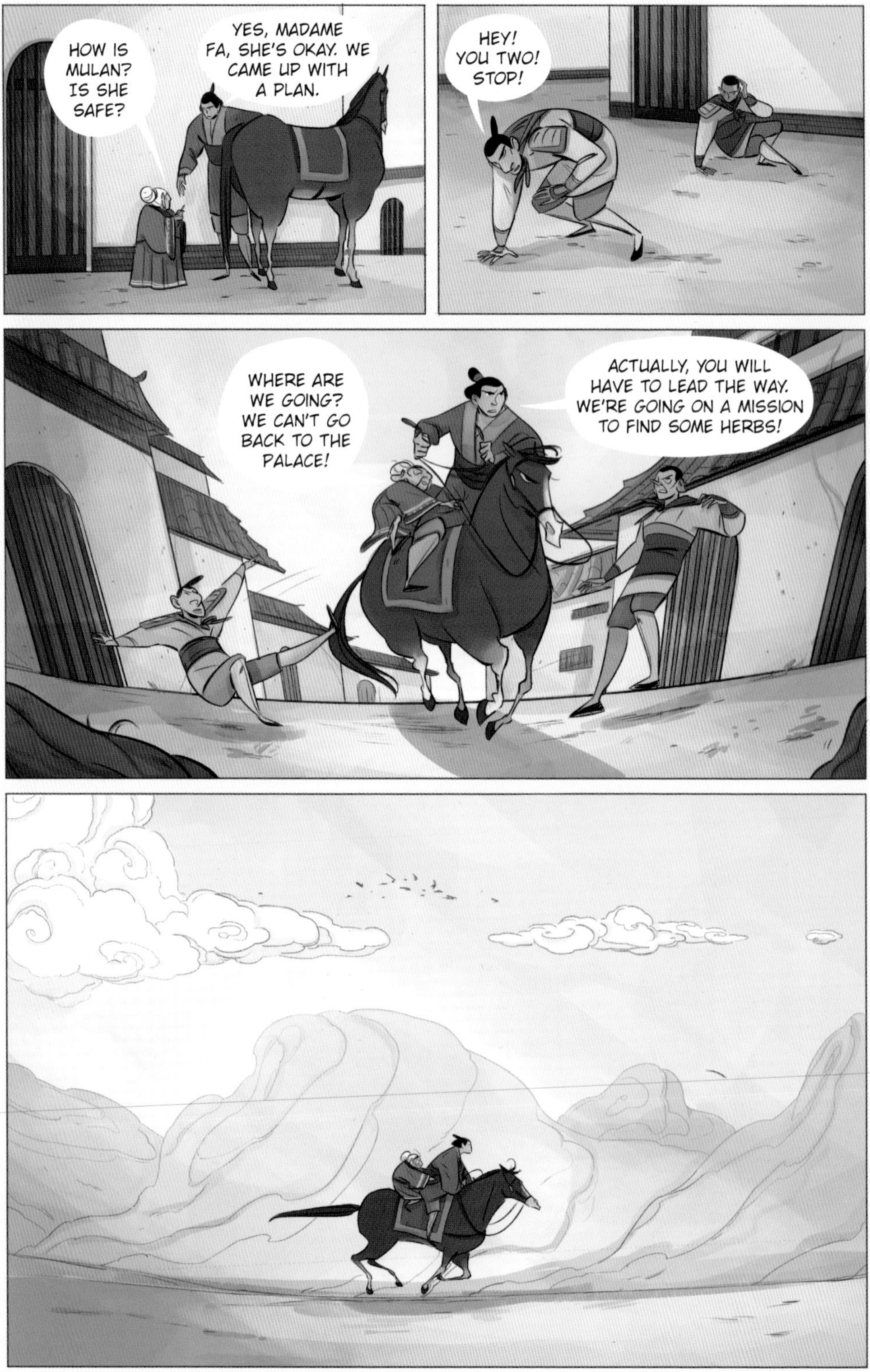
HOW IS MULAN? IS SHE SAFE?
YES, MADAME FA, SHE'S OKAY. WE CAME UP WITH A PLAN.
HEY! YOU TWO! STOP!
WHERE ARE WE GOING? WE CAN'T GO BACK TO THE PALACE!
ACTUALLY, YOU WILL HAVE TO LEAD THE WAY. WE'RE GOING ON A MISSION TO FIND SOME HERBS!

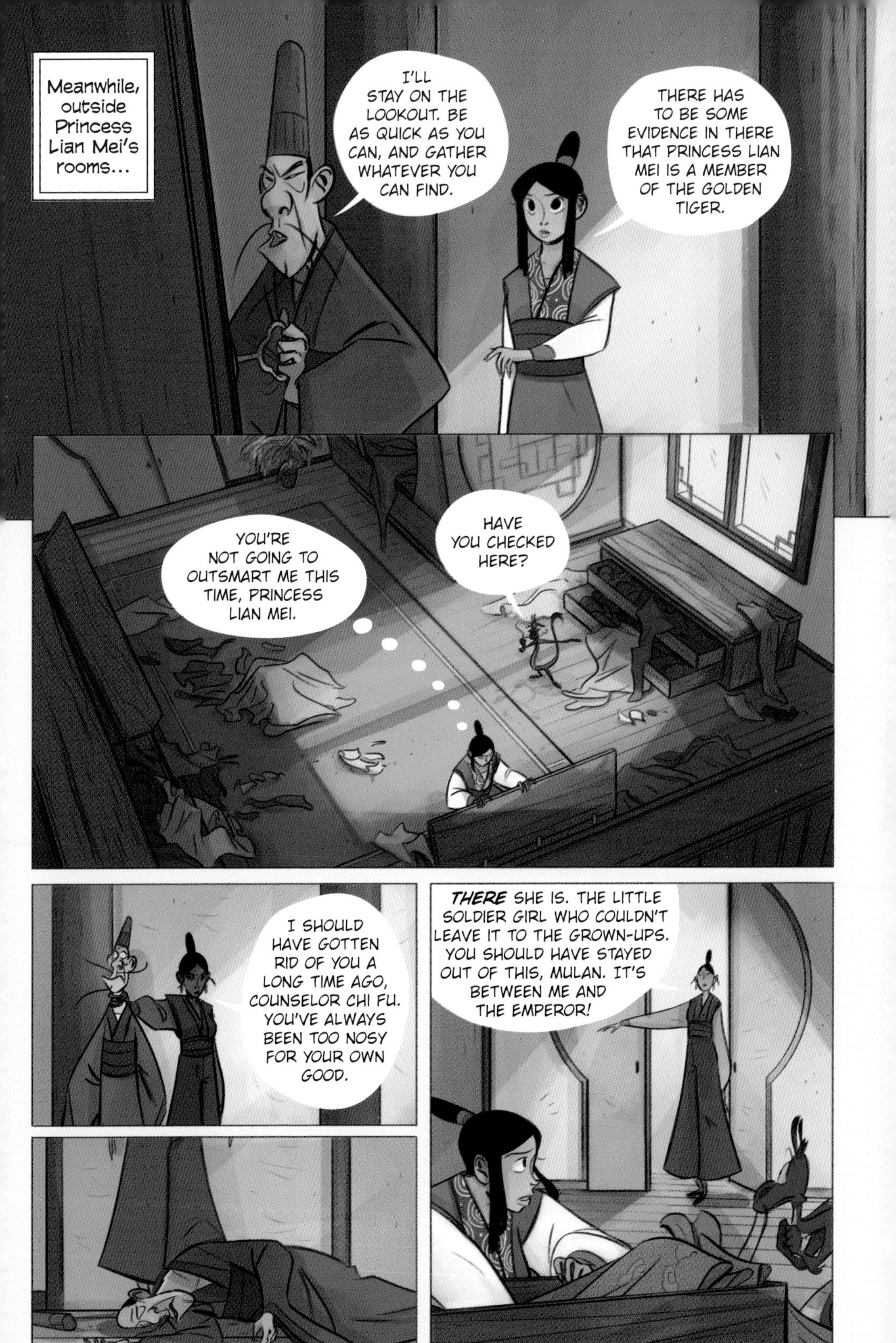
Meanwhile, outside Princess Lian Mei's rooms...
I'LL STAY ON THE LOOKOUT. BE AS QUICK AS YOU CAN, AND GATHER WHATEVER YOU CAN FIND.
THERE HAS TO BE SOME EVIDENCE IN THERE THAT PRINCESS LIAN MEI IS A MEMBER OF THE GOLDEN TIGER.
YOU'RE NOT GOING TO OUTSMART ME THIS TIME, PRINCESS LIAN MEI.
HAVE YOU CHECKED HERE?
I SHOULD HAVE GOTTEN RID OF YOU A LONG TIME AGO, COUNSELOR CHI FU. YOU'VE ALWAYS BEEN TOO NOSY FOR YOUR OWN GOOD.
THERE SHE IS. THE LITTLE SOLDIER GIRL WHO COULDN'T LEAVE IT TO THE GROWN-UPS. YOU SHOULD HAVE STAYED OUT OF THIS, MULAN. IT'S BETWEEN ME AND THE EMPEROR!

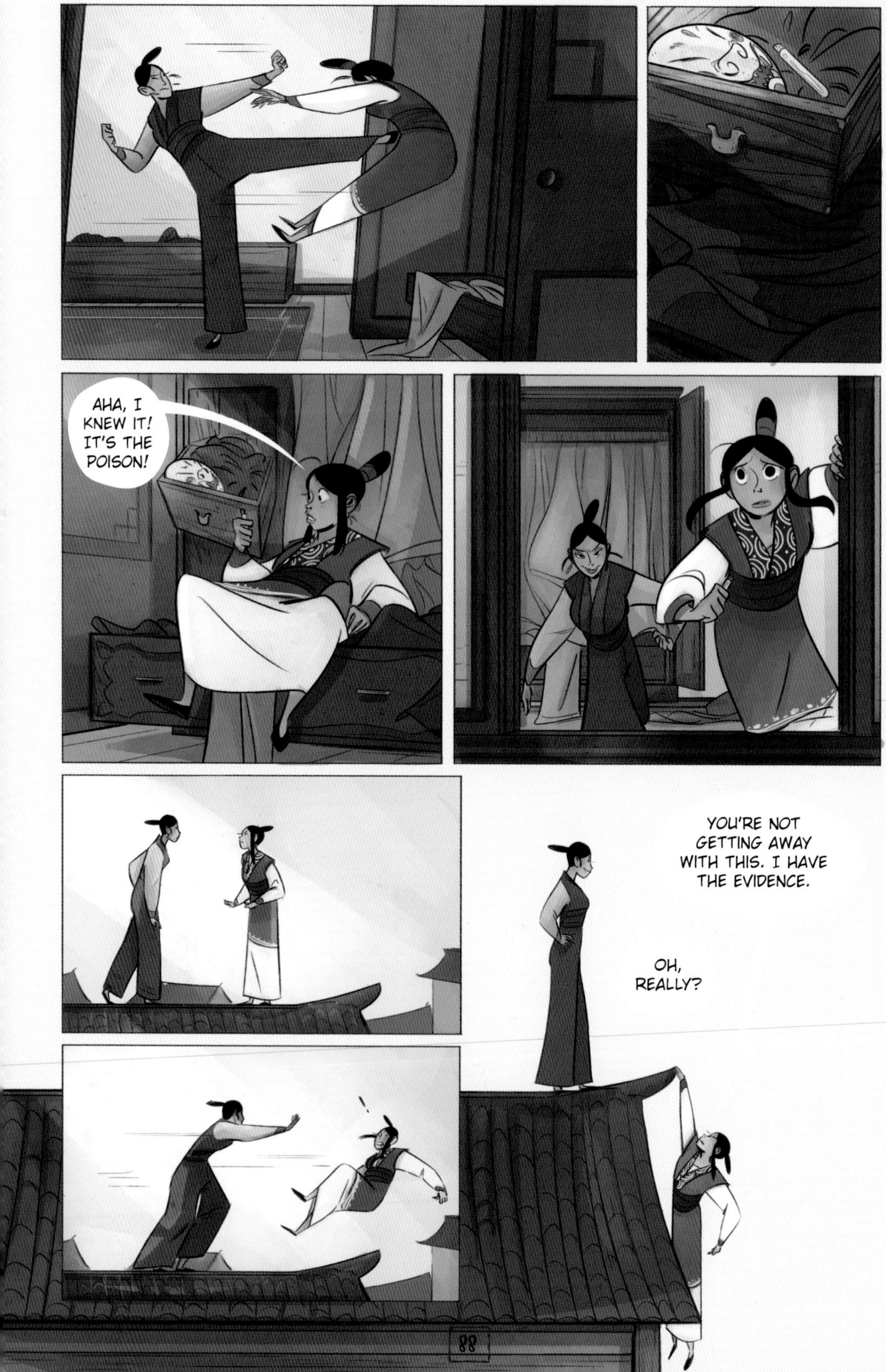
AHA, I KNEW IT! IT'S THE POISON!
YOU'RE NOT GETTING AWAY WITH THIS. I HAVE THE EVIDENCE.
OH, REALLY?
!

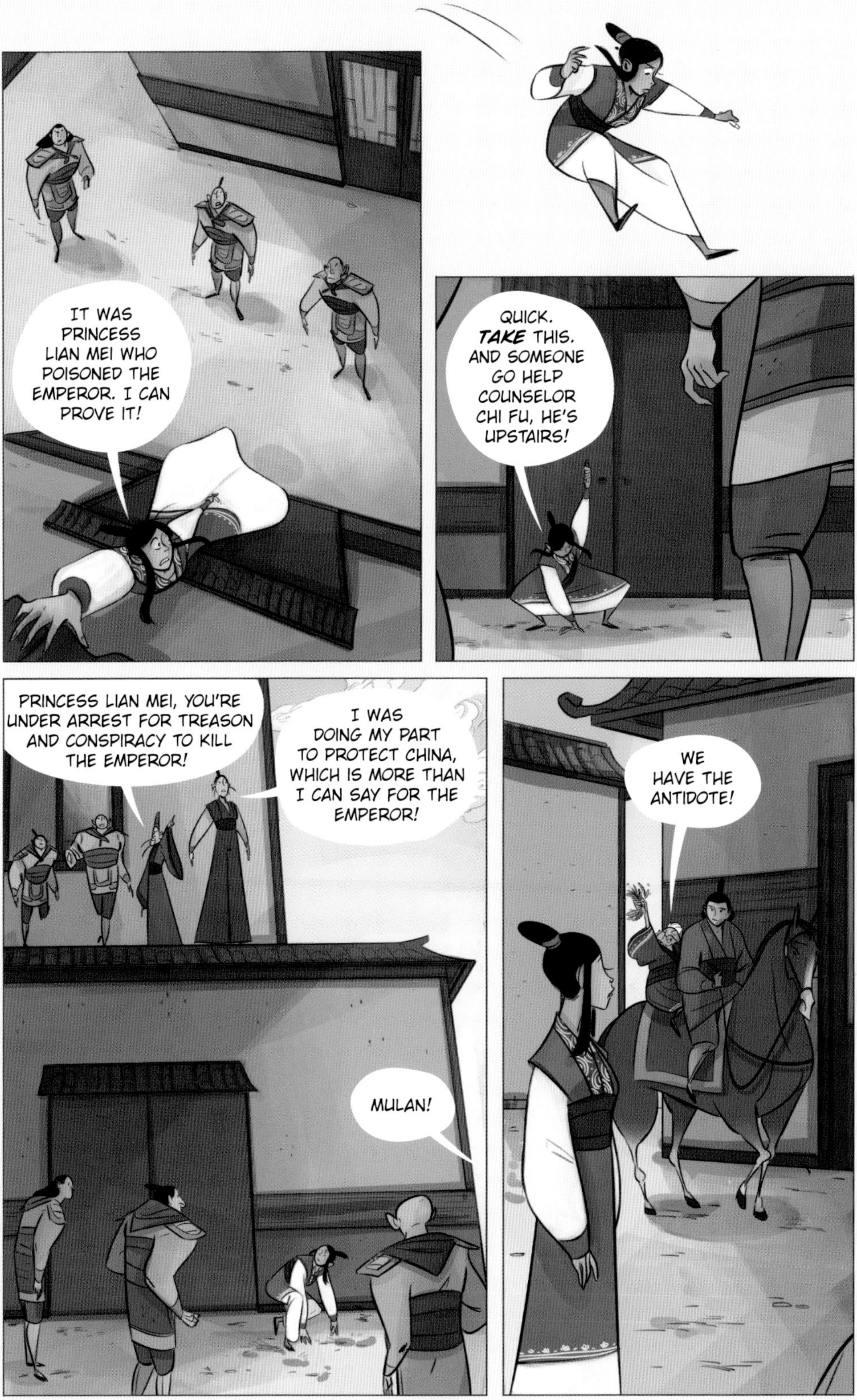
IT WAS PRINCESS LIAN MEI WHO POISONED THE EMPEROR. I CAN PROVE IT!
QUICK. **TAKE** THIS. AND SOMEONE GO HELP COUNSELOR CHI FU, HE'S UPSTAIRS!
PRINCESS LIAN MEI, YOU'RE UNDER ARREST FOR TREASON AND CONSPIRACY TO KILL THE EMPEROR!
I WAS DOING MY PART TO PROTECT CHINA, WHICH IS MORE THAN I CAN SAY FOR THE EMPEROR!
MULAN!
WE HAVE THE ANTIDOTE!

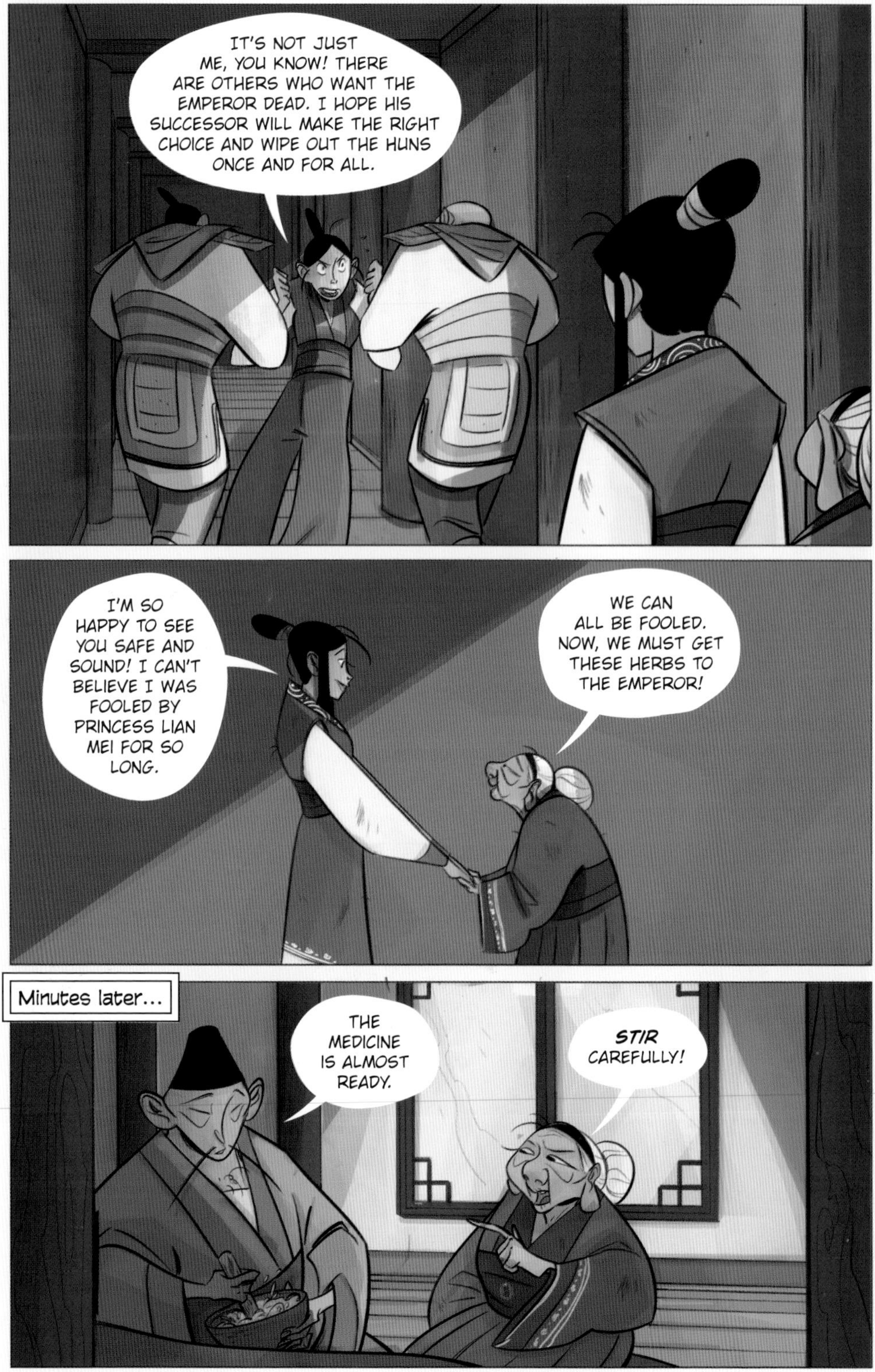
IT'S NOT JUST ME, YOU KNOW! THERE ARE OTHERS WHO WANT THE EMPEROR DEAD. I HOPE HIS SUCCESSOR WILL MAKE THE RIGHT CHOICE AND WIPE OUT THE HUNS ONCE AND FOR ALL.
I'M SO HAPPY TO SEE YOU SAFE AND SOUND! I CAN'T BELIEVE I WAS FOOLED BY PRINCESS LIAN MEI FOR SO LONG.
WE CAN ALL BE FOOLED. NOW, WE MUST GET THESE HERBS TO THE EMPEROR!
Minutes later...
THE MEDICINE IS ALMOST READY.
STIR CAREFULLY!

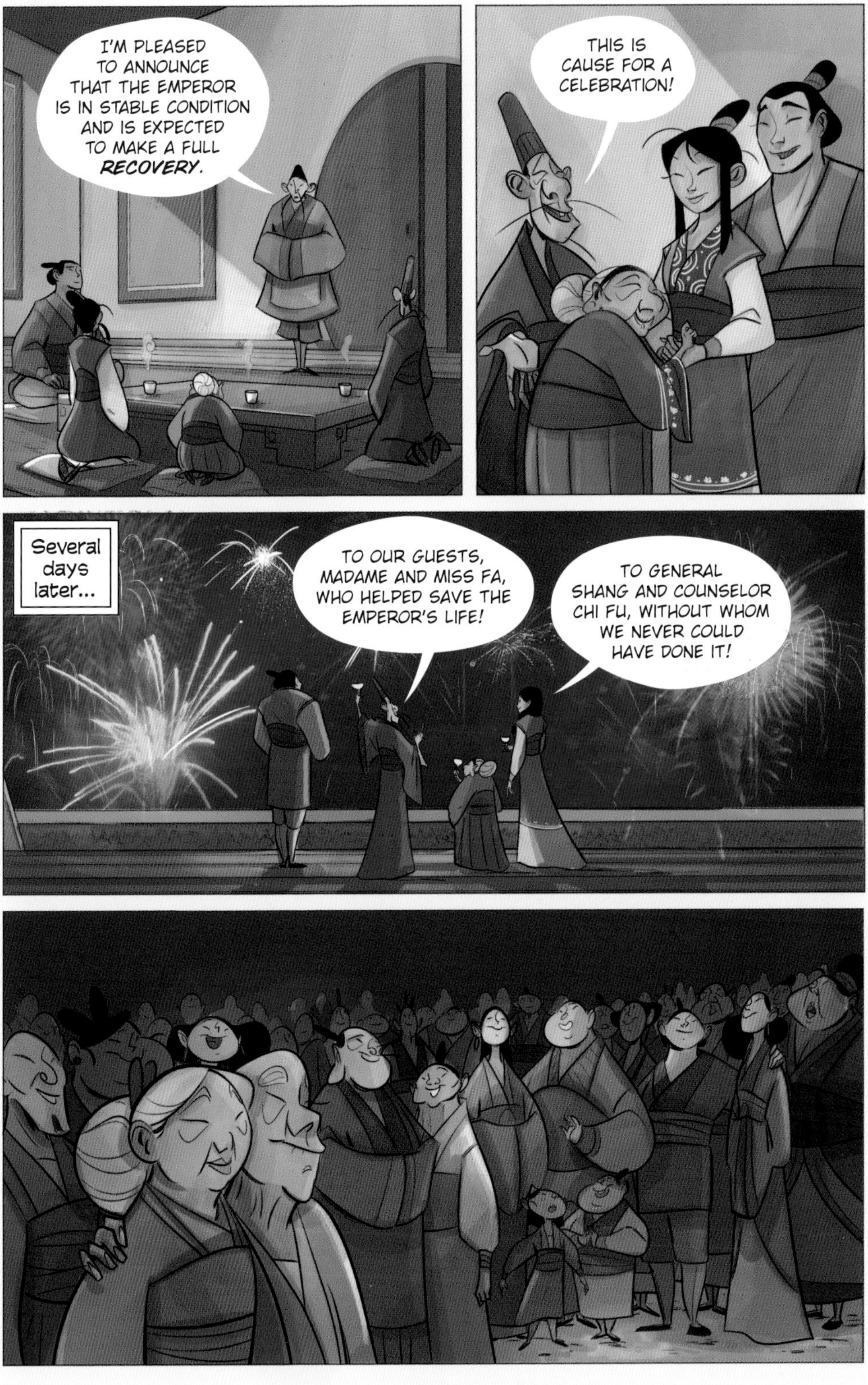
I'M PLEASED TO ANNOUNCE THAT THE EMPEROR IS IN STABLE CONDITION AND IS EXPECTED TO MAKE A FULL RECOVERY.
THIS IS CAUSE FOR A CELEBRATION!
Several days later...
TO OUR GUESTS, MADAME AND MISS FA, WHO HELPED SAVE THE EMPEROR'S LIFE!
TO GENERAL SHANG AND COUNSELOR CHI FU, WITHOUT WHOM WE NEVER COULD HAVE DONE IT!

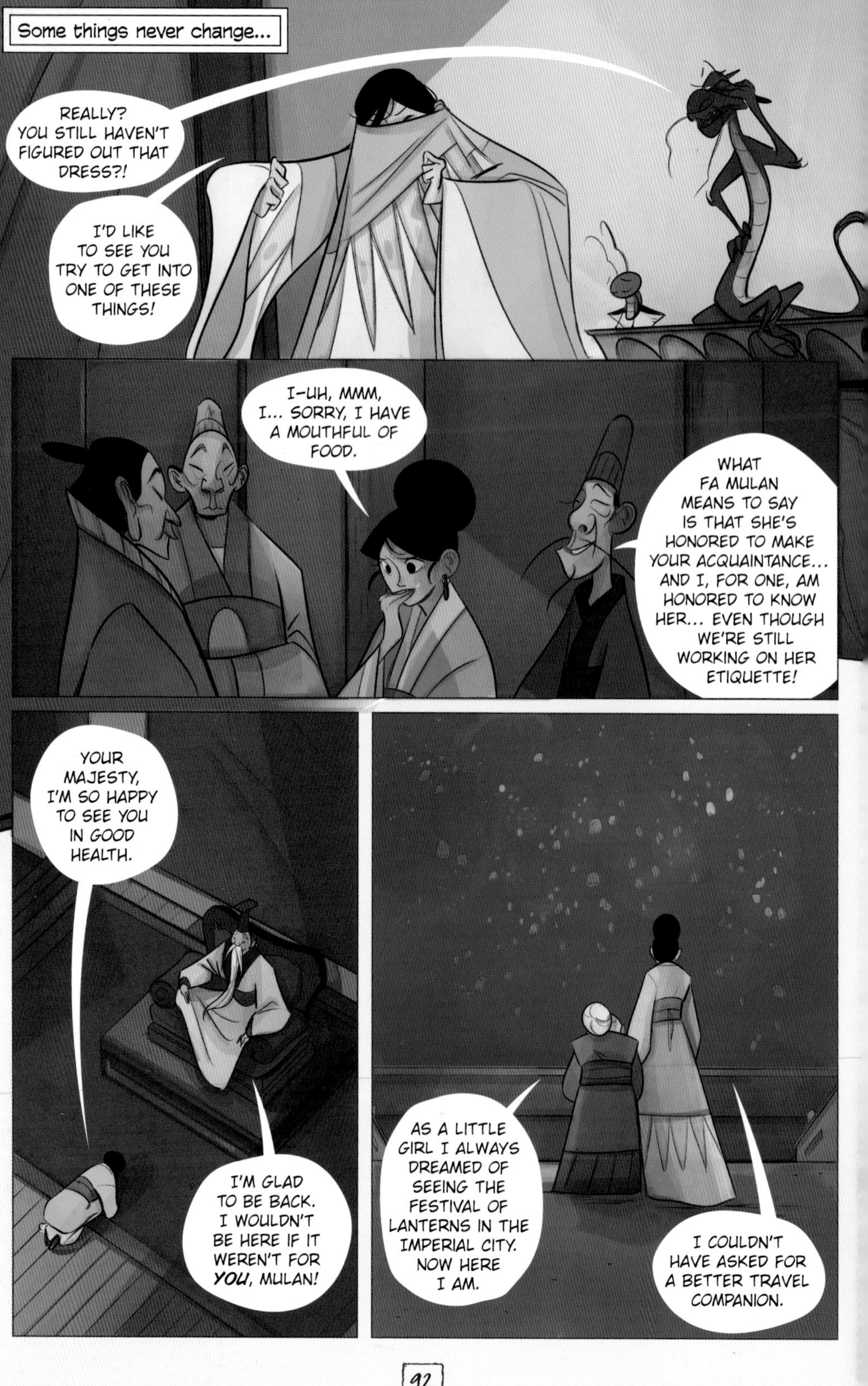
Some things never change...
REALLY? YOU STILL HAVEN'T FIGURED OUT THAT DRESS?!
I'D LIKE TO SEE YOU TRY TO GET INTO ONE OF THESE THINGS!
I-UH, MMM, I... SORRY, I HAVE A MOUTHFUL OF FOOD.
WHAT FA MULAN MEANS TO SAY IS THAT SHE'S HONORED TO MAKE YOUR ACQUAINTANCE... AND I, FOR ONE, AM HONORED TO KNOW HER... EVEN THOUGH WE'RE STILL WORKING ON HER ETIQUETTE!
YOUR MAJESTY, I'M SO HAPPY TO SEE YOU IN GOOD HEALTH.
I'M GLAD TO BE BACK. I WOULDN'T BE HERE IF IT WEREN'T FOR *YOU*, MULAN!
AS A LITTLE GIRL I ALWAYS DREAMED OF SEEING THE FESTIVAL OF LANTERNS IN THE IMPERIAL CITY. NOW HERE I AM.
I COULDN'T HAVE ASKED FOR A BETTER TRAVEL COMPANION.

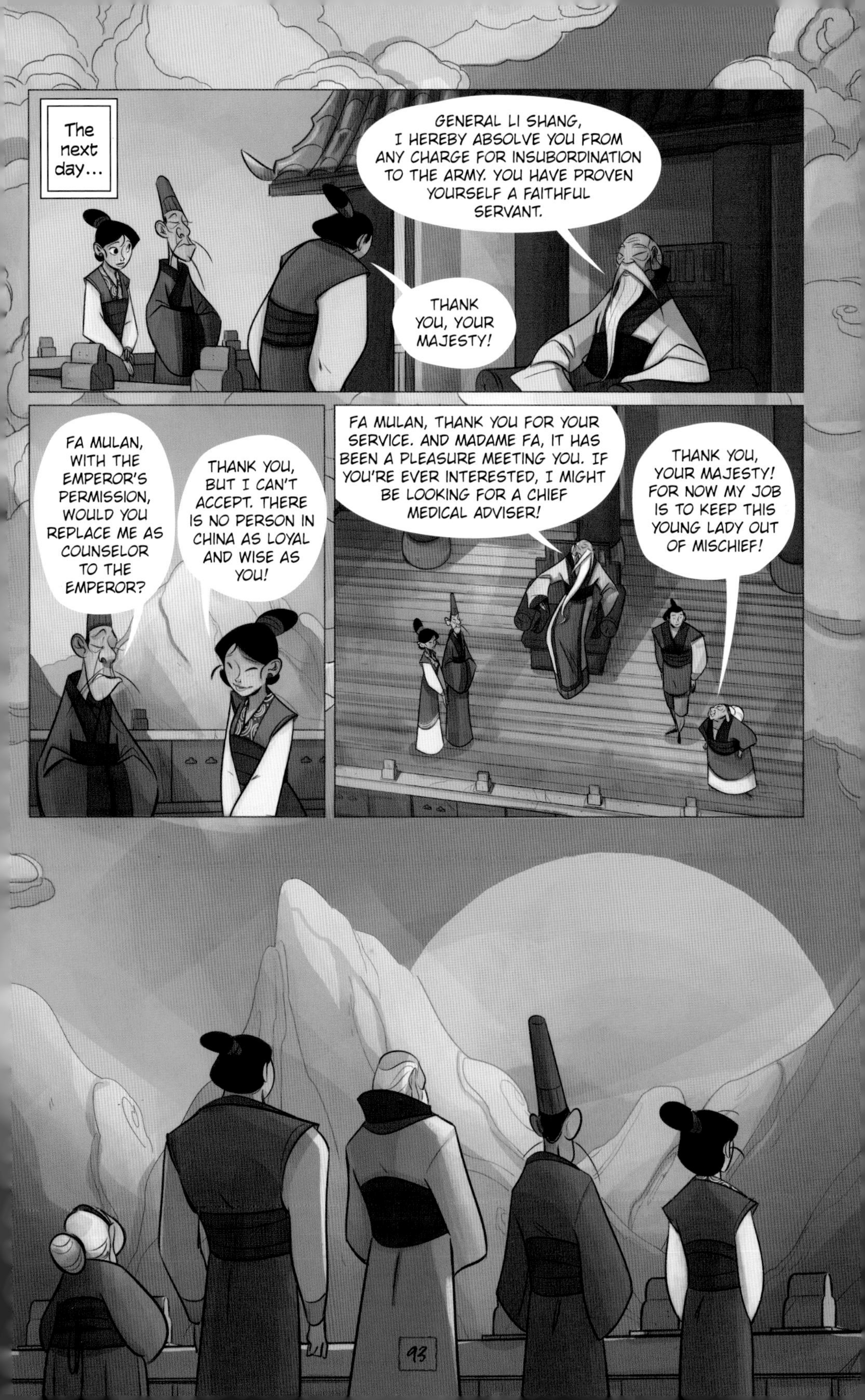
The next day...
GENERAL LI SHANG, I HEREBY ABSOLVE YOU FROM ANY CHARGE FOR INSUBORDINATION TO THE ARMY. YOU HAVE PROVEN YOURSELF A FAITHFUL SERVANT.
THANK YOU, YOUR MAJESTY!
FA MULAN, WITH THE EMPEROR'S PERMISSION, WOULD YOU REPLACE ME AS COUNSELOR TO THE EMPEROR?
THANK YOU, BUT I CAN'T ACCEPT. THERE IS NO PERSON IN CHINA AS LOYAL AND WISE AS YOU!
FA MULAN, THANK YOU FOR YOUR SERVICE. AND MADAME FA, IT HAS BEEN A PLEASURE MEETING YOU. IF YOU'RE EVER INTERESTED, I MIGHT BE LOOKING FOR A CHIEF MEDICAL ADVISER!
THANK YOU, YOUR MAJESTY! FOR NOW MY JOB IS TO KEEP THIS YOUNG LADY OUT OF MISCHIEF!

It's been quite an eventful trip, but Grandma, Shang, and I are heading back to the countryside tomorrow morning. I'm just happy everything worked out in the end and the Emperor is safe. I still get sad when I think about Princess Lian Mei. You just never know who will prove to be the enemy and who will turn out to be your greatest ally.

I've learned a lot of valuable lessons during my stay at the palace. But I'm not sure I'll ever get the hang of those fancy clothes. I definitely won't miss all the formal dinners and court rituals!

On the other hand, I'm quite looking forward to spending some time with Mother and Father back in the peace of the village. I think I've had enough adventure for several lifetimes... Just kidding!

Go: A strategy board game, similar to chess but more complex. The game is played on a much larger board laid out in a grid, with game pieces called stones. The objective of the game is to surround more territory on the board than your opponent. Go was invented in China over 2,500 years ago and is still played throughout the world.

Spring Festival: The centuries-old traditional Chinese New Year celebration, which lasts for fifteen days and is one of the world's biggest festivals. The Spring Festival celebrations begin with the new moon in late January or early February. Many of the ancient customs and traditions associated with it are still observed today, such as cleaning out homes prior to the festival and decorating them with red lanterns, flowers, and colorful pictures for good fortune.

Imperial City: This is a section of the Emperor's capital city that is surrounded by high walls. The Imperial City contains gardens, shrines, and the ancient palace, where the Chinese emperors and their courts once resided and carried out national business.

Chinese Theater Masks: Colorfully decorated masks used in Chinese opera and theater to identify different characters and their emotions. Certain mask colors are associated with specific character traits; for example, a red mask suggests intelligence and bravery, a white mask indicates an evil character, and a yellow mask signals weakness and betrayal.

DARK HORSE BOOKS

president and publisher Mike Richardson / collection editor Freddye Miller / collection assistant editor Judy Khuu / collection designer Scott Erwert / digital art technician Allyson Haller

Neil Hankerson Executive Vice President • Tom Weddle Chief Financial Officer • Randy Stradley Vice President of Publishing • Nick McWhorter Chief Business Development Officer • Dale LaFountain Chief Information Officer • Matt Parkinson Vice President of Marketing • Cara Niece Vice President of Production and Scheduling • Mark Bernardi Vice President of Book Trade and Digital Sales • Ken Lizzi General Counsel • Dave Marshall Editor in Chief • Davey Estrada Editorial Director • Chris Warner Senior Books Editor • Cary Grazzini Director of Specialty Projects • Lia Ribacchi Art Director • Vanessa Todd-Holmes Director of Print Purchasing • Matt Dryer Director of Digital Art and Prepress • Michael Gombos Senior Director of Licensed Publications • Kari Yadro Director of Custom Programs • Kari Torson Director of International Licensing • Sean Brice Director of Trade Sales

DISNEY PUBLISHING WORLDWIDE GLOBAL MAGAZINES, COMICS AND PARTWORKS

PUBLISHER Lynn Waggoner • EDITORIAL TEAM Bianca Coletti (Director, Magazines), Guido Frazzini (Director, Comics), Carlotta Quattrocolo (Executive Editor), Stefano Ambrosio (Executive Editor, New IP), Camilla Vedove (Senior Manager, Editorial Development), Behnoosh Khalili (Senior Editor), Julie Dorris (Senior Editor), Mina Riazi (Assistant Editor) • DESIGN Enrico Soave (Senior Designer) • ART Ken Shue (VP, Global Art), Manny Mederos (Senior Illustration Manager, Comics and Magazines), Roberto Santillo (Creative Director), Marco Ghiglione (Creative Manager), Stefano Attardi (Illustration Manager) • PORTFOLIO MANAGEMENT Olivia Ciancarelli (Director) • BUSINESS & MARKETING Mariantonietta Galla (Senior Manager, Franchise), Virpi Korhonen (Editorial Manager)

Published by Dark Horse Books
A division of Dark Horse Comics LLC
10956 SE Main Street
Milwaukie, OR 97222

DarkHorse.com

To find a comics shop in your area, visit comicshoplocator.com

First Dark Horse Books edition: March 2020
ISBN 978-1-50671-653-4
Digital ISBN 978-1-50671-654-1

10 9 8 7 6 5 4 3 2 1
Printed in China